"Lily!" Zane's face lit up. "I was thinking about you earlier."

"Really?" Despite Lily's best intentions to stay in the friend zone, her smile widened. "Did you think of me because your mother sent you more Christmas cards?"

"No." Zane ordered a cup of coffee. Large, black, and with a shot of espresso. He paid and moved to one side, allowing Lily access to the barista behind the cash register.

"One small hot chocolate, extra whip, extra marshmallows," she said.

Zane released a long, slow whistle. "That's going to get you more wired than my shot of espresso."

"It's for my nephew." Cheeks heating, Lily gestured to Ford before paying.

"Sure it is." Zane smiled mischievously. Sobering, he produced what looked like something official from his back pocket. "I got your name added to the guest list for the Twelve Parties of Christmas here in Clementine. I sure hope you're free."

Dear Reader,

Life has a way of throwing curveballs. So does the craft of writing. I've learned to laugh when they come my way and use them to comedic advantage. Nowhere has this been more true than in this story.

Zane Duvall and Lily Smith have something in common. They've always been on the outside looking in—Zane as a foster kid, Lily as a girl who was never accepted by the man she called Dad. But this holiday season, this pair of friends is front and center because Zane's mother and foster mother are determined Zane be engaged by Christmas. Zane isn't interested in all the attention at this season's many holiday parties. Zane's only shield? Using Lily as his fake date until Christmas, which would be great except those casual feelings start to seem like the real deal.

I hope you enjoy Zane and Lily's unexpected romance, and come to love the cowboys and cowgirls of The Cowboy Academy series as much as I do.

Happy reading!

Melinda

THE CHRISTMAS COWBOY

MELINDA CURTIS

HEARTWARMING

If you purchased this book without a cover you should be aware that this book is stolen property. It was reported as "unsold and destroyed" to the publisher, and neither the author nor the publisher has received any payment for this "stripped book."

Harlequin® **HEARTWARMING**™

ISBN-13: 978-1-335-46023-3

Recycling programs for this product may not exist in your area.

The Christmas Cowboy

Copyright © 2025 by Melinda Wooten

All rights reserved. No part of this book may be used or reproduced in any manner whatsoever without written permission.

Without limiting the author's and publisher's exclusive rights, any unauthorized use of this publication to train generative artificial intelligence (AI) technologies is expressly prohibited.

This is a work of fiction. Names, characters, places and incidents are either the product of the author's imagination or are used fictitiously. Any resemblance to actual persons, living or dead, businesses, companies, events or locales is entirely coincidental.

For questions and comments about the quality of this book, please contact us at CustomerService@Harlequin.com.

TM and ® are trademarks of Harlequin Enterprises ULC.

Harlequin Enterprises ULC
22 Adelaide St. West, 41st Floor
Toronto, Ontario M5H 4E3, Canada
www.Harlequin.com

HarperCollins Publishers
Macken House, 39/40 Mayor Street Upper,
Dublin 1, D01 C9W8, Ireland
www.HarperCollins.com

Printed in U.S.A.

Award-winning *USA TODAY* bestselling author **Melinda Curtis**, when not writing romance, can be found working on a fixer-upper she and her husband purchased in Oregon's Willamette Valley. Although this is the third home they've lived in and renovated (in three different states), it's not a job for the faint of heart. But it's been a good metaphor for book writing, as sometimes you have to tear things down to the bare bones to find the core beauty and potential. In between, and during, renovations, Melinda has written over forty books for Harlequin, including her Heartwarming book *Dandelion Wishes*, which is now a TV movie, *Love in Harmony Valley*, starring Amber Marshall.

Brenda Novak says *Season of Change* "found a place on my keeper shelf."

Books by Melinda Curtis

Harlequin Heartwarming

The Cowboy Academy

A Cowboy Worth Waiting For
A Cowboy's Fourth of July
A Cowboy Christmas Carol
A Cowboy for the Twins
The Rodeo Star's Reunion
Cowboy Santa
The Cowboy's Wedding Proposal
Country Fair Cowboy

The Blackwell Belles

A Cowboy Never Forgets

Visit the Author Profile page
at Harlequin.com for more titles.

To the many branches of my blended and found
family. May all your dreams come true.

CHAPTER ONE

Here we go.

On the Saturday after Thanksgiving, the entire Smith family—*or what was left of them*—was waiting on the front porch to greet Lily Smith upon her arrival in Clementine, Oklahoma.

Inside Lily, uncertainty fluttered and banged about, like a firefly caught in a jar.

Taking a deep breath, Lily stepped out of her truck and positioned her cowboy hat more firmly on her head, still undecided about what, if anything, she'd tell her brother Beau about a letter she'd received two weeks ago. This was the first time Lily had seen Beau and his family since they'd buried their parents six months earlier, a tragedy caused by a drunken driver.

My parents...

Lily bit her lip as the nippy November wind swirled around her.

The man we buried might not have been my biological father.

At least, that's what the letter claimed.

A feeling of bittersweet grief crowded into

Lily's chest, making it hard to draw a full breath. Rather than dwell on the turbulent emotions, Lily focused on the small ranchette Beau and his wife, Nora, owned while waiting for them to cross the expansive front yard to reach her.

The single-story house had received a fresh coat of paint since her last visit—soft gray with white shutters. The front porch was outlined with large, colorful Christmas lights. What looked like an inflatable Santa Claus sat crumpled on the front lawn in front of a pair of floodlights. The south side of the yard was devoted to raised beds that had once produced the summer's bounty. Now stalks and leaves in those beds had curled and yellowed. Beyond the vegetable garden, a stout brown pony stood in a small pasture and whinnied a greeting.

A part of Lily knew she should aspire to this life. To home and family. To a garden and a horse pasture. To love and heritage. But whenever she thought about settling down, a little voice in her head whispered: *This isn't for you.*

Five year-old Ford raced ahead of his parents on quick, jean-clad legs. "Whoop-whoop! Auntie's here!" Ford tossed his straw cowboy hat into the air, revealing straight, sunny-blond hair. And then he was slamming into Lily with a hug so fierce and loving it squeezed the grief right out of her.

Ford stared up at Lily with mischievous gray eyes. "Is that Jet in your trailer, Auntie? Can I ride him? Will you teach me how to rope? Can we build a fort in the pasture? Do you remember how to play checkers? Can we play later?"

"Give your auntie space," Beau cautioned his son, drawing Lily in for a warm hug with Ford between them. It was a steadfast, familiar embrace. "I'm glad you came, Lily."

"Me, too," Ford piped up, squirming his way out from their tangle of legs. "Hey. My hat!" He ran over to pick it up off the lawn as if just realizing it wasn't on his head.

"Same old Ford." Lily loved her nephew. Even though most days, his enthusiasm for life outweighed his youthful take on common sense.

Lily eased out of her brother's arms, taking inventory of his broad frame, straight blond hair and soft gray eyes that were a contradiction to his strong cheekbones.

Physically, Lily looked nothing like her older brother, Beau. She had a tall, slight frame, wavy brown hair, dark brown eyes and what their mother used to call *happy dimples* in her cheeks. Staring at Beau, she'd never felt like such an imposter.

It must be true. We have different fathers.

Her heart sank.

Beau peered at her, always in tune with her moods. "What's wrong?"

"Nothing." *Everything.* But Lily waved his concern aside and turned to give his wife, Nora, a gentle hug, careful of the newborn baby girl bundled in her arms. "I'm here to help, Nora. Don't be shy about asking me to do dishes, change diapers or take out the trash."

"You know me. I won't be shy," Nora promised with a laugh, long blond hair ruffled by the chill, prairie wind. "And I can't wait to catch up."

Lily smiled, grateful that she and her sister-in-law had bonded upon first meet and every meeting since.

"You'll have plenty of time to help Mom." Ford marched up in front of Lily once more, hands on hips, resolve in those gray eyes. "*After* we have our time together, Auntie."

Lily bent her knees, dropping down until her face was at her nephew's level. "Ford, sometimes babies come first. That means you need to learn to be patient."

"That's what Dad says." Ford kicked a patch of dirt with the toe of his brown cowboy boot.

"Your dad would know all about being an older brother." Lily smiled, adjusting the set of Ford's cowboy hat. "He was your age when I was born. Older brothers are important to their little sisters."

"That's right, son." Beau grinned. "*I'm* the reason your sister is so cool."

Ford's eyes widened. "Not Grandma and Grandpa Smith?"

Lily sucked in air, still grieving over the loss.

"Nope. Not our parents." Beau held on to his holiday sweater where jacket lapels might have been had he been wearing one. "Lily's coolness is all from her knowing me."

Love outmuscled the bittersweet feeling in Lily's chest.

No matter what, Beau will always be my brother.

Lily hugged Beau a second time.

Inside Lily's horse trailer, Jet stomped a hoof, impatient to get out.

"We'll talk about whatever is bothering you later," Beau promised in a whisper before releasing Lily. "Come on, Ford. Let's get this horse out of the trailer and into the pasture with Mouse."

"That's my cue to get you inside where it's warm, Nora." Lily ushered her sister-in-law toward the house.

"I'm fine," Nora protested, albeit weakly. "You should unload and unpack."

"Beau will get my suitcase and backpack." Lily didn't have many possessions. It made her nomadic life as a seasonal ranch hand easier. "Stop being a hostess. I'm here to see to your needs. And by the look of you, the first thing you need is a nap."

"Oh, Lily. I'm so glad you came," Nora gushed. Blond hair glinting in the winter sun, she led Lily inside.

A few years ago, when Beau and Nora had moved back to Clementine and purchased the ranchette, the first thing they'd done was take down the walls separating the kitchen and dining room from the living room to open things up. A kitchen island, an oak dining set and overstuffed, tan living room furniture and a wooden granny rocker defined the spaces. There was a small fireplace in the corner and the wall next to it was devoted to family photographs. One face popped out of those pictures—Sonny Smith, the man Lily had assumed was her father until recently when that letter had arrived, claiming otherwise.

"No Christmas tree yet?" Lily asked, turning to face Nora.

"I was hoping you could take Ford to pick one out this week," Nora admitted. "Beau's been busy at the office." He ran a small accounting firm by himself.

The baby made a soft whimpering noise.

"Let me hold that little ray of sunshine." Lily eased the baby from Nora, fitting Cady into her arms as if her appendages had been made to cradle babies, not rope ranch stock. "Hello, Cady."

Newborn Cadence was swaddled in a pink blanket from shoulders to toes. Wispy blond hair fringed a pink knit hospital cap.

"She's adorable, Nora," Lily whispered, already in love.

"Isn't she just?" Nora cupped Cady's head with her palm. "Someday we'll coo over your babies the way we've cooed over mine."

I wish.

But Lily wasn't going to hold her breath. As a seasonal ranch hand, she'd learned to blend in with her male counterparts. No rancher liked his roosters fighting over the one hen in the coop.

And since Lily fit in so well with the men—*just one of the guys*—she hadn't had a date in... She couldn't remember when.

"You don't believe you'll ever have a baby," Nora continued gently, reading Lily as well as Beau had. "But it'll happen."

"Stop with the romance nonsense," Lily gently chided. "Grab a nap before this angel decides she's hungry."

"You don't have to tell me twice." Nora pressed a kiss to Cady's forehead and then disappeared down the hallway, leaving Lily to gaze at Cady and entertain sappy thoughts about finding Mr. Right Cowboy and having a family.

Which is better than thinking about my questionable parentage.

To avoid looking at all those family photos on the wall, Lily faced the front window and watched a tenacious Ford open the pasture gate. Beau led Lily's black gelding inside.

Jet pranced, swiveling away from Beau. Most seven-year-old ranch horses would wait patiently for their halter to be removed before jostling and kicking up their heels. But Jet was a handful.

Even so, Beau was able to calm Jet down. He removed the gelding's halter, and let him loose. Jet wasted no time taking a lap around the pasture followed at a slower pace by Ford's little brown pony. And Ford.

Her nephew ran determinedly after the faster creatures, shouting something Lily couldn't make out before giving up and stumble-running back to Beau, who swung Ford into his arms and tickled the disappointment out of him.

Ford's shrieks of joy made Lily smile and relax a little bit more.

The baby squirmed, making those same faint noises Ford had made when he was a newborn.

Lily fussed with Cady's blanket, tucking in the corners while she tucked away a longing for family of her own.

Beau and Ford raced to the front porch. Of course, Beau let his son win. Not only had he been the best older brother a girl could ask for, he was the best of dads, too.

"You'll never doubt your daddy loves you, Cady," Lily whispered as Beau and Ford clambered up the porch steps and through the front door.

"Someday, I'll be as fast as Jet and Mouse," Ford proclaimed, hanging his cowboy hat on a hook, then plopping on the floor to tug off his boots.

"It's good to have dreams," Beau told his son before taking Ford into the kitchen, where they washed their hands. "Since Mom is resting, whatever we do needs to be quiet."

"I'll be quiet," Ford promised, nodding with exaggerated movements. "If I can have a piece of pumpkin pie and watch a movie."

"Deal." Beau shook on it.

Lily tsked. "What happened to waiting to eat

dessert until *after* a meal?" That had been a strict rule in the Smith household. "It's half past three. Won't pie spoil Ford's appetite?"

"Who cares? It's the holiday weekend." Beau smirked. Then he bent to Ford's level to say, "Besides, what happens when Mommy's napping is our little secret."

Ford's grin spilled over into a knowing giggle. "Because I'm a big brother now."

Lily bet a lot of rules were going to be broken before Cady learned to walk, and she was all for it. "I'll take a slice of pumpkin pie, too."

"Heavy on the whipped cream, Dad." Ford skipped around the kitchen.

The pie and extra whipped cream made a good treat, bolstering Lily's spirits enough that when she was done, she felt up to studying the wall of family photographs next to the fireplace.

Ford spread out on the floor, watching a video on a tablet with headphones on, and Beau rocked the baby, who was starting to fuss.

"Are you going to tell me what's wrong?" Beau asked.

"Yes." She'd been waiting for him to ask again. Lily took a folded envelope from her jeans pocket and handed the letter inside to Beau. "I got this in the mail shortly after the Clementine newspaper published that nice article about Mom and…*Dad*." They'd both grown up in Clementine.

"*Rowdy Brown*," Beau muttered after scanning it. He crumbled the paper in his hand, only stopping when Lily snatched it away, smoothing out the wrinkles before returning it to the envelope, then her pocket. "This is nonsense, Lily," Beau said in a louder voice. "Rowdy Brown isn't your father. Mom would never have cheated on Dad."

"I thought so, too, at first. But... Forget how unbelievable it sounds." Lily took a small framed photograph from the wall and held it toward Beau. "Look at this. Three-of-four people in this photograph have straight blond hair and gray eyes. I don't."

"Mom said you looked like her aunt. What was her name?" The baby fussed. Beau shifted Cady onto his shoulder. He frowned. "Dorothy, wasn't it?"

Lily had looked at those faded pictures of her great-aunt over the years, never seeing the resemblance. She returned the photograph to the wall. "Come on, Beau. You can't stare right at the truth and deny it."

"That's my story, Cady, and I'm sticking to it." Beau rocked his daughter faster.

"If it's true, it would explain everything." Lily returned the photograph to its place on the wall. "Why Dad didn't love me and—"

"He loved you," Beau said with whispered venom, getting to his feet when Cady let out a low sob.

"Not the way he loved you." Lily took the baby from him. Cady's little face was scrunched, as if she was gathering her strength to tell them she was hungry. They'd have to wake Nora soon. "Dad never hugged me. He didn't take me on fishing trips or to football games."

"You don't like fishing or football." Beau took Lily's spot at the wall, analyzing the photographs.

"He didn't read me bedtime stories or pick me up after school to get a milkshake," Lily pointed out.

"That's no proof," Beau grumbled, glancing around the room as if looking for something to justify his position. "Dad just… He didn't know how to raise a girl. Or…or how to express emotions."

"That much is true. He never told me he loved me." Lily came to stand next to her brother. Her *half* brother.

They looked intently at the photographs—none of which had the man that Lily called Dad near her. Zero. Nada. Not even on her birthday.

"Do you think he knew Mom had an affair and resented me?" Lily whispered. "Was that why we moved away before I was born?"

"I think…" Beau turned to face Lily, placing his hands on her shoulders. "I think Rowdy Brown has finally lost his grip on the reins of sanity. His son moved away before our parents died. He's the town hermit now. A crab apple. I heard he had a heart attack recently. He must have looked around and realized he was alone and—"

"Chose me? *A woman he's never met* to claim as family? In a letter, where he says he's my biological father?" Uncertainty gripped Lily's throat and gave it a good squeeze.

Am I being made a fool of? By a stranger?

That seemed unlikely.

Cady gave a strained cry.

"It's a lot of trouble to go through," Lily said, jiggling the baby. "That is, if it's *not* true." It was why she tended to believe Rowdy.

Beau let his hands fall to his sides. "And now, you want to meet Rowdy." A statement. Not a question. Beau took the baby back from Lily. "Don't do this. We have a family."

"I know." Lily's arms felt empty, the way her heart felt when she looked at those pictures.

"If you talk to Rowdy, he'll plant a seed of doubt in your head." Beau tucked the baby close to his chest.

"It's already planted. The letter did that." Lily stared up at a picture of the man she'd called Dad. The man she'd spent most of her life trying to please. "The letter made sense. It made sense on a lot of levels." Without saying a lot of words. "But if it's true... Who am I?"

Cady released another displeased cry.

"You're my sister." Beau rocked Cady from side to side. "You'll always be my sister. But if what Rowdy claims is true... There's a reason our parents didn't tell us. What was it Dad used to say? *Knowing the truth doesn't always make life any better.* You should reject anything to do with Rowdy."

Lily shook her head slowly. "I need to know the truth." For good or ill.

"Even if it means our mother..." Beau didn't finish. Perhaps he couldn't.

Lily had no words, either. Just a jumble of thoughts in her head. About Mom. About herself. About the future.

What does it all mean?

The tension in the room was as thick as Oklahoma low country fog on a cold winter day.

Lily had to get out of there before she broke down and cried.

She turned, heading toward the front door.

"Where are you going?" Beau asked.

Lily didn't answer. She didn't know.

CHAPTER TWO

"Happy Holidays, Zane! I saw one of your moms earlier and she asked me to give you this."

Zane Duvall turned around on his barstool at the Buckboard Bar & Grill in Clementine, Oklahoma, to find an attractive cowgirl tapping her booted foot to the beat of the country song the band was playing. She had long blond hair, wore a small, fancy cowboy hat the same ice blue color as her dress and had big blue eyes.

If she hadn't handed him a small red envelope, Zane might have been tempted to ask her for a dance.

"Hey, Evie." Zane took the missive and set it down on the bar on top of the five other red envelopes he'd received in the past hour, before turning back to his beer. "Thanks."

"Aren't you going to open it?" Evie asked in a super-polite voice. "It's from your real mom."

As opposed to his foster mother, whom he called Mama Mary.

Fact was, Zane considered both women his mamas.

"Here's the thing, Evie." Zane hung on to his smile as he straightened the stack of envelopes. "I'm not opening my mother's holiday cards here." There was no telling what was inside. His gaze found Evie's pretty one in the bar mirror. He tried to look apologetic, not annoyed.

But he *was* annoyed. His biological mother had blown into town mid-November after more than twenty years of being mostly AWOL and, finding him still single and still childless, had immediately put her head together with Mama Mary's and devised ways to remedy that.

Like giving every single woman in Clementine a Christmas card to deliver to me.

That was their strategy this week. Last week, they'd given women a small box of chocolates to deliver. In cowboy terms, his mamas were driving him toward the chute leading to matrimony, whether he was ready for it or not.

After two weeks of this nonsense, even the most patient of cowboys would be annoyed. And considering what he'd put his mamas through when he was a teenager, Zane needed to be patient. He owed them. And yet...

My mamas and I need to have a talk about personal boundaries.

In the mirror, Zane watched Evie flounce, pouting attractively. She was a flouncer by nature and a frequent pouter, as if someone had once told her she was irresistible when she pouted. Zane supposed if he hadn't known Evie most of his life, he might have smiled at her flouncy-pout performance. There was a challenge there. Whoever was in a relationship with Evie would be in a power struggle involving Evie's desire to be in charge and have her way 24/7. Ultimately, she was too self-centered for the likes of Zane.

Evie tossed a hand toward the dance floor, where couples were having a whirl. "Your mom told me you'd ask me to dance."

Of course she did.

"My mother fancies herself as Cupid." But instead of a refined, targeted approach, like the woman he'd hired last summer had used to find him true love—*which had turned out to be a dead end, romance-wise*—his mother considered any single woman a candidate for a march down the aisle to Zane—*which was turning out to be a black hole, romance-wise*. Unfortunately, his mother had convinced his foster mother, a woman normally steady as a newly set fence post, to get on board with the idea. "My mamas are hoping we'll hit it off, get married and have babies before next Christmas."

"Would that be so bad?" Evie said carefully and with less pout.

"*Evie...*" Zane did the polite thing and turned in his barstool to face her, searching for the right words to explain how unsuited they were for each other. Truth be told, he wished he could just skedaddle.

"*Zane...*" Evie smoothed her ice-blue skirt before continuing. "Hear me out. Last summer, you hired Ronnie to match you, same as I did. And then she had a baby before either of us found our one true love." She drew a long, slow breath, as if this was a trial for her to admit. "We're still alone."

The trial had been the matchmaking process itself. With Ronnie having her attention on other important personal matters, he'd ended up agreeing to dates with more than one woman he wasn't suited for. Ginni Trelawney didn't want kids, for instance. Zane couldn't rule them out. Louise Kingston was dead set on life in the city. Zane would never permanently leave Clementine. This was his home. His family was here. They meant everything to him.

After just a few weeks of that, Zane had backed away from his search for love and decided to work on solidifying his economic future instead. Not that he had a plan for that…

He was more of an instinctual guy when it came to the future, following his gut, not his head or heart. And unlike many of his peers, he wasn't a planner.

"And now," Evie continued, "you'd rather spend the holidays alone just because someone else has taken up the matchmaker reins?"

"Yep." There was more to it than that, but he didn't want to get into it with Evie.

"You'd cut off your nose to spite your face."

That said, Evie stomped off, presumably to join her friends at a table in the back.

The band wrapped up one song and launched into a classic holiday tune.

Zane returned his attention to his beer, but his teeth were on edge. He expected another red envelope any minute.

"Is this seat taken?" And without waiting for Zane to answer, a tall, lanky cowgirl wearing blue jeans and a shearling jacket sat next to him and ordered a beer from Chet, the gray-handlebar-mustached bartender.

Zane tried not to stare at the cowgirl directly in case she was delivering another red envelope. But he did sneak a peek in the bar mirror, taking in a well-worn, brown cowboy hat, thick, shoulder-length brown curls and a thin face mostly hidden by that hat brim.

Zane didn't recognize her. But that didn't mean anything where his mamas were concerned.

All I wanted was a quiet moment at the bar to imagine how things would improve in the new year. Is that too much to ask for?

"Pretzels?" Chet asked the woman next to him, raising his voice to be heard above the band's rendition of "Holly Jolly Christmas."

"I was looking for something more substantial." The woman next to Zane tilted her cowboy hat back, fully revealing a fresh-faced look with large freckles plastered across her nose and cheeks. "Something like chili cheese fries or loaded nachos."

"The nachos," Zane said without thinking. "Always."

She turned her head his way, empty hands resting on the bar. "You don't say? Are they good?"

Zane nodded. "The best around." And instead of looking away, he took another long look at her.

The woman had a friendly smile with a hint of dimples, soft brown eyes and a way of engaging Zane that spoke of confidence, not come-ons.

"Nachos it is. Thanks." And then, she turned to the beer that Chet put in front of her, dismissing Zane the same way he'd tried to dismiss Evie earlier.

It was like drinking next to a stranger minding their own business.

Nice.

Zane breathed a sigh of relief.

"Hey, Zane," came a female voice from behind him, setting him back on edge. "I saw your mother in the feedstore this afternoon and she asked me to give you this."

A red envelope came into view, proffered by a hand with fingernails striped with red and white polish.

Zane slowly spun around in his seat to face another delivery. "Hey, Cassie. Nice of you to do my mom a selfless favor."

The attractive redhead frowned, undoubtedly sensing Zane's sarcasm. Or perhaps it was the stack of red envelopes near his beer that got her goat. Cassie tossed the envelope onto the stack, smirked at Zane and then walked off.

"Is there something going on with those red envelopes?" the cowgirl next to him asked.

"Nope. Must be one of those new holidays."

"Like National Christmas Card Delivery Day?" she quipped, not at all put off by Zane's curt reply. "Took me by surprise. Guess I'll have to make due texting all my contacts holiday emojis."

Zane glanced at the cowgirl to see if she was flirting with him—giggling, or smiling knowingly, or beaming at him, looking for attention.

She wasn't. She simply sipped her beer.

Again, Zane got the vibe that she could blend into any crowd.

Someone tapped Zane's shoulder. A flash of red caught his eye.

Girding himself, Zane slowly spun to face... "Hey, Mallory. Thanks." He took the dreaded red envelope, placed it with the others and then turned back to the bar, not even trying to be polite.

"Your mama is one busy woman," the cowgirl next to him noted dryly.

"*Mamas.* Plural." Zane straightened the stack of Christmas cards. "I was in foster care on and off in my teens. So I have a biological mom and a foster mom in my life." Double the nurturing and the meddling. "Most biological parents hold resentment toward foster parents. But not my mother. She and Mama Mary are like two peas in a pod when they get together." As if they knew how much he needed them both.

Or had, until now.

"Two matchmakers with one beloved client." The cowgirl smiled wryly.

The more they talked, the more blanks Zane was filling in about this tall cowgirl. She was self-assured, with a dry sense of humor, along with good taste in beer and bar food.

He smiled right back at her, as if they'd been friends for more than a minute. "Mostly, my biological mom runs point. She was the one handing out all the Christmas cards the past two days, instead of shopping those Black Friday deals." Zane tapped the red stack with one finger. "Last weekend, she invited me to breakfast at the Buffalo Diner and proceeded to arrange for six women to stop by our table. Every one of those women brought me a cup of coffee from Clementine Coffee Roasters. Picture it." He paused, making sure the irony of the situation sunk in for his seatmate. "These women brought me a cup of coffee from *Clementine Coffee Roasters* while I was at the *Buffalo Diner* with my own cup of joe sitting in front of me." He held up his hands in a gesture of surrender. "By coffee delivery number four, Coronet, the owner of the diner, told me she was *this close*—" he held his thumb and forefinger an inch apart "—from banning me until the new year. *Me.* Not my mother. Or the women she recruited."

"Six women bringing you coffee? And now

eight more have delivered you holiday cards?" The cowgirl next to him laughed, not in a sarcastic or superior way. No. She laughed as if she appreciated a good story, deepening those dimples. "The local gals must consider you a catch."

But not her.

He wasn't picking up an ounce of interest from her.

Frowning, Zane took another good look at his seatmate, suddenly suspicious of a setup.

She was pretty but not in a flashy way. Not like most of the women his mother maneuvered into his path. If his foster mother had a look at his seatmate, she'd classify the cowgirl's looks as down-to-earth. There was a callus on the thumb of her left hand, the one that loosely curled around her beer, as if she worked with her hands for a living. No jewelry. No wedding ring. No sparkles and glitter. No nonsense. But there was a friendly aura about her. It wasn't just that splash of large freckles or the wayward curl of her hair beneath that cowboy hat. No... It was that dimpled smile. It lit up her entire face and turned her from plain pretty into something more...*extraordinary.*

Zane hid a scoff in his beer. He wasn't prone to romantic thoughts, which was probably why he was leaving his twenties without a single significant relationship under his belt. Maybe she was the same way.

"I came here for some peace and quiet," she told him, as if reading his thoughts. "So, if you think you'll get more red envelope business coming through, I should move." She glanced up and down the bar, but there were no empty seats left. And then she glanced around the room, but there were no available tables, either. It was the Saturday night after Thanksgiving. The Buckboard was packed.

"Or you could just sit here and bear these matchmaking efforts with me," Zane offered, having the sense that he could do worse in choice of a wingman.

"Zane, honey..."

At the sound of another woman's voice, Zane and his wingman simultaneously turned in their barstools.

"Thanks, Polly." Zane plucked the envelope from Polly's fingers, then swung back around.

As did his cowgirl. She sipped her beer as Polly stomped away. "Dedicated, your mamas. Are you up to ten cards yet?"

Zane counted them. "Nine. What does ten signify?"

"Holiday cards come in boxes of ten or twenty, I think."

"Let's hope she only bought a tenner."

His wingman laughed, a full-throated sound without censure. Sitting with her was just like hanging out with one of his foster brothers.

"You won't laugh when my mother very sweetly asks *you* to do something for her," Zane promised. "She's a retired nurse and used to convincing even the most ornery patients and egotistical surgeons to bend to her will." He extended his hand, telling her his first name.

"Lily." Her hand twitched in his, as if she felt shocked by his touch. He might have thought he'd imagined it except afterward Lily ran that hand over the leg of her faded blue jeans. "I'm here visiting my brother, Beau Smith."

"I know Beau." Zane smiled. "He's an accountant in town."

"That's him." Lily grinned. "Good man to know if you need your taxes done."

"Excuse me, Zane?" It was another woman holding a red envelope.

"Your mom bought a pack of twenty," Lily told Zane thirty minutes and several more envelopes later. She was halfway through her loaded nachos and her beer, progressing slowly because this was the most fun she'd had since receiving that letter from Rowdy Brown two weeks ago. Plus, she'd almost forgotten her argument with Beau. "Zane... With your luck, your mother bought two boxes of holiday cards."

Frowning, Zane straightened the stack. "Merry Christmas to me."

He was a good-looking, guileless cowboy, the kind that went through life without much of a plan. As a seasonal ranch worker traveling throughout the West every year, Lily had met dozens of cowboys like him and called most of them friend.

And if she'd felt a jolt of attraction when she and Zane had shaken hands earlier, she knew how to keep her distance and guard her heart, having learned the hard way.

"How does anyone eat this alone?" Lily eased her nachos plate toward Zane. "Want to help me finish them off?"

"A few will do me." Not shy, Zane dug right in. "I haven't seen you around before. Do you visit Beau much?"

"No, sir. Once or twice a year. But Beau and his wife, Nora, had a baby last week. And since my job at a ranch in Texas ended before the holiday, I thought I'd stay awhile to help out." Lily refrained from mentioning Rowdy's letter. That man's invitation to visit hadn't come in a red envelope but it had provided Lily with the same level of curiosity and dread as Zane seemed to have toward that stack of Christmas cards in front of him.

Why is Rowdy contacting me now? And why didn't Mom tell me the man I called Dad wasn't mine after all?

Lily stuffed those questions to the back of her mind.

"You're a ranch hand? Me, too." Zane was well on his way to finishing her nachos. "Full time again at the Done Roamin' Ranch, although I've tried several other jobs at different places. Are you looking for work? I could put in a good word for you."

"Thanks, but I won't be looking until spring. I

figured I'd hang out and help the family with the baby this winter." She'd saved a little and her inheritance was coming soon, although she'd much rather have her parents than their money. Just the thought of having Christmas without them made her teary. Lily shook her head, blinking and bringing herself back to the present. "If you hear any leads come spring, let me know. I have references. I'm good on the range, fixing fences and the like. I've even participated in a few mustang round-ups."

"You bounce around?" Zane gave Lily a searching look.

She recognized that expression, having seen it on dozens of other faces. Zane wanted to know why she was a ranch hand, why she didn't settle in one place, why she didn't get married, why she didn't have kids.

"I prefer to say I move on when the mood suits me." Lily reached for her drink, having no intention of answering any personal questions.

Mostly because she didn't know the answers herself. She just listened to the same voice with the often-repeated phrase: *This isn't for you.*

"Zane?" Another woman approached them.

Saved by a Christmas card.

Lily sipped her beer while Zane dealt with delivery number eighteen. When he'd thanked the woman and she went on her way, Lily ventured to say, "I think your mother has good taste in dating candidates. I haven't seen one clunker." All the women were beautiful and well-turned-out. Dressed up when compared with Lily's holiday sweater and blue jeans.

"You and I might label clunkers differently," Zane said cryptically.

Is he trying not to hurt my feelings because I'm not a girlie-girl?

Lily chewed on that thought for a moment but... *naw.*

She knew she cleaned up nicely if she straightened her hair, applied some makeup and wore a dress. But on the daily, she was most comfortable with air-dried, curly hair, no makeup, jeans and a T-shirt, just like any other ranch hand.

Basically, he was seeing her the way she intended male coworkers to. And that meant any dreaming about Zane romantically was destined for a dead end. Fine by her.

The band took a break. Chatter blended with the canned echo of Elvis singing "Blue Christmas."

Another woman appeared behind them holding envelope number nineteen. "Zane? I met your mother at the gas station. She told me you were back in town and she asked me to give you this." When Zane turned, extending his hand, the woman hesitated. "I was wondering if you're doing the Twelve Parties of Christmas."

"Wouldn't miss it, Carlene," Zane said carefully, gaze shifting toward Lily and then back to the delivery woman.

She handed over the envelope, smiling coyly. "I look forward to seeing you there." And then, she was gone.

"The plot thickens," Lily said, intrigued. "What is the Twelve Parties of Christmas?"

Zane straightened his stack of holiday cards. "It's Clementine's new holiday tradition. Or so some folks hope. The twelve largest ranches in the area are each holding a shindig in December, all with the goal of nurturing a sense of kinship in Clementine. The organizers believe single folks in their twenties and thirties aren't embracing the community the way they did when they were our age. And you can bet my mothers will have a matchmaking strategy for each party." He turned up his nose.

"You don't have to go." Although Lily was curious to witness what his mothers came up with next. Their ideas so far seemed rather brilliant.

"Oh, but my presence has been requested," Zane countered. "My foster mother is on the committee that organized the whole shebang. Wouldn't look good if one of her foster boys didn't show."

"The old guilt trap. Do they also tell you stories about when they were younger and dating?" Lily leaned closer, continuing in a conspiratorial whisper, "Did they both marry their high school sweethearts? Or…" and here, she gasped dramatically "…did they walk miles through the snow to meet their dates? Barefoot? During a blizzard? All in the pursuit of love?"

"Something like that." Zane lightened up, as she'd meant him to. A smile spread across his chiseled cheeks and he bent his head toward her to whisper, "You forgot to mention how they fell in love at first sight and wouldn't have if they hadn't shown up in that blizzard."

Oh. He smells good. Woodsy.

It brought to mind a walk through the pines. She imagined holding this cowboy's hand on a trail strewn with pine needles and—

I've strayed outside the friend zone.

Feeling her cheeks heat, Lily sat back on her stool, reminding herself that Zane wasn't attracted to her. Thankfully, he didn't meet the basic requirement she used to set for potential suitors— that they were attracted to her on the get-go, not just seeing her as one of the guys.

Lily drew a calming breath. "That still doesn't mean you have to attend these Christmas parties."

"Oh, but I do. The organizing committee sweetened the deal this year." Zane swirled a triangular corn chip through the last swath of melted cheese. "There will be prizes awarded at each event, like for the best ugly Christmas sweater and best line dancer. But they're also giving out raffle tickets to Clementine residents at every party for one special drawing. The grand prize winner will be chosen at our Santapalooza Parade on Christmas Day." There was a wistful note in his voice that Lily took to mean he really wanted that grand prize.

She'd heard of the Santapalooza Parade, where all riders wore Santa suits. But it was the giveaway, whatever that was, that Zane seemed to want so badly and made her so curious. "The grand prize being…"

"A plot of land." His gaze softened, turning wistful. "Ten acres plus a modest house."

"That's some grand prize." Made Lily wish she'd set down roots here, if only for a chance to win her own spread.

Zane smiled at her, warm and welcoming. "If you like, I can get you an invitation to the parties. You might win one of the smaller prizes."

"Can you do that? Invite me, I mean?"

Zane tapped his chest with one hand. "Remember me? My foster mom is one of the organizers. I'll swing by Beau's place this week with an invitation and party schedule."

"Thank you." Smiling, Lily raised her nearly empty beer glass. "Now I have something to look forward to this holiday season besides snuggling a baby."

And meeting my biological father.

Not smiling, Zane clinked his glass to hers. "Forgive me if I don't feel the same enthusiasm," Zane said, right before the twentieth red envelope was delivered. And when the woman departed, he added, "The only good thing about these parties are the increased entries I earn for that grand prize. I'm dreading my mamas' matchmaking efforts."

In a gesture of solidarity, Lily clapped a hand on his shoulder—his solid, muscular, off-limits shoulder.

She quickly withdrew her hand. "If you can handle twenty Christmas cards and six coffee deliveries, you can handle whatever your mamas throw at you next, including a partridge in a pear tree."

Her phone pinged with a message from Beau, asking where she was.

"That's my cue to leave." Lily paid her bill and wished Zane a happy holiday season.

She smiled all the way back to Beau's, thinking about Zane being a target of his matchmaking mothers, wondering what they'd throw in his path next, safe in the knowledge that it wouldn't be her.

But kind of wishing…

CHAPTER THREE

MONDAY MORNING FOUND Zane working at the Done Roamin' Ranch, where he'd spent his foster years and had learned how to pick himself up when he was tossed into the dirt, rodeo-style.

Life did that more often than he'd like it to.

While he moved stock through a shoot into the arena, one at a time, Zane's thoughts bounced from imagining winning the Twelve Parties of Christmas grand prize to the unusual cowgirl he'd met Saturday night. One dream filled him with longing and the memory of Lily's laughter brought a smile to his face.

All around the ranch yard, cowboys were setting up holiday decorations—red and green garland, Christmas trees (real, plastic, inflatable), lights upon lights upon lights—all under the supervision of Mama Mary. She loved the Christmas season and went all out on making everything—inside and out—look festive. She had Christmas carols playing from a speaker on the front porch where she sat with Zane's biological mother. Their heads were together—scheming about matchmaking, no doubt—and their laps were full of stark white yarn.

It was nippy out. Somewhere, bells were jingling.

Zane wasn't in the holiday spirit. He wasn't on decorating duty. He and a small crew were training livestock for rodeo competition. The Done Roamin' Ranch supplied roughstock for top-quality rodeos near and far—bucking bulls and broncs, steers and calves for roping. This morning, they were working with young wrestling and roping steers so that they'd be easy to handle once they returned to the official circuit.

With cold fingers, Zane tugged a horn wrap onto a fidgety steer in the arena chute. The nylon webbing helped protect the animal's head and horns during roping competitions from bruising, chipping and horn breakage. And even though the Done Roamin' Ranch was on a brief hiatus from rodeo for the holiday season, important jobs and tasks hadn't ceased.

Zane angled his forearm against the steer's neck and gave the stretchy webbing another yank just as the steer tossed his big head, blocking Zane's efforts. "This guy doesn't like to be wrapped."

"He doesn't like it?" Chandler, one of Zane's oldest foster brothers and the Done Roamin' Ranch foreman, moved closer, seemingly intent upon helping. "Or maybe you've lost your touch."

Zane elbowed Chandler back. "Listen, old man—"

"*Old man?* How about *wise* man?" Chandler used his longer arm reach to get the horn wrap into place. "I'm about ten years your senior."

"Remind me to get you the seniors' discount pass at the feed and seed for Christmas." Zane stepped back, chuckling. He moved the lever to release the steer into the arena, watching him bolt for the exit gate on the chute's other side. Then Zane closed off the exit and picked up another webbed horn wrap before the next steer moved into the chute.

Chandler reached down to pet his son's brown labradoodle, Rusty, who squished a weathered tennis ball in his mouth. When Chandler's son was in school, Rusty never left Chandler's side.

The ranch foreman straightened, moving closer to inspect Zane's work. "How do you feel about your old ranch being the grand prize for the Twelve Parties of Christmas?"

Something hot and wild burst through Zane's veins, causing his blood to pound harder, faster.

Zane focused on deep breaths, on work, on trying to tamp down his helpless resentment. "How would you feel if Rowdy Brown bought your parents' ranch out from under them when they were declaring bankruptcy? And then twenty years later, Rowdy decides to just…give the ranch away?" Without so much as contacting Zane to see if he wanted to buy it first.

His pulse refused to stop its frustrated beat.

"I'd be angry," Chandler admitted, setting his

cowboy hat back farther on his head. "But maybe grateful, too."

"Grateful?" Zane finished wrapping the steer's horns and let it through the chute. "Why grateful?"

"Because of local legend, of course." Chandler slapped the next steer on its haunches to encourage it to move forward. "They call it—"

"The Bad Luck Ranch?" Zane scoffed, familiar with the local nickname. "I don't believe that." His family had been happy there. Besides the Done Roamin' Ranch, it was the only other place he'd called home. The only place where he'd felt he'd fit in.

"There's plenty of proof of its power of misfortune." Chandler looked thoughtful. "Your parents got divorced after living there. Rowdy Brown left it vacant for years until his son moved in. Lucas Brown didn't last more than a few years before he and his wife left town. And I heard there are half a dozen stories that established that legend before your dad bought the place."

"It's not cursed, Chandler," Zane insisted. "It's just a ranch." A property he wanted back.

"Look! It's Solomon!" someone on the other side of the arena shouted.

Cowboys around the ranch stopped what they were doing and moved to get a look at the infamous wild horse, some climbing wooden fences for a better view.

Zane did just that, spotting a white stallion galloping by the ranch proper and toward the pastures beyond. "What I wouldn't give to put a rope around Solomon's neck."

"You and hundreds of others," Chandler told Zane, tugging the back of Zane's jacket to encourage him to put his feet and his dreams back on the ground. "Although many have tried, no one's been able to catch him."

"I bet he'd make a good bucking bronc." In Zane's eyes, a good bucker was steady income.

"Solomon would be more trouble than he was worth." Chandler snatched the wet tennis ball from Rusty's mouth and tossed it across the ranch yard. The dog streaked after it. "That horse jumps fences. He'd pitch a rider to the dirt and leap over the rodeo fence into the crowd. And then what?"

"You don't have to be glass half empty," Zane grumbled. "Let a man dream." Of easy victories and a more prosperous future.

Several cowboys headed out at a gallop after the white horse. Wishing he was with them, Zane returned to his task and picked up another horn wrap.

Across the ranch yard, feminine laughter rippled through the air above the chorus of "Rocking Around the Christmas Tree." Mom and Mama Mary were having the best time together.

Zane's shoulders stiffened as he imagined his mothers were planning their next romantic move. He tugged the wrap on another steer, wrangling it into place.

"You want to win a ranch," Chandler said loftily, as if this was a fresh epiphany he was having about Zane's life. "And you want to capture a wild horse. Both things seem like shortcuts to riches. But what if you fail at both? Are you going to be a jack-of-all-trades, moving about forever?"

"Here we go," Zane murmured. Chandler was as regular with life-lesson speeches lately as their foster father had been when they were growing up. "Give it to me."

"You're nearing thirty, and from experience, I'd say you're looking at your life differently than you did at twenty. Or even twenty-five." When Zane opened the chute gate, Chandler roused the steer. The steer trotted obediently toward the exit gate on the far side. "You thought you'd have a home of your own by now, perhaps with a wife, maybe with kids. And you'd be set on a path—ranching or rodeo or something else that provided you with a steady income to keep a roof over your head. And instead, you still have a suitcase under your bed in the bunkhouse, ready to leave if something new catches your fancy."

"Yeah, but..." Zane closed the chute gate as the next steer banged his way forward. "I'm not critical of my choices. I took chances in the past decade dreaming and pursuing things that interested me." But nothing stuck. Zane picked up another horn wrap. "You can't fault a man for not knowing what he wants to do *when he grows up*. I've tried a little of this and a little of that." But always in the back of his mind was the idea that he'd earn enough money to buy the Bad Luck Ranch someday. Somehow.

Not that he had substantial savings to show for it. But he had savings.

"You've tried more careers than anyone else I know." Chandler had a way of looking at a person that made you think he saw more than you wanted him to. "Let's see... You've been a rodeo roper, rodeo announcer, stock car driver, boot salesman, long-haul truck driver, horse breeder, horse trainer and ranch hand, obviously. Oh, and Solomon horse hunter, if that hungry look in your eye a few minutes back is any indication."

"You forgot carpenter's apprentice," Zane griped, setting the mechanism to hold the steer in place before picking up another horn wrap.

"And yet, no matter what you've tried, you always show up here after things don't work out." Chandler's gaze held a judgy shine. "As your foster brother, I want to tell you there will always be a place for you at the Done Roamin' Ranch. But as ranch foreman, I feel like I should point out that you can't always expect us to have a job open for you when your other gigs fall apart."

Zane glanced over his shoulder at the bunkhouse, which was full this month. "What are you saying?"

"What I'm saying is this, Zane." Chandler tugged the ball free from Rusty's slobbery mouth and tossed it across the ranch yard. And then he fixed Zane with a stare that was all business. "Will there always be a bed for you if you need it? Of course. Will we always have a spot for you on the payroll? I don't know. It's time to settle into the life you want for the next decade or so."

"You're as bad as my mothers," Zane mumbled, feeling the expanse of the Done Roamin' Ranch close in on him.

"Speak of the devils..." Chandler pointed toward the approaching women. "Good thing this is the last steer. Why don't you take a break when this one is done? Give your mamas a few minutes of your time." Chandler strode off, tossing over his shoulder, "I see the riders who went after Solomon are coming back empty-handed."

"Like I would, too, if I went after him, you mean," Zane muttered, making quick work of the horn wrap. He released the steer and then he turned to face his mothers, going on the defensive. "What new plan have you hatched to torture me now?"

"Oh, Zane. This isn't about that." His mother winked at Mama Mary, belying her words. She wore a red sweatshirt with Santa's face on it over mom jeans and boots not made for riding. Her shoulder-length, dark hair rippled in the breeze. He loved his mother, but she had a calculated smile on her face that created a knot of worry in his gut. "The theme of the first Christmas party is Ugly Boots, Sweaters or Ties. We got you an ugly sweater to wear, Zane."

"We know how competitive you are." Mama Mary was a more traditional cowgirl, preferring cowboy boots and hat, plus a blue-checked shirt and lined denim jacket for warmth rather than a sweater of any kind. Her silver hair was too short beneath her straw cowboy hat to be upset by any prairie breeze. "You'll win a prize for wearing this." Mama Mary handed him a large, brown paper bag with twine handles. The contents of the bag jingled and she wasn't shaking it.

Uh-oh.

Zane peeked inside. "It's white." And not a soft white, either. It was look-at-me white. Wedding dress white. The white flag of surrender white.

"And it has bells, like streamers." Mom seemed happy about this feature. Proud, even. "We just finished attaching them."

"I bet not everyone will take the theme seriously at this first party. It'll be easier to win a prize." Mama Mary glowed. "You'll wear it, won't you?" And since she'd had a cancer scare over a year ago, when she glowed nowadays, Zane would do anything to keep that smile on her face.

"If it'll make you happy." Zane sighed, coming to terms with the forthcoming embarrassment. "I'll wear it." And hope it was homely enough to keep women at bay and to nab him a prize of some sort.

"Say thank you!" Chandler teased from the other side of the arena and making Zane want to march over there and slug him in the shoulder.

"Thank you, Mamas," Zane said dutifully instead.

"Now, Zane. I need a favor." Mama Mary took the opportunity of that small win to push for more. "I volunteered to work the Holly Scouts Christmas tree lot in town Tuesday afternoon, but I forgot I have a dentist appointment. Could you cover for me?"

"If it's okay with the ranch foreman. Chandler?" He was about to face his foster brother but quickly peered at Mama Mary in suspicion. *Hmm, she looked sincere.* Or it could have been that she was distracted from setting him up by a big gust of wind that threatened to blow her straw cowboy hat off. "I'll work the Christmas tree lot as long as it doesn't involve meeting single women."

Mama Mary was quick to assure him that would be the case. But her hands were behind her back and he wouldn't put it past her to be crossing her fingers.

"By the way." Mom edged Mama Mary aside, smiling like she hadn't a care in the world. "I think you should give the tickets you earn for the grand prize at each event to someone else. The Bad Luck Ranch has never been anything but trouble and—"

"You know I don't believe in superstition," Zane reminded her.

"But your future wife might not want to be a rancher," Mom pressed, still smiling.

No clunkers. That's what Lily had said about the women his mamas had sent his way.

Understanding dawned. "You've been picking a certain type of woman for me."

They'd been sending city cowgirls his way. Women who dressed like cowgirls but didn't own a horse and probably never had, unlike Lily. He had no use for a princess, no room for one in his dream future of owning his childhood home.

"Listen up, Mamas." Zane put his hands on his hips. "I'm going to win the grand prize from the Twelve Parties of Christmas—the old Duvall Ranch. And whoever I marry will love living there. The least you could do while playing Cupid is to honor the vision I have for my life."

"Pfft." Mom waved aside his declaration. "The way you've been drifting through your days so far, it's clear you don't know what you want. Let us help you decide."

Mama Mary didn't look as if she was on the same page as his biological mother, but she remained silent.

"This is going to be the best Christmas ever." Mom hooked her arm through Mama Mary's and led her away. "Our boy is finally going to fall in love. Then, he'll move up to Tulsa to be closer to me and his sister."

Zane scoffed. "I'm not moving to Tulsa."

Mama Mary glanced over her shoulder, an apologetic look in her eyes. She may have been in league with his mother, but she wasn't on the same page entirely, which was encouraging.

They moved out of earshot.

Zane stared at the white sweater they'd given him, reliving some of the many awkward moments they'd put him through lately—chocolate boxes, coffee cups, Christmas cards. If he wore this sweater, he knew he was in for another night of being a target for romance.

Loud voices and laughter brought him back to the present. The cowboys who'd tried to chase down the white stallion had no luck, other than to return with a good story to tell.

Zane headed their way, wanting to learn from their mistakes.

LILY DROVE ON a dusty dirt road that cut through the Rolling Prairie Ranch, heading toward the main house where Rowdy Brown lived.

Where my dad lives?

Lily was nervous about this meeting and driving too fast. Dust billowed behind her, obliterating the rear view. She came over a rise with roller-coaster speed, taking a bit of air. Her stomach dropped.

Zane would appreciate that. He seemed like the type of guy who enjoyed roller coasters.

But Lily didn't. Heart pounding, she slowed down.

A tall, lanky old man was waiting for her on the front porch. He was so tall, in fact, that he had to bend over to lean on his black cane. He wore rumpled blue jeans, a rumpled blue-checked shirt and a blue-quilted coat vest, all topped with a white, ten-gallon hat. "You're either behind schedule delivering something or you're my long-lost daughter here to see me. Either way, you don't speed on my drive."

How very unwelcome.

Lily climbed the six porch steps slowly, unsure of how to greet him.

"Name's Rowdy," the tall man said gruffly. He was older than her mother had been. Or at least, he looked it. Life had drawn long, disapproving lines on his thin face. "And seeing as how you don't have a package or anything like that, you're late." And without another word, he turned and entered the ranch house, as if expecting Lily to obey.

He had a slow, rolling gait, his legs bowed from years in the saddle.

Lily hesitated.

Rowdy reminded her of the man she'd called Dad. He'd had a brusque demeanor and a lifelong cowboy's gait, too.

Emotions swirled inside her, unsettled by a disappointing truth.

Knowing the truth doesn't always make life any better.

Lily glanced back at her truck, tempted to drive away. Dust still swirled around it, unsettled by her arrival.

She glanced through the open door. Sunshine illuminated dust motes, unsettled by Rowdy's passing.

Lily felt foolish for thinking this would be a sentimental first meet. That Rowdy would welcome her with open arms. Perhaps, to him, she was just as disruptive to his equilibrium as she'd been to the man she still thought of as Dad.

Lily stepped over the threshold, pausing there to take in the home's aesthetic. The woodwork was handcrafted and stained dark except where it was worn on the grand banister rail. Wallpaper hung above the paneling, faded and peeling at the seams. A large oil painting of a bouquet of roses on a black background had a gaudy, gold frame with cobwebs cutting each corner. Hooks fashioned from what looked like deer antlers lined the wall closest to the front door. There were coats there and Rowdy's oversize cowboy hat.

"Quit gawking and get in here," Rowdy snapped from a room on her left. He was as friendly as a prickly stalk of milkweed.

Lily hurried to join him.

It was an office in the same state of sadness as the entry. A dark wood bookshelf spanned the floor to ceiling on one wall. The books had a layer of dust. A brown couch sat opposite the desk, its leather arms cracked and splitting.

Rowdy sat behind a large walnut desk with two framed pictures on top, both facing a single guest chair. He studied her with beady eyes from behind what looked like a pair of narrow reading glasses.

He was the second person she'd met in Clementine, and unlike Zane, Rowdy didn't make her want to get to know him better.

"I'm not one for small talk so let's get down to business," Rowdy grumbled.

"You had an affair with my mother," Lily blurted, sounding judgmental. Feeling judged, although none of this was her fault.

Her outburst seemed to ruffle Rowdy's feathers. He took a moment to run his bony fingers around the edge of the clean blotter on his desk. "We had a *relationship*."

Lily scoffed the way her brother, Beau, would have scoffed, as if, in this case, *affair* couldn't ever be translated to *relationship*.

Rowdy's cheeks reddened. He leaned forward, shaking a finger in Lily's direction. "Dawnice and Sonny—*your parents*—were separated and—"

"No." Lily sat back in her chair and said again, "No. I never heard of any trouble in their marriage. This is…just a cruel joke." The way Beau had said.

"A joke?" Rowdy seemed to shudder in his chair before collecting himself and continuing. "My wife had just left me for my ranch foreman. Your mother and I…fell in love. Or I thought we had." The old cowboy rubbed a hand through his short, white hair as if saying the words out loud made his head hurt. "But then Sonny came around to collect Dawnice, apologizing and spouting flowery words, and that was the end of that." Rowdy pinned Lily with a cold stare. "At least, it was what I thought until I saw the death notice and the accompanying picture of the *Smith* family. And then I realized that you…" He hesitated, seeming to gather himself for the most incriminatory fact. "*You* look exactly like *my* mother."

Lily frowned, disliking his reaching for a connection.

Rowdy turned around one of the small framed photographs on his desk and plunked it in front of Lily.

She gasped.

It was a black-and-white, square-shaped photograph. The woman in the picture had her hair up in a loose, rippling bun. But her face…those freckles…that smile…those happy dimples…

She's my grandmother.

"I… I…" Lily went cold inside when faced with such powerful evidence. She didn't know who she was if she wasn't a Smith. Were Browns upstanding citizens? Known to volunteer in the community? True to their word? Lily didn't know what to say.

Oh, but Rowdy did. "That resemblance isn't enough for me. I need to be sure. You'll have to take a DNA test."

"No," Lily murmured. Then louder, "No. I'm not related to you. I'm a Smith."

"Pfft." Rowdy shifted in his seat. "What has being a Smith ever gotten you? You'll take the DNA test and be grateful."

"Grateful?" To a prickly curmudgeon? "I don't want anything from you. I came here to see if you were my father because…"

Rowdy waited for her to finish.

Lily swallowed, looked away, lowered her voice and admitted the truth, "Because if you were my father, we'd have some sort of connection. Some feeling… Some way of knowing that we belong together. Like a natural affinity for each other." The feeling that had been missing between Lily and Sonny Smith. "And right now… I feel nothing for you that tells me you're my father." Or that she wanted him to be.

Rowdy laughed. Paused, then laughed harder. "Feelings? What poppycock."

Disappointment again burned inside Lily, the same way it had burned inside Lily whenever she'd felt the man she'd called Dad be distant and impossible to please.

She got to her feet. "I came here out of courtesy. But now I'm leaving." Her gaze drifted toward the picture of Rowdy's mother. "Because even if we share some type of genetic sequence, I have no need for another bad father in my life."

Lily stomped out of the room, out of the house and down the porch steps.

Beau was right. It was idiotic to do this.

CHAPTER FOUR

AN AFFAIR?

Rowdy sat at his desk for a long time after Lily left, numb. He hadn't expected Lily to know nothing about him, much less to denigrate what he'd had with Dawnice by calling it *an affair*.

We were in love.

And maybe their love hadn't been strong enough to hold on to when Sonny showed up and told Dawnice, "I'm sorry I haven't tried harder, but we both should, for the sake not just of our future but our child's, as well. Think about it." But it had been real.

Rowdy opened a desk drawer and carefully withdrew a small acorn, running his fingers over its smooth, brown surface.

It's beautiful out here, Dawnice had told Rowdy as they walked through a pasture toward an oak tree sitting on a hill. *So peaceful.*

You can breathe easy out here, Rowdy had said, taking Dawnice's hand. Her palm was warm and smooth. Her hold gentle.

Rowdy remembered thinking: *I can trust her with my heart.*

He didn't remember what else they'd said as they'd approached that old oak tree. But once they were sheltered beneath its branches, they'd turned toward each other and exchanged their first kiss.

Rowdy had picked up two acorns, giving Dawnice one and tucking the other, the one he kept in his desk, into his pocket, telling her, *Someday, we'll plant these acorns and tell our children why the trees that grow there were nourished by our love.*

They'd never planted those acorns. Or at least, Rowdy hadn't. He had no idea what Dawnice had done with hers.

Months after that first kiss, Rowdy's romantic rival had convinced Dawnice to uphold her promise to him at the altar, leaving Rowdy's already bruised and broken heart in pieces.

It was still in pieces today. And not just because his daughter thought she was a product of an illicit affair. But because Lily said Sonny hadn't been the best father.

If I'd known you existed, I would have fought for you.

He would have made certain she had a father in her life who loved her.

CHAPTER FIVE

"WE BROUGHT YOU LUNCH." Zane's mother was waiting in the bunkhouse with Mama Mary when Zane came inside to clean up before he went for ranch supplies.

No one else was in the bunkhouse, possibly having been scared away by the two maternal figures in Zane's life.

I should hightail it out of here, too.

Earlier, he'd been tempted to saddle up and see if he could track down Solomon. But then Chandler had asked him to run errands in town.

Something Lily said came back to Zane: *I've even participated in a few mustang roundups.* Maybe she'd like to ride down that stallion with him. The more he thought about it, the more he liked the idea.

But before Zane could flee his mamas to find Lily, his gaze caught on a thick-sliced ham sandwich on the bunkhouse dining table and a large slice of three-tiered chocolate cake beside it.

"This is sad," Zane said, coming to sit down

across from the pair. "I'm just now realizing that I can be bought. With food."

His mothers laughed.

"Mary made the chocolate cake," his biological mother said.

"And Rita made you the ham sandwich," his foster mother said.

"I'm surprised you didn't have the food delivered by one of Clementine's single ladies." Zane took a bite of the ham sandwich, savoring the sweet honey mustard and spicy pepper jack cheese.

"There's no need to do such a thing to you here at the ranch," his foster mother said, earning a grateful smile from Zane.

"Nope. We've got those Twelve Parties of Christmas coming up," his biological mother said, earning a disapproving frown from Zane. "No sense encouraging ladies to visit the ranch when you're dirty and dusty and not looking your best."

"You'll be dressed in your Saturday night clothes at those parties," his foster mother chimed in, grinning from ear to ear. "Wednesday, Friday and Saturday for the next four weeks."

Trapped.

Zane imagined he heard Lily's full-throated laughter echoing in his head.

"Yes, sir. You will surely look your best during the festivities, except for this Wednesday when you wear that adorable ugly Christmas sweater," Mom added.

"There's nothing as endearing as a man getting in the holiday spirit," Mama Mary said.

Zane was no different from any other working cowboy in Clementine—making ends meet but not making much headway. The prizes being given away were tempting, especially the chance to win the ranch that he'd once called home. But...

The reality of his situation sank in.

For the next four weeks, Zane was a target for his mothers' romantic machinations. He needed to thwart their plans.

Somehow.

"I LIKE IT when you pick me up from school, Auntie." Ford buckled himself into the back seat of Lily's truck. "Is it milkshake time?"

Still smarting from her meeting with Rowdy, Lily had to work hard to smile at her nephew. Milkshakes had been a special treat shared by Beau and Sonny. She wanted to create different traditions with her nephew.

"How about a hot chocolate?" When she'd bought a coffee at Clementine Coffee Roasters on her way to see Rowdy, she'd noticed hot cocoa on the menu.

"Only if you ask for double whip and double marshmallows. *Please.*" Ford had learned the art of bargaining since her last visit. "Can you see me? I'm smiling."

Catching his grin in the rearview mirror, Lily laughed, easing forward in the pickup line toward the school exit. "That's a lot of sugar. Your mother might not approve."

Maybe this shouldn't be a new tradition.

Lily tried to mentally calculate the sugar difference between a chocolate milkshake and a hot chocolate with double whip and double marshmallows. Unlike Beau, math had never been her strong suit.

"And when I've had my hot chocolate," Ford continued as if she hadn't spoken, "then I'd like to go riding. I'll ride Jet and you can ride Mouse."

Lily laughed again, with more humor this time. Her nephew was good medicine for the blues. "I'm too big to ride your pony, Ford." She pulled onto the road heading toward Main Street.

Lily's family had left Clementine before she was born. She'd only been to town a few times since Beau moved back here. But Clementine was small enough that navigating wasn't an issue.

"Auntie, I'm not too small to ride Jet." Ford sounded pleased with his logic. "If you don't want to ride Mouse, you can watch me."

"I don't think so. Jet is a horse boss." Lily needed to squash her nephew's desire to ride him. The black gelding was too headstrong for a kid.

"What's a horse boss?"

"That means if Jet doesn't think you can control him, Jet does whatever he wants." That had been why she'd been able to purchase the gelding so cheap. He'd been too much horse for the elderly rancher she'd worked for a few years back.

Ford was silent for a while before asking, "Could Dad ride him?"

"Maybe. Your dad was a good rider when we were kids." Although he'd been more interested in riding the range of nearby government land while Lily had been absorbed by roping contests. But she'd never been able to afford a quality roping horse to do more than win local competitions.

Lily parked on Main Street and they entered Clementine Coffee Roasters. It was a small shop with a few mismatched tables and chairs for customers. A large Christmas tree sat in front of the window decorated with white crocheted snowflakes, silver garland and soft twinkle lights. There was a short line of cowboys waiting to order, including one Lily recognized.

With Ford intent on admiring the Christmas tree near the front window, Lily greeted the man she'd shared nachos with on Saturday night with a tap on the shoulder and a smile. "Hey, Zane."

"Lily." Zane's face lit up. "I was thinking about you earlier."

"Really?" Despite Lily's best intentions to stay in the friend zone, her smile widened. "Did you think of me because your mother sent you more Christmas cards?"

"No." Zane ordered a cup of coffee. Large, black and with a shot of espresso. He paid and moved to one side, allowing Lily access to the barista behind the cash register.

"One small hot chocolate, extra whip, extra marshmallows," she said.

Zane released a long, slow whistle. "That's going to get you more wired than my shot of espresso."

"It's for my nephew." Cheeks heating, Lily gestured to Ford before paying.

"Sure it is." Zane smiled mischievously. Sobering, he produced what looked like something official from his back pocket. "I got your name added to the guest list for the Twelve Parties of Christmas. I was going to swing by Beau's office later. This is the invitation with the dates, times and themes for each but..."

"Black coffee with a shot." The barista handed Zane his coffee.

"But?" Lily prompted Zane.

"Let's sit." Zane led Lily to a table, sat down, but didn't say more. He glanced toward the Christmas tree where Ford was singing softly to himself as he adjusted a lace star. "What's your nephew's name?"

"Bufford. But we call him Ford."

"*Bufford?*" Zane rubbed the stubble on his chin. "That's a mouthful."

"It's a tradition in my father's family to have a name that's a throwback to olden days and a nickname that isn't." She hurried to provide examples. "Beauregard is Beau. My dad was Hutchinson but most folks called him Sonny. And the new baby is Cadence. Cady for short."

"And Lily is short for…"

"Lily. It says Lily on my birth certificate." A fact that only reinforced that she wasn't a Smith, that Sonny had known she was Rowdy's child and had insisted her name didn't fit the Smith tradition.

Zane frowned. "Not Lillian or Elizabeth or…"

"Just plain old Lily." Lily clung to her smile, thinking of Rowdy and his own personal brand of unwelcome. She didn't plan on taking a DNA test. What was the use of that when she didn't plan on trying to have a relationship with him?

"You're not plain old anything," Zane said in a low voice, looking serious.

Lily's cheeks began heating again. This wouldn't do. They were friends. She tugged her cowboy hat brim lower. If they'd been working on a ranch together, she'd have formed some excuse to work elsewhere. But there was no graceful way to exit after that compliment since Ford's drink wasn't up yet.

Zane cleared his throat. "I was wondering if you'd do me a favor." He rubbed a hand around the back of his neck. "I want to—"

"Hot chocolate. Double whip. Double marshmallows," the barista called out.

"That's mine!" Ford ran to the counter, thanked the barista, then turned. "Auntie, we've gotta roll. We're going horseback riding when I finish this."

Zane chuckled.

And her nephew pulled Lily out of the coffee

shop before Zane had a chance to say anything more than, "*Goodbye*."

Leaving her with no idea what he wanted to talk to her about.

"JET'S HOOVES ARE too heavy." Ford gave up trying to clean the black gelding's hooves, which was a condition of him earning a ride on Jet.

A condition Lily had known Ford wouldn't meet. She held Jet's lead rope and stroked her horse's velvety nose.

"Auntie, why can't you groom him, saddle him and let me ride him?" Ford leaned against Jet's front leg. "Let me ride him and I'll get you the best Christmas present ever."

Lily crossed her arms and set her expression on negative.

Before Ford could restate his plea, Jet lifted his front leg, backing away from Ford without warning, which meant—

"*Ay-yee!*" Ford tumbled to the ground on his backside, expression a cross between fear and verge of tears. "What did Jet do that for?"

Jet blew a raspberry, not helping Ford's mood.

"Jet, bad horse." With a poor attempt at a growl, Ford pushed himself upright.

"What did you expect?" Lily helped her nephew, brushing dirt off his backside. "I told you. Jet is a horse boss. If you were the boss, would you let anyone lean on you?"

"No. But still…" Ford put his hands on his hips,

hinged his torso forward and repeated, "That wasn't nice, Jet."

The big black gelding ignored him.

Mouse ambled to Ford's side. The sweet, little brown pony rubbed her cheek against Ford's shoulder the way a cat might rub against its favorite person, over and over.

Ford slung an arm over her neck. "Mouse would never do that to me." He dug in his pocket for a baby carrot. Then he held another toward Jet.

"Where'd you get those carrots, Ford?" Lily asked suspiciously.

"From my lunch box."

Lily should have known. She'd packed his lunch box this morning. "Did you eat any?"

"No. I don't like carrots."

Jet slowly extended his neck toward the boy and gummed the baby carrot from Ford's hand.

"He likes me," Ford crowed. "That means he'll let me ride him, Auntie."

"No. That means he likes carrots." Lily hurried to add, "I've found that friendship with a horse isn't the same as proving you're a horseman worthy of a ride on a horse boss."

Just like she'd found friendship with a cowboy didn't mean deeper feelings would bloom on his part. It was best to set your expectations realistically from the start.

Her heart was safer that way.

CHAPTER SIX

ON TUESDAY AFTERNOON, Zane finished tying a Christmas tree to the top of an ancient gray sedan, then moved toward the driver's window. "You're ready to go, Mrs. Carter." She'd been his kindergarten teacher. "Are you sure you have help getting the tree inside your house?"

"My grandson promised he'd swing by. Here's a little something for your trouble, dear." Mrs. Carter handed him a wrapped red peppermint. "Merry Christmas!"

"Merry Christmas." Smiling wryly, Zane unwrapped his candy and dropped his tip into his mouth.

Working the Christmas tree lot for the Holly Scouts was like solving a unique puzzle for each customer. They wanted a pretty tree for a designated spot in their house while also taking into consideration what would fit in or atop their vehicle at a price that wouldn't break the bank.

Kept a man on his toes.

Not to mention, sap on his gloves, checked shirt, vest jacket and cheek, by the feel of it.

The tree operation was located in a corner of the grocery store's parking lot. Christmas music played from beneath the pop-up awning, which sheltered a table and two canvas camp chairs. Zane had assumed he'd be sitting beneath that awning and fighting boredom on this sunny school day afternoon, but there'd been a steady stream of customers. He'd been moving nonstop.

Thankfully, none of his tree-shopping customers had been sent his way by his mothers.

And while he'd held up trees and pounded their trunks onto the pavement at several tree buyers' requests, Zane had thought about Lily and the proposition he'd been unable to present yesterday—*helping him find and catch Solomon.*

Several trucks turned into the parking lot and came to a stop nearby. Children spilled out, running toward the tree lot and chattering excitedly.

"School's out," his coworker Izzy Powell announced. She was a parent of a Holly Scout and engaged to Done Roamin' Ranch foreman Chandler. They were getting married this February. "It'll get busier now."

"Busier?" Zane hadn't had a chance to get a drink of water since he'd arrived two hours ago.

"Auntie, I want the biggest tree on the planet!" A small cowboy raced past Zane.

"Ford, I don't think the biggest tree on the planet will fit in your house."

That familiar female voice had Zane turning. And smiling. "I was just thinking about you."

Lily stopped a few feet away and gave Zane a guarded look that wasn't encouraging. "You were thinking about me? Again today? Why?"

"Auntie!" Ford called, standing at the base of what had to be a fourteen-foot pine. "I found our tree!"

"Oh. Not that one, Ford." Lily excused herself and hurried over to attempt to head off trouble.

"Hey, Zane. This is a strange question but do you flock trees here?" It was Coronet from the Buffalo Diner. "I saw a pink-flocked tree on TV the other night and now I'm fancying one for the diner."

"We do flock trees." Or so Zane had been told. "Let me ask Izzy if we have pink flocking."

"Yes." Izzy appeared from between the tree aisles, apparently having heard Coronet. "We have flocking in many colors, Coronet. We do charge extra, though."

"Sometimes, the joy brought by getting just what you want is worth that extra penny or two." Coronet smiled dreamily at the big tree Ford had been eyeing, not that it would fit in her diner, either. "When I find the right tree, I'll let you know."

"I've never flocked a tree before," Zane admitted to Izzy.

"Same," Izzy said, gathering her white-blond hair behind her neck. "But they told me it's like applying hair spray. You cover everything. How hard could it be?"

Zane wasn't consoled. He had no experience with hair spray.

"The other Holly Scout mothers are supposed to be here soon," Izzy told him. "Hang in there." She hurried off to help the town doctor select a tree.

"We only have room for a small tree this year, honey," Willa Tarkenton said to her little girl, while holding the scraggliest, smallest tree on the lot—a three-footer. It had been marked down to five dollars.

"Mama, small doesn't mean tiny." Her little girl held on to a branch of a fuller, four-foot tree. The tree she held was twenty dollars. All the trees had been donated and were priced to be affordable.

Willa looked stricken. She had been through a nasty divorce this year and rumor had it that she was struggling to make ends meet.

Without thinking, Zane moved to stand next to the four-foot tree. "There's a special on this tree, Willa. It's only five dollars." He'd cover the extra fifteen.

Willa looked as if she wanted to refuse but her little girl danced around with the tree. Shaking her head, Willa caught Zane's gaze and mouthed the words, "*Thank you*," before handing over a five-dollar bill.

"Do you need help getting it in your car?" Zane asked.

"No. We walked over. We're staying at the Sunny Acres." Which was just a block away, a small motel used mostly as transitional housing for those in need. Willa recovered somewhat to smile. "It sounds like a really nice retirement home, doesn't it?"

"We live in a clubhouse," her little girl piped up. "It's cute."

"I live in a bunkhouse. I bet it's not as cute as yours." Zane walked them out. And then he headed down the tree aisle where he'd last seen Lily and Ford.

"That tree is no good, Auntie." Ford wandered farther down the aisle. "The tree has to be taller than you."

"That's not what your mother said." But Lily didn't sound as steadfast as she might have. "Why on earth do you want a really tall tree?"

Ford stopped in front of another big fir. "Because Grandma and Grandpa Smith always had a ginormous tree. And since they aren't here anymore, we should get a tree they'd like."

"*Oh*," Lily said in a small voice.

Zane was reminded that Lily's parents had died this year. He removed one of his work gloves as he approached, then rubbed a hand commensurately across Lily's back before tugging on his glove again. "Ford, that's the best reason I've heard yet for buying a larger tree than planned."

"It is, isn't it?" Lily said in a faraway voice. "My parents loved Christmas." She looked into Zane's eyes. For once, her brown gaze was unsteady.

Zane had the strongest urge to rub Lily's back a second time and reassure her that everything would be all right.

She managed a smile for him. "My parents would have loved the Twelve Parties of Christmas. They wouldn't even have needed the grand-prize drawing as an enticement to attend."

Before he could answer, a feminine voice called out, "There he is! Santa's helper."

Zane turned to look for Santa's elf but all he saw was a well-dressed cowgirl bearing down on him. She carried a large, fancy leather purse in the crook of her arm and wore a smile that implied she'd just won something special. Simply by finding him?

Oh, my mothers!

Zane gritted his teeth.

"Zane, I was told that you could help me pick out the perfect tree." Tawny Marable blinked rapidly at him, a coy grin on her face, which somehow managed to throw him off.

Her lashes were so long. And so thick. He was surprised Tawny could open her eyes at all.

Zane managed to collect himself enough to say, "Define *perfect*."

"Well," Tawny said smoothly. "It has to be large enough to make a statement but not so large that it's a fire hazard when I have a date in front of my fireplace."

"You make dates with your fireplace?" Ford asked, seemingly equally flabbergasted by Tawny.

"I meant that I don't want my tree to catch fire." She leaned closer to Zane. "Although my date should emanate heat *and* feel it, too."

Oh, I feel the heat. And it's telling me to hightail it out of the kitchen before I get burned.

"You'll be wanting a skinny tree." Zane led Tawny away from Lily and Ford. "We've got several options over here for you to choose from." And while he patiently held up tree after tree, another wave of customers flooded the lot.

Females. Every one.

And every one of them headed his way.

"Zane, thank you for the most romantic gesture I've had since my prom-posal." A young blonde who looked barely beyond her prom years showed Zane a small, red felt heart with three words stitched on it: *Return to Sender*.

Uh-oh.

"Or, it would have been romantic if I'd been the only one he sent this heart to," said another woman, frowning and clenching a similar red felt heart.

"I thought I was the only one who got this," said a third, hanging her felt heart on the branch of a fir tree. "It came in the mail with instructions to return it to you. XO. XO."

"What are all those cowgirls doing with Zane, Auntie?" Ford scampered up to the young prom princess. "Hi, cousin Ava. What are you doing here?"

"Hey, Ford." The young woman beamed at Ford. And then at Zane. "I'm…shopping."

"Oh, hey, Ava. Good to see you again." Lily appeared at Zane's side, hefting a seven-foot tree. Without warning, she stumbled into him, biting back a smile that let Zane know her clumsiness was an act. "Oops. This tree is just too heavy for me, Zane. Can you carry it to my truck?"

My hero.

"Of course." Trying not to smile, Zane mumbled his excuses to the women with felt hearts and then carried Lily's tree out of the lot. He deposited their Christmas tree in her truck bed. "Thanks for the rescue, Lily. I can't believe my mothers would do such a thing."

"Oh, I can. And no need to thank me. As friends, I know you'd do the same for me." Lily handed him cash for the tree, looking amused. "Aren't your mamas running out of single cowgirls in Clementine?"

"I wish." Zane smiled at Lily, preparing to ask her about joining him to hunt for Solomon.

"Is Zane gonna marry cousin Ava?" Ford interrupted before Zane got a word out. He climbed up on the truck's rear bumper with the speed and agility of a squirrel. "Ava's staring at him the way Mommy stares at Daddy sometimes."

Zane glanced back. Sure enough, Ava was fixated on him, smiling dreamily. "I'm too old for her."

Lily laughed. "You don't even know how old she is."

"I don't need an exact figure to know I'm too old for her." She looked to be barely out of high school.

"Auntie, we have to hurry up home." Ford jumped to the ground and took hold of Lily's hand. "This tree needs water and I need one of those chocolate chip cookies you baked yesterday."

"Just one?" Lily teased her nephew.

"Auntie," Ford said in a voice as serious as Zane had ever heard the kid use. "No one can eat just one of your cookies."

"You're just saying that so you can have two," Lily countered, smiling broadly.

Her smile was infectious. Zane was smiling, too.

"Auntie, I'll have three cookies," Ford bargained, holding up three fingers. "Please and thank you to my favorite aunt ever."

"You're his only aunt, aren't you?" Zane asked between chuckles.

"Yep. Sorry we can't stick around to protect you any longer, Zane." Lily grinned wider. "We've got a tree to water and cookies to eat. But I'm sure you'll be fine on your own."

Zane assured her he would be.

As they drove away, Zane realized he'd missed his chance to ask Lily to join him on the search for Solomon.

When Lily and Ford arrived back at the house with the Christmas tree, Nora had managed to clear an area in front of the living room window and placed the tree stand on the floor.

"Mom! You'll never guess what happened to Auntie's cowboy." Ford removed his boots in the foyer, letting them clatter to the floor. "He had all his hearts returned to him, even by Ava."

"Auntie's cowboy?" Nora sat in the wooden rocking chair with Cady in her arms. But her attention was riveted on Lily, who could feel the weight of her sister-in-law's inquisitive gaze.

"Zane isn't *my* cowboy," Lily clarified, resting the tree just inside the door so she could remove her boots and hat.

"Zane *is* your cowboy, Auntie. We see him everywhere. At the coffee place. At the Christmas tree lot. I bet we see him again tomorrow after school." Ford ran into the kitchen and opened the cookie tin. "I'm having my three cookies now."

"Three cookies?" Nora raised her slender brows.

"Yes. Three cookies. Your kid is one heck of a negotiator," Lily said, carrying the tree toward the tree stand. The top scraped the ceiling. "Even Zane said so."

"Am I going to have to call Beau to get rid of your cowboy stalker?" Nora teased.

"Zane isn't a stalker." Lily managed to get the base of the tree into the red metal stand. "Nora, I need an assist to lock this tree in place."

Nora carefully laid the baby on a blanket on the floor before coming over to help.

When she was done, both women stepped back to admire the tree.

"It's pretty but… I thought we were getting a small tree," Nora said.

"Ford thought different."

"Ah." Nora scooped the baby up. "That's like the time I sent Beau and Ford to the store for a small container of ice cream and they returned with three large cartons, each a different flavor."

"Got to hand it to your son. He lives life large." Lily turned the tree a bit to the right so that its fullest branches were facing the room. "Where are your lights and decorations?"

"In the garage." Nora shifted the baby to her shoulder, immediately eliciting a burp. "But I'll have Beau bring them in later. In my family, we decorate the tree a little each day. Tomorrow, we'll put on lights and the star. The next day garland. And finally, all the ornaments. I like to stretch out my holiday."

Whereas Lily's parents had dived in headfirst, putting their tree, outdoor lights and other decorations up before Thanksgiving. The last few years, Lily hadn't made it home in time to help decorate. Regrets clogged her throat. She would have done so many things differently if she'd known…

"Cousin Ava is here." Ford came to stand at the front window near Lily, eating a chocolate chip cookie while a small, yellow sedan pulled into the driveway. "We saw her at the Christmas tree lot but she didn't buy a tree from Zane, like we did."

"How do you know that? Her tree could be small and in her trunk." Lily enjoyed teasing Ford.

He rolled his eyes. "She has a no-mess rule, Auntie."

"In her car?"

Ford shrugged. "About everything."

"Did Ava say she was stopping by when you saw her earlier?" Nora returned to the rocking chair. "I haven't seen or heard from her in months."

"Do you want me to tell her to go?" Lily moved toward the door. Ava was an odd duck and Nora might not be in the mood for her.

"No," Nora said quickly, almost too kindly. "It's good to see family, isn't it, Ford?"

"I guess." Ford shrugged.

Ava breezed in without knocking, all smiles and heavy perfume. She hugged Lily and Nora. She snuggled Cady—until the baby spit up. She wanted to snuggle Ford—but only after he'd cleaned melted chocolate from his fingers and face. And then Ava settled on the couch and fixed Lily with a no-escaping stare. "Tell me about Zane. Did you get a felt heart from his mamas, too?"

"Oh. No," Lily was quick to say. "I've never met his mamas. I've only just met Zane. He's not my type."

Or more accurately, I'm not his.

"What is your type?" Nora said softly, having rocked the baby back to sleep.

Ford was crawling beneath the Christmas tree, pausing occasionally to look up through its branches. "Her type is Zane."

"*Ford*," Lily whispered a warning.

"You have nice teeth," Ava said to Lily out of the blue.

"Thank you?" Lily stopped smiling and glanced at her sister-in-law for clarification.

"Ava just graduated from dental hygienist school," Nora explained.

"I like teeth. I'm ahead of most of my friends on the adult track," Ava said proudly. "They're either still mucking about with part-time jobs or away at college. It's not surprising that I'm ready to find a man and get a family started. I'm only nineteen but I'm an old soul."

Nora's expression questioned that last statement.

"What's an old soul?" Ford wiggled out from under the tree. "Do old souls cry after riding roller coasters? Spill nail paints on the couch when they babysit me? Or kiss boys underneath the bleachers at the rodeo?"

Ava frowned at him.

"That's a lot to unpack, Ford," Lily said, trying not to smile.

"Not to mention, I was never told about spilled nail polish," Nora murmured, staring at Cady instead of Ava.

But Ford paid no one any mind. "I'm *not* an old soul. I love roller coasters, don't like to paint anything and you won't catch me kissing girls. *Ever.*"

"*Ford*," Ava said in a put-upon voice that truly did sound like an old soul. An impatient one at that. "I didn't realize I was an old soul until recently. People like me are more introspective and mature. We see what others don't." Ava sought out Lily's gaze while visibly putting on her old-soul composure, which came across closer to Rowdy's disapproving countenance than Lily thought Ava might have wanted. "I think Zane likes you, Lily."

Lily laughed, shaking her head. "I don't think Zane likes me the way you think he does." But there was the way he'd told her—*twice*—that he'd been thinking about her. And the way he'd started to ask her something—*twice*—only to be interrupted by Ford.

"I like Zane. And I think he likes me." Ford rolled onto his back and laced his fingers behind his head as he stared at the ceiling. "Does Zane have a horse? Do you think I could ride his horse? Cuz you won't let me ride yours, Auntie."

"Seriously, Lily," Ava said in that controlled, superior way of hers. "There are so many pretty women chasing after Zane and he left them to help you with your Christmas tree."

"We're friends," Lily insisted, albeit gently. "And I think he's vowed not to date anyone his mamas send after him. I get the feeling he doesn't like to be chased."

"Oh? That puts a new light on things." Ava sounded pleased. She studied Lily's face long enough to count Lily's freckles, before adding, "We should be friends."

Lily and Nora exchanged glances.

Lily bet her sister-in-law was thinking the same thing Lily was: *This friendship feels as if it comes with strings attached.*

The same way Rowdy's demand of parentage did.

"Well?" Ava prompted.

"We should try being friends," Lily said carefully, if only to placate the teen.

CHAPTER SEVEN

First Party of Christmas:
Ugly Boots, Sweaters and Ties
Hosted by: Rowland Ranch

THE FIRST OF the Twelve Parties of Christmas was being held in the Rowland Ranch's newly built barn. Ellie Rowland-Oakley and her husband, Tate, raised sheep and alpaca, the latter of which were proving to be highly profitable and, along with Ellie's catering business, were funding the newly married couple's ranch expansion.

Rumor had it that Tate had seen the white stallion somewhere on the Rowland Ranch this week. His spread bordered a stretch of rear acreage of the Done Roamin' Ranch. Zane wanted to ask Tate about the sighting. And tonight, he was determined to ask Lily if she wanted to ride along with him to capture Solomon.

Zane parked along the lane that led to the Rowland Ranch proper and got out with a ringing of jingle bells from his snow-white sweater.

He grabbed the tin of cookies Mama Mary had baked for the potluck.

His was one of many trucks parked along the lane. The stars were out and shining in the black-velvet sky above him. Ahead of Zane, the main ranch buildings were outlined in blinking red and green lights. Loud holiday music blended with many voices and was interspersed with laughter.

Zane used to look forward to parties. To dancing and flirting and letting nature take its course for the brief time attraction lasted. But he knew his two mamas were inside that party. Nature wasn't going to take its course tonight. His mamas were.

His sweater bells rang softly.

Was it too much to hope that the ugly sweater would be a put-off to women?

The bright white sweater he wore was covered in white ribbons that were each tied to round bells of various sizes. He sounded like Santa's sleigh every time he moved. And he looked like a lounge singer when he raised his arms, as the ribbons and bells dangled a foot below his arms. He didn't appear to be a catch by any means. More like a poor man's Elvis impersonator.

A truck pulled up behind Zane and a pair of former Done Roamin' Ranch cowboys hopped out.

"Oh, this is fitting." Fletcher Sunday carried a six-pack of soda. He wore a white dress shirt with a black bolo tie. It wasn't until he came closer that Zane realized Fletcher's tie clasp was a big, gaudy gold cowboy hat and the tie ends were oversize, equally homely gold boots. "Three single cowboys headed into a party full of single cowgirls. I can't wait for the dancing to start."

"I'm looking forward to the food." Calvin Cowser came around from the passenger side of the truck. He carried a bottle of soda water and wore a black Christmas sweater with stars that twinkled. "And if there happens to be mistletoe... Well, I'll tell whatever pretty cowgirl is closest that it was fate we ended up beneath it."

Zane laughed, feeling a bit relieved. Assuming his mothers were going to ambush him with single ladies was paranoia talking. There'd be plenty of single women at the party but plenty of single men, as well.

The trio walked toward the barn, Zane's sweater jingling all the way.

"If we lose Zane, all we have to do is listen," Fletcher teased. "If he's moving, he sounds like the school janitor carrying his room keys."

Something clanked on the lane.

"You lost one." Calvin picked up a bell and ribbon from the dirt and handed it to Zane. "One less bell isn't a bad thing."

"I'm hoping it won't hinder my chances at winning a prize for the best ugly sweater." Zane tucked the bell into his pocket, not that he planned to fix the sweater or wear it again, for that matter. But littering was a no-no.

They passed the central ranch house where couples were dropping off kids. He wondered if Ford was inside. The kid was a dynamo and brought a smile to Zane's face whenever he came to mind, same as his favorite aunt, Lily. Zane wouldn't mind stopping to say howdy.

Finally, the men reached the barn. A country version of "Happy Holidays" was playing. It was loud enough to cover the jingle of Zane's bells.

Or so he hoped.

"Merry Christmas, boys." Mama Mary greeted each of them to the right of the door with a small candy cane. She wore blue jeans, boots, a fancy green cowboy hat and a tan sweatshirt with Santa sunning himself on a tropical island.

"Thank you for coming. This is your grand-prize entry." On the left-hand side of the doors, Zane's biological mother wore a green-fringed sweater that looked like a decorated Christmas tree. The fringed hem dipped below her waist and Zane noticed the long, flowing white skirt she wore. She gave Fletcher and Calvin each a raffle ticket to fill out with their names and then drop them into a very large glass pitcher. She patted Zane on the back. "Move along, Zane. You don't want to win the grand prize."

"I do." With a ringing of bells, Zane took a ticket and filled it out with his name, then dropped it into the glass pitcher, earning a smirk from his mother.

"Let him choose, Rita," Mama Mary said gently.

After a moment, Zane's biological mama nodded.

Entries made, the men proceeded to the tables where food and drinks were being dropped off. Zane set his cookie tin on the table between a fir bough and a bowl of red-and-white-frosted cupcakes, then he removed the lid.

Someone tapped Zane's shoulder.

He turned, smiling guardedly at the cowgirl in front of him. "Hey, Nia."

"Merry Christmas." She wore a shimmery teal blouse over a pair of powder blue jeans. No ugly Christmas sweater for her. Her half boots were high-heeled, gray and glittery, not of the ugly variety, either. Nia held up a small silver bell attached to a bright white ribbon. "You dropped this."

"Thanks." Zane shoved it into his jeans pocket with the bell that had dropped on the lane.

"I haven't seen you in a long, long time." Nia smiled instead of moving on. Normally, she didn't give Zane the time of day. "Haven't seen you at the Buckboard lately. Are you dating anyone special?"

Uh-oh.

"Still single. Still sitting at the bar at the Buckboard solo, which is probably why you haven't seen me." Zane tucked his hands in his back pockets. A beribboned bell attached to his elbow dropped to the ground. Zane bent to pick it up, shoving it into the pocket with the other bells. "How about you? I heard you were married."

"Married. Divorced. Just ended another relationship." Nia tilted her head, still smiling at Zane as if trying to decide her level of interest. "I remember you tagging along with the older Done Roamin' Ranch boys in school. You were cute back then and you're even cuter now."

Feeling trapped, Zane shifted his feet, creating a jingle of bells barely audible above the music.

Thankfully, another cowgirl joined them, one who also hadn't embraced the ugly sweater, boots or tie theme. She wore a burgundy velvet dress and dangled a jingle bell by its ribbon. "Zane, is this yours? I found it by the door."

By the door? Where the mamas greeted me? Double uh-oh.

A suspicion began to build in Zane's head, even as tension built in his chest. While Nia and Enid made small talk, Zane tucked the latest dropped bell in his pocket, gaze seeking out his troublemaking mothers.

Were they handing out bells along with candy canes and raffle tickets to single ladies? He couldn't tell.

Another cowgirl joined their circle, returning another one of Zane's jingle bells. She greeted Nia and Enid. Like the other two women, Kiki wore nothing ugly that would win her a prize at the party. Her black pantsuit was elegant, as were her fancy black boots.

Zane sent a dark look toward his mothers, who didn't so much as look his way.

Guilty, as charged.

The three women circling him stopped chit-chatting and stared at Zane expectantly, as if it was his turn to speak. Or decide a course of action.

Triple uh-oh.

"Um…" Zane laughed nervously. Another bell dropped, bouncing off the top of his brown boot. "I'm shedding worse than a barn cat on the first warm day of spring." He tried to make a joke, shaking his arms like a scarecrow, hoping his dorkiness would scare them off. Two more bells dropped to the ground. He bent to scoop all the bells up.

"Look, there's Willa," Nia said, while he was gathering bells. "I heard the bank evicted her last week."

"It wasn't her fault," Enid added as Zane got to his feet. "Her deadbeat ex never pays child support or comes to visit his daughter."

"Thank goodness for the county's transition housing," Kiki commented. "I hope Willa wins the grand prize on Christmas Day. She needs a roof over her head."

All three women were nodding as they looked across the dance floor toward Willa.

Zane didn't nod. Sure, he felt selfish for disagreeing but he wanted his home back.

A tall cowgirl chuckled as she walked past, catching Zane's eye and murmuring, "*Bells?*"

Lily.

The tension in Zane's chest eased.

"Excuse me, ladies. I need to talk to that cowgirl about a horse." *Solomon.* Zane strode after Lily, who stopped at the punch bowl to get a drink.

She wore a black sweater with pink cats wearing Santa hats on the front, blue jeans, that worn brown cowboy hat and a truly ugly pair of black-and-white-checked cowboy boots. She smiled at Zane when he joined her, clearly amused. "I should have known I could count on you for entertainment. Your sweater is like a waterfall of—"

Clunk-clunk. Another bell fell to the floor.

"—jingle bells." Lily's grin widened, deepening her dimples and highlighting those bold freckles of hers. She bent to retrieve the bell, holding the white ribbon and giving it a little shake. *Ding-a-ling-a-ling!* "Is this the work of your mamas?"

Zane rolled his eyes. "Of course it is."

"You have to admire their determination. Not to mention, their creativity." Lily reached over, grabbed hold of a white ribbon on his sweater and gave it a gentle tug.

The ribbon easily popped out of the white weave.

Zane made a frustrated noise.

Lily laughed, holding up both bells. "They threaded the ribbon through the sweater and tied a little knot on the end. It wouldn't take much to pluck you like a goose for Christmas." She laughed again. "The only thing they could have done better was to write your phone number on the ribbon."

"Yikes. Don't give them any more ideas."

The young blond cowgirl who'd referenced a prom-posal yesterday at the Christmas tree lot approached. She wore a gold sweater dress and gold cowboy boots with very high heels. And, of course, she carried a bell attached to a white ribbon.

"Incoming," Zane warned Lily. He needn't have bothered.

"Hi, Ava." Lily welcomed Ford's cousin. "You look very pretty tonight. Doesn't she, Zane?"

He nodded, not wanting to encourage Ava with words.

"Have you danced yet, Lily?" Ava's question was directed toward Lily but her sparkling smile was aimed at Zane.

Zane grunted.

"Hey, Ava." A slim cowboy who looked to be the same age as Ava eased into their group. He wore a simple blue holiday sweater with snowflakes across his chest. "I haven't seen you in forever."

"Hey, Stu." Ava didn't take her eyes off Zane.

Stu tipped his cowboy hat back, rubbing the top of his forehead and looking uneasy. "I was hoping we could have a dance, Ava. For old times?"

Ava shrugged, her shoulders stiff.

Lily leaned closer to Zane and whispered in his ear, "Old times probably means when she kissed Stu under the rodeo bleachers. That's what Ford told me."

Zane choked back a laugh, earning a few back slaps from Lily. "I'm good." If only he could stop the urge to laugh.

Ava waved a hand to snag Lily's attention. "I love to dance, don't you, Lily?" But again, Ava only had eyes for Zane.

"And I'm ready to take you for a whirl," Stu said in a louder voice.

Ava turned to Stu with a composure that belied her age. "I'm talking to my friends, Stu."

"Oh." Stu's cheeks turned beet red. "Sure." He disappeared in the crowd.

"Sorry for the interruption." Ava clasped her hands over her abdomen, like the church ladies who manned the snack table after church service. "We were talking about dancing. I love it. How about you two?"

"The world is better off with me only dancing in the privacy of my room," Lily deadpanned.

"You can't two-step at home by yourself," Zane said, feigning outrage. "You need a partner."

"Who said I was two-stepping at home?" Lily released a self-deprecating laugh. "I'm talking line dancing. Without a partner, I'm like a bull in a china shop, taking out everything in my path when I miss a turn."

"We're going to have to two-step now. Just so I

can verify those statements, Lily." Zane held out his hand toward Lily. "And when the line dancing starts, we'll do that, too."

Lily didn't take his hand. She glanced at Ava. "Maybe you should take a spin on the dance floor with someone more coordinated than me, Zane."

"I'd love to," Ava said eagerly.

A woman headed toward them. A woman wearing a fancy dress and holding another jingle bell.

Feeling stalked, Zane blurted, "No offense, Ava, but Lily did throw down a challenge and now she's coming with me to the dance floor." He took Lily by the hand and led her into the center of the barn, not waiting for Ava's reply.

The opening guitar chords of "Jingle Bell Rock" filled the air.

Zane took Lily into his arms and began to dance. Only then did he realize several odd facts.

Lily fit into his arms perfectly. She was the right height, the right build and held herself just the right way—not too close, not too far away. She smelled like a combination of freshly bathed baby and Christmas tree, two aromas he'd never have admitted before this moment as being appealing.

And then, he realized something else. "You're a good dancer."

"When I confessed my lack of skill, it was with line dancing, remember?" Lily's brown eyes were even with his. They sparkled with amusement but her tone was a scold. "Ava really wanted to dance with you."

"That's not going to happen," Zane assured her. "I'm at least ten years older than she is."

"She claims she's an old soul." Lily's eyes were still sparkling.

"If I were to dance with her or show any interest beyond friendship," he said crisply, "people would claim I'm a dirty old man."

Lily laughed.

"If she wants to dance, Stu is her man."

"She doesn't want Stu," Lily said with a nod toward Zane.

Zane chose to ignore her. "Besides, now that we're on the dance floor, I'm safe from the Bell Squad." He gestured toward the refreshment table where they'd left Ava. Two women had joined Ava and were watching them while holding beribboned bells. "Have you heard the legend of Solomon?"

Lily's brow furrowed. "Solomon's mines?"

"No. Solomon is a wild white horse in the area. A stallion. Rumor has it he was too much horse for his owner and jumped a fence to get away. He's been roaming around this county and the next for as long as I can remember. No one can catch him."

His mothers beamed at them.

A bell fell from Zane's sweater. Not wanting to let go of Lily, Zane kicked it toward the wall so that no one would trip on it and get hurt.

"Why do I have a feeling that you want to catch him?"

"Because you're a mind reader." Zane grinned. "Look. I've been wanting to ask—"

"Shoot. I didn't think he'd be here." Lily spun Zane around and danced him toward the far corner of the dance floor.

"Who? Which he?" Zane craned his neck, trying to spot the man who'd upset Lily. "Did someone make a pass at you?" Deep inside Zane, something leaped up, ready for defensive action.

"Don't turn this into something dramatic." Lily subtly fought Zane's efforts to spin her around. "Can we just dance without talking for a minute?"

"Sure." Zane used that time to scan the ever-increasing crowd but none of the cowboys he knew were single seemed to be fixated on Lily.

The music ended. Zane and Lily stopped dancing and stared at each other.

Not romantically, thank goodness. Because that would be just as bad as the jingle bell seekers. Not that he didn't find Lily attractive and intriguing.

No. They stared at each other with an understanding. Of what, Zane had no idea. He hadn't known her long. Truth be told, he didn't know her well at all. But Zane was sure that she'd be a steadfast friend, come what may. He liked that about her.

The music started again. *It's the Most Wonderful Time of the Year.*

"We should get a lemonade while I pitch you my idea." Jingling, Zane took Lily by the arm and led her to the table with drinks. He poured her a glass of lemonade, and then another for himself.

"Lily." A gruff voice came from behind him.

Zane turned, surprised to find Rowdy Brown. He was the man who'd destroyed Zane's family when he'd snapped up their ranch. Zane scowled. "What do you want?"

Rowdy waved Zane aside. "Lily, we have unfinished business."

"As far as I'm concerned, we don't," Lily said, looking pale.

That was all Zane needed to become her knight in shining armor. "Yes, over and done with." Zane led Lily away from the old man. "I hate that guy."

"Why?"

"Other than the fact that he's Scrooge reincarnated? Because he stole my family's ranch." Zane's gut clenched. "Things snowballed after that. My parents divorced. My mom moved me to Tulsa. I ran away, hitchhiked back here to find my dad but he was gone and I ended up in foster care. Never heard from him again." There was so much more to the story but now wasn't the time for sad tales.

"So... Rowdy has a history of breaking up families?" Lily gnawed on her lower lip.

"Yeah. Stay away from him. Far, far away from him."

She nodded.

CHAPTER EIGHT

"WHAT'S THIS I hear about you and Zane Duvall dating?"

Beau and Lily were walking down the lane away from the party. Nora was ahead of them, carrying the baby, with Ford beside her. The lane was lit by all the holiday lights.

"Moving kinda fast, aren't we?" Beau asked Lily in a low voice.

"Beau…" Lily wrapped her coat tighter around her, still unsettled by Rowdy saying they had unfinished business. Not even winning a pair of movie tickets for wearing Nora's ugly boots had lifted her spirits. "I'm twenty-nine. I don't have a curfew and you have no right to grill me about men. Besides, we're not dating. Zane and I are friends."

There had been a moment just as they'd started dancing when she'd imagined Zane saw her as more than a friend. But that moment was short-lived. That was good. Great, even. He wasn't the right man for her. She'd known that from their first meeting.

"Lily," Beau began.

But, at the same time, another voice cut through the night uttering her name as well, "*Lily.*"

She turned, recognizing the gravelly voice—*Rowdy's*.

When Beau would have stepped in front of her, Lily held him back. "We can't run from this."

Rowdy's gait was stiff. He didn't have his cane. That didn't slow him down. But he did pause a few feet away from them to steady himself on someone's tailgate. "We still have things to discuss."

Her brother scoffed.

"Rowdy, I think you're confused because I've told you I'm done with our conversation," Lily said in a calm voice.

Rowdy smacked his lips. "Sometimes, young lady, you have to be persistent to get what you want."

"Beau? Can you unlock the truck, please? It's getting cold," Nora called from the end of the lane.

"Yes, honey. Let's go, Lily." Beau turned away, heading toward his family.

Lily stayed put, facing an unwanted branch of her family. "I'll catch up. I know what it is to really want something, so I'll hear what Rowdy has to say."

"I don't have much to say other than this." Rowdy tottered closer, holding out a small white box. "Take the DNA test."

Lily kept her hands in her jacket pockets. "Why?"

"Because…" Rowdy's stance became solid. Certain. But his voice… His voice was pitted with vulnerability. "Because I loved Dawnice. Because the fact that she gave birth to you means on some level that she loved me, too."

Just not as much as she loved Dad.

"And that means…" Lily prompted, still uncertain what Rowdy really wanted from her or if she wanted anything to do with him.

"Take the test." Rowdy thrust the box forward. "Don't make me ask again."

"*Please?*" she suggested.

"Please," Rowdy echoed without inflection or enthusiasm.

Lily accepted the DNA test. "To be clear, I'm only doing this because I want to prove I'm *not* yours."

"Then you'll be disappointed." Rowdy turned and walked back toward the barn and the happy party still happening inside. "And stay away from that Duvall boy."

"That Duvall boy?" Lily repeated softly. She turned and hurried to join the family loading up Beau's truck. "Hey, Beau, didn't you say Zane's last name was Duvall?"

"Yes." Beau heaved a sigh. "This only proves my point. You can't date someone when you don't even know their last name."

"I'm not dating him. We're friends."

But Zane wouldn't approve of Lily being related to Rowdy any more than she did.

"Congratulations on winning the ugly sweater contest tonight." Tate Oakley, one of Zane's older foster brothers and part owner of the property the party had been held on, patted Zane on the back, causing a few more bells to drop to the floor.

While Tate found it amusing, Zane had reached his limit for his flaking jingle bells. He hurried to pick them up, then decided to pluck the remaining bells free. All without losing sight of one burning question. "Is it true that you've seen Solomon on your ranch?"

"Yeah." Tate tugged a ribbon free of Zane's sweater, laughing once more. "Solomon makes the rounds. I know Ryan's seen him over at his and Jo's spread, too." Ryan was Tate's twin brother. "Are you thinking of going after him?"

"Yeah." Briefly, Zane explained how he thought Solomon would be a good bucking bronc, still pulling ribbons free of his white sweater. "If I catch him, that is. And if he can be trained not to hurt himself in a rodeo chute or jump an arena fence."

"That's a lot of *ifs*." Tate grinned. "But then again, you were always willing to take on risks most of us wouldn't. I noticed you hanging out with Beau Smith's sister." Tate's grin widened into a knowing smile. "Your interest put a kink in the plans of a lot of women attending."

"Not to mention my mamas." Zane smiled at the memory of hanging out with Lily, although she'd rejoined her family soon after Rowdy Brown had confronted her. And they'd left after the prizes were announced. All in all, the party had only lasted two hours. "You wouldn't want to ride out with me to find Solomon sometime, would you?"

Tate shook his head. "My days of chasing dreams are over. I'm a responsible father of three now and loving every minute. Never a moment alone."

Tate's wife called him over to the refreshment table. She held a baby in her arms that looked to be about the same age as Cady.

"See what I mean? Good luck with Solomon." Tate hurried off, looking happy, not harried.

Never a moment alone.

That was something Zane appreciated about living at the Done Roamin' Ranch. There was always someone around to talk to. On his excursions to try new jobs, he often lived on his own.

Someone jostled Zane on their way out. The party continued to dwindle.

"You only danced with that one tall cowgirl." Zane's mother came to his right side, taking hold of his arm and slowing the plucking. "What's her name?"

"Lily." Out of nowhere, the instinct to protect Lily arose once more, hardening his words. "And you can leave her alone." Zane dropped a tangle of beribboned bells into his mother's free hand. "You owe me after your bell plot."

"Oh, but you wouldn't have won those country music festival concert tickets without our sweater." Mama Mary came to his left side, taking hold of his other arm. "And you have to admit it was fun."

He shook his head, not willing to admit any such thing.

"We're curious about Lily," his mother said, steamrolling over Zane's boundaries. "Do you know her, Mary?"

"Haven't had the pleasure of meeting her, Rita," Mama Mary said politely. "Although she left with one of Zane's jingle bell ribbons wrapped around her finger."

Had she? Zane hadn't noticed.

"Like an engagement ring," his mother said in a swoony voice. "How romantic."

"Slow the train," Zane told them. "In fact, come to a full stop. I should have known when you gave me this sweater that I should never have put it on. It's only encouraged you to continue torturing me."

"But you look adorable in that sweater." Mama Mary plucked a bell from his sweater and rang it, smiling at him fondly.

"Not to mention all the single ladies who returned your jingle bells to you," his mother pointed out. "That was a brilliant idea, Mary."

"I can't take credit for the internet, Rita," Mama Mary said.

"It's like I'm not even here," Zane lamented, plucking a few more bells.

Ava walked past on her way out, slowing when she caught Zane's eye. "You and Lily make a cute couple."

"So true," Mama Mary echoed.

His mother looked thoughtful.

"I'll walk you out, Ava." Stu trotted after his blond fixation.

Seeing the pair, Zane was reminded once more of Lily. He smiled.

"You like her," Mama Mary surmised, looking pleased.

His biological mother looked as if the jury was still out.

Zane extricated his arms from theirs. "I love you both but why can't you use your powers for good?"

"We are," Mama Mary said, looking shocked.

"We're using our powers on *you*," Mom added. "And we've still got a job to do."

His mothers exchanged smiles. High-fived each other. And then, they traipsed off, clearly very happy with themselves. Meanwhile, Zane stewed all the way back to the Done Roamin' Ranch. He still hadn't been able to ask Lily if she'd help him catch Solomon. That he'd protected Lily from his mothers and their matchmaking was small consolation.

But there was one thing that confounded him. Why was Rowdy Brown bothering Lily?

CHAPTER NINE

EARLY THURSDAY MORNING, Lily delivered a glass of water to Nora, who sat nursing Cady, surrounded by pillows and covered by a red Christmas blanket.

The morning had dawned bright and sunny. Beau was getting Ford ready for school, moving slowly since they'd stayed out past Ford's bedtime last night at the party. Their voices blended together in the back of the house.

Lily gently fluffed her sister-in-law's pillows. "What else can I get you?"

"Oh, you shouldn't ask." Nora adjusted the baby in her arms. She looked better than she had in days. There were no more bags under her eyes. And her smile was the brightest ray of sunshine in the room. "I have a long list and you should be afraid."

Lily chuckled, settling into a seat nearby and picking up her coffee. "Consider me your not-so-secret Santa. I'm here to help, remember?"

Nora rested her head on the couch back. "Well, I wouldn't want to crimp your love life—"

"Don't make assumptions about me and Zane." Lily smiled reassuringly. "After you finish feeding Cady, I want you to go take a long, hot bath, and then a longer nap."

Finished eating, Cady made a mewling noise and stretched, loosening the blanket wrapped around her.

"And look, that's your cue to take a rest." Lily swooped in to take the tiny bundle of joy, intending to shoo Nora back to bed but there was something about holding a baby that stopped her every time. Lily brought the baby more firmly into her arms, staring at that angelic face and experiencing a bolt of unexpected yearning.

"I recognize that look on your face." Nora came over to put her arm around Lily's waist. "I wore that same expression when I held my friend Vickie's baby over a year ago. That's when I knew it was time to have another one. You should think about your future, what you want out of life. What makes sense for you."

"I guess I should." The idea of settling down, having a baby, was confounding, cluttered with images of babies with Zane's dark eyes and wholehearted laughter. A baby? Lily wasn't certain that day would ever come. She had no business daydreaming about babies. Especially, Zane's babies. "I haven't found Mr. Right Cowboy."

"I think you and Zane make a cute couple." Nora wiped down the kitchen counter.

"He's not the one, Nora."

"What makes you say that?"

"The man I fall in love with is going to see me as a woman first, not as a friend or coworker." Lily fussed with Cady's blanket. "I think your mommy is a hopeful romantic." Lily had no such delusions.

Nora chuckled. "As long as we both believe in love, we can agree to disagree."

Quick footsteps sounded in the hallway. Ford appeared. All fifty pounds of rambunctious cowboy slammed into Lily's legs. "Daddy said we'd ride after school today." The cherubic face of her nephew beamed up at her. His blond-brown hair was slicked into place except for a cowlick at his crown. "Daddy said you'd keep teaching me to rope. And—"

"Did your daddy also say you needed to keep your voice down in case your sister was sleeping?" Lily moved the little thing to her shoulder to burp.

Still clinging to Lily's legs, Ford hung his head. "I can't keep my voice down all day."

"Sure you can. And if you do, I'm sure Santa will know how good you've been."

"Santa?" Ford flopped onto the couch dramatically, arms spread. "My friend Shay says Santa goes easy on kids in Oklahoma."

"Is that because she's nice when you get in trouble?" Lily teased.

A distant sound of water tumbling into a tub

reassured Lily that Nora was taking good care of herself.

"Time to leave." Her brother, Beau, entered, smiling broadly. "Can't be late for school, Ford."

Beau came to take Cadence, pressing a gentle kiss to the slumbering baby's forehead. "Can you believe I'm a father of two?" He gestured toward the pictures of family on the wall. "You know, I'm keeping a space for pictures of you and your family on there. I just..." His demeanor changed, shifted, hardened. "I'm worried about you and..."

"My wandering lifestyle?" she guessed, misunderstanding him on purpose.

"No... Yes, that, too." He handed the baby back to her. "You and... Honestly, I can't decide which makes me more nervous. You dating a man you just met or you and..." He glanced at Ford over by the door and then to the unopened DNA test kit on the dining room table. "You fraternizing with *Rowdy Brown*."

Lily scoffed. "Don't worry about Zane. And Rowdy Brown isn't family or father material." Rowdy was a much worse option as a father figure than Sonny Smith had ever been. "I won't disappoint you."

"You never have, Lil." Beau moved to the foyer and shoved his feet into his boots while standing.

"Auntie..." Ford opened the front door, hat on his head, backpack on his shoulder. "Don't forget to pick me up after school."

"Gotcha," Lily said.

"I'll need another hot chocolate, Auntie."

"Consider it done, Ford," she promised.

Beau and Ford left. The house was quiet except for the muted thunder of water tumbling into the bathtub.

The DNA test on the dining table drew Lily's gaze, sent a shiver of trepidation down her spine.

What if it's true? What if that ornery grump is my father?

Lily took a breath, a beat, a second look at that DNA test.

What does it matter? Nothing will change.

She'd move on come spring and Rowdy would just be a bad memory.

Lily's gaze went to the wall of family photographs next. She may not have had an ideal relationship with Sonny Smith but at least he hadn't stomped around as if the world was against him and he didn't care.

The water in back stopped running.

Cady made a small snuffling noise, stretched one arm into the air, sighed and slowly lowered her arm.

"I'll take the test when you go down for your afternoon nap, Cady," Lily whispered. "And drop it off when I'm in town to pick up more baby wipes and Ford."

ZANE CAME OUT of the feedstore, having picked up a large container of saddle soap and another of dewormer for the Done Roamin' Ranch.

It was a crisp winter day. The sun was bright. Its rays glinted off a vehicle windshield, making it impossible for Zane to see.

He tugged down the brim of his tan cowboy hat and searched for the source of the glare.

Instead, he spotted a tall, lanky cowgirl crossing Main Street, heading toward Clementine Coffee Roasters. Her short, brown hair floated in thick curls beneath her worn, brown cowboy hat. She rolled her shoulders as if she'd just come out of the tax man's office, not the post office.

Lily.

Zane took a step toward her. But then he remembered how his mothers had latched onto the idea that they were a couple.

He stopped, considered returning to the ranch without saying hello. He was taking the rest of the afternoon off to ride out in search of Solomon. And yet...

Lily.

Talking to her always lifted his spirits. And he hadn't been able to ask her last night if she'd help chase down that wild stallion.

Decision made, Zane stowed his purchases in his truck before walking through the center of town. Each step brought a stronger aroma of fresh ground coffee.

Zane entered the coffee shop, gaze finding Lily in the short line to order. He approached, then tapped her shoulder. "Hey, fancy meeting you here."

Lily's expression went from pinched and tense to relaxed at the sight of him. "I was running errands and decided a strong coffee was in order. What brings you to town?"

"Picking up the ranch's feedstore order. Thought I'd grab a cup before heading back." Zane noticed her smile didn't quite reach her eyes. "I have time to sit and drink it here if you'd like."

Lily checked her phone. "No messages from Nora. And I have thirty minutes before I have to pick up Ford."

They ordered their coffees—his black, hers a vanilla latte—and found a table by the Christmas tree. Lily was unusually quiet.

"Are you okay?" Zane asked quietly. "You seem…" *Guarded.* "…distracted."

"Family stuff." Lily tried to smile. Didn't quite succeed, which tugged at his heartstrings for some unknown reason.

Zane sipped his black coffee, trying to think of something to say, finally landing on, "I didn't get to finish telling you about Solomon."

"Vanilla latte for Lily," the barista called.

Lily went to retrieve her drink, returning with the same somber smile. "Is there more to the legend? Don't tell me whoever catches this runaway stallion gets to be the grand marshal of the Santapalooza Parade on Christmas Day."

"No. Nothing like that." Zane leaned forward, wanting this next question to be their little secret.

"I want to make a run for Solomon. And I want you to ride along with me."

"Me?" She set down her coffee cup. "Don't you have several cowboys you work with who could do this with you?"

"Yes. But you have experience catching wild mustangs." Zane was suddenly struck by a thought. "Is it…that you don't want to do this… *with me*?"

"It's not that." Lily held on to that coffee cup with both hands, as if it was her anchor. "I like you, Zane. We're friends. But I'm here to support my family. Chasing down wild horses is a several-day activity."

"I thought we'd just ride out in the direction Solomon was last spotted. I'm taking my horse out to look for him on that property where the party was last night. He was spotted there earlier in the week."

"You're just looking? Hoping to get lucky?" She shook her head. "That's counterproductive. When I was on the roundup crew, there were spotters in the air—planes, helicopters, even drones. We mobilized when a herd was spotted. Trailered our horses as far in as we could before pursuing on horseback."

Zane frowned. "That's a bigger operation than I was thinking."

Lily nodded, reaching over to touch his hand briefly. "Not to mention, it's easier to spot a herd than a single horse. Why do you want to catch Solomon?"

"No one's ever caught him before."

Her hand still covered his. "You want the accolade of bringing him in?"

"No. I..." How could he make her understand? "My parents divorced when I was twelve." Zane gently tapped his coffee cup on the table. "No. It started before that." Zane drew a deep breath. "My dad mismanaged our ranch. Everything from cattle breeding programs to leasing grazing land. Meanwhile, my mom mismanaged the household finances. Outfitting herself and my older sister in the latest trends. Our family's bankruptcy wasn't just the result of one thing. But because of it, in the eyes of Clementine, there's a stigma attached to the Duvall name."

"That's rough," Lily said consolingly. "I'm sorry."

"All my life, I've tried to find something where I can excel. Where I can make the Duvall name associated with good things." Wow. There was an epiphany Chandler hadn't thought of.

Chandler would be proud of my growing self-awareness. Amused by it, too.

"I don't suppose being targeted by two mamas playing Cupid counts as a good association," Lily gently teased.

"It doesn't."

Ava entered the coffee shop. She wore scrubs beneath a fancy, knee-length black jacket. She approached them and sat down next to Zane. "Your mother said you'd buy whoever found you a cup of coffee. Brown sugar, oat milk espresso, please." She turned to Lily. "Hi. Did you find him for the scavenger hunt, too?"

"No. He found me." Lily frowned, drawing her hand away from Zane's. "When did this scavenger hunt begin?"

"Rita just posted on social media in the past hour." Ava grinned at Zane. "Fun, right?"

"Not from where I'm sitting." Zane tugged his phone from his jacket pocket and scanned through social media. He found his mother's post almost immediately. His jaw clenched. "She hinted I'm downtown. She says I'll ask one lucky scavenger to the next Christmas party."

"In addition to buying them a coffee for all who find you," Ava reminded him. "Should I place my own order before the rush of other scavenger hunters arrive?"

Heat gathered in Zane's chest and blazed a trail to his face. He couldn't speak. At least, not anything civil.

"Place your order, Ava, and tell the barista to start a tab for Zane." Lily placed a hand over his once more. "Take a breath."

Zane stared at Lily, taking in her kind expression and all those big, bold freckles. "How can I breathe when I don't know when they'll strike next?"

Two women he didn't recognize entered the coffee shop and hurried to their table.

"Order your coffees," he told them, chastising himself for his tone, and gesturing with the hand untouched by Lily.

"What about the next Christmas party?" the brunette asked, making note of Lily's hand covering his. "Are you still looking for a date? Or are we too late?"

"I've already got a date," Zane said without thinking. "With Lily." It made sense. She got a kick out of his mamas' devious schemes. Now she'd have a front row seat.

And yet, it didn't seem to make sense to Lily. She gently retracted her hand from his, cheeks turning a soft shade of pink that highlighted those unique freckles.

Zane was…disappointed.

Funny thing that.

Zane had dated his share of women—the delicate, the daring and, yes, also the girl next door. But no one had made him want to hang on when they retreated.

"I should be going." Lily scooted her chair back, smile long gone. "I need to pick up Ford."

And then she, too, was out of there.

"CONGRATULATIONS." AVA FOLLOWED Lily out of Clementine Coffee Roasters. "You got a date with the most eligible bachelor in Clementine."

"You know that's not true." Lily was being used

as a shield. A part of her wanted to march back inside and make it very clear that she and Zane had no date. But another part of her wanted to let the ruse continue. She liked Zane. Their *friendship* would go on if she agreed to play her part in his scheme. And, admittedly, she was curious as to how a date with Zane would play out.

It's only one night. What harm is there?

Ava tsked. "I saw you holding hands back there."

"Zane was upset. I offered him some *friendly* comfort." Had that been a mistake?

Lily's gaze roved Main Street. The vintage brick buildings, the town square decorated for the holiday, the smiling cowboys and cowgirls walking hand in hand.

I could be one of them.

If Zane's romantic interest in her was true.

Lily knew it wasn't.

Not yet, that inner voice counseled. *Not him.*

Ava tsked. "I heard Zane say you have a date, Lily. You're the only one he danced with last night. Believe what he says. He's a dedicated cowboy, honest and true. You should give him a shot. Best buy a fresh tube of lipstick."

"Why?" Lily had been to this rodeo before and lost. Also, she wasn't a lipstick or lip gloss type of gal.

"Why not? Do you like being alone? There's nothing more tempting to a cowboy than pretty lips." And as if to prove her point, Ava pointed to cowboys and cowgirls paired up all around them, then took out a tube of lipstick and applied it.

"You should get back to your coffee." Lily hugged Ava, trying to distract her. "I've got to pick up Ford from school." But it wasn't going to be a hot chocolate day. No way was she returning to the coffee shop. With her luck, Zane would still be there juggling all his admirers and clinging to the ruse that he had a date with Lily.

But before she returned to her truck, Lily darted into the drugstore for a tub of diaper wipes and also bought a new lipstick: Glamberry.

She'd probably never wear it. Ever.

It was like buying a prom dress before anyone asked you to go.

CHAPTER TEN

FORD WASTED NO time submitting his demands when Lily picked him up after school. "Hot chocolate and horseback rides, Auntie."

"Let's mix it up today. We'll get milkshakes for me, you and your dad." Lily had the strongest urge to talk to her brother.

"Hey!" Ford cried. "What happened to horseback rides?"

Lily assured her nephew they'd have time to ride and practice roping before dark. She silently commended herself for not looking toward Clementine Coffee Roasters as they drove past on their way to Tasty Freeze.

A short time later, they entered Beau's office carrying their milkshakes—chocolate for Ford, festive eggnog for Lily and Beau. He was an accountant of one with room to grow.

Ford found a vacant desk chair and proceeded to spin himself around.

"What's wrong?" Beau asked Lily, tugging on his Western tie. "You never bring me milkshakes unless something is wrong."

No way was Lily going to confess that she had a date with Zane, real or otherwise. She needed to mentally reframe her relationship with the sought-after cowboy. And the only way she knew how to do that was to focus on the aspects of their relationship that were friendly—laughing about his mamas and their matchmaking efforts or chasing down this phantom horse.

"Tell me about the legend of the uncatchable Solomon." Lily sipped her milkshake.

Beau held up his milkshake cup, staring at her with suspicion in his eyes. "You bought me a milkshake to ask about a local myth?"

"Just answer the question."

He closed his laptop, sat back in his desk chair, and stirred his milkshake with his straw. "There's not much to tell. This time of year, a white stallion shows up in the area. There's always a cowboy or two who fancies they can capture him. They head out looking. But no one ever succeeds in catching him." He slurped his milkshake, giving her a speculative look. "Seems like someone spots him out near Rowdy's land first. Did you see him the other day?"

Lily shook her head.

"Do you have a wild hair, Lily?" Beau smiled indulgently. "Think you can capture Solomon?"

"Not alone," Lily began slowly, suddenly realizing if she joined forces with Zane that they'd be spending lots of time together.

Not the wisest move when she was at risk of

falling for the cowboy. But the thought brought a ray of joy anyway.

"If you catch him, will you stay in town?" Beau's brow clouded with worry. "I've never understood your need to roam."

"Maybe I'm like Solomon, roaming and looking for a place to call home." The words... Unplanned... But they resonated within Lily with a clear note of truth. Before Lily could admit it was Zane who wanted the stallion, Ford joined their conversation.

"I'll help catch him, Auntie!" Ford leaped out of his chair, interrupting and flexing his muscles. "That white horse is for me, isn't he?" Ford's grin spanned from ear to ear. "I'll help you catch him. Then I'm going to rename him Lightning because he's fast." Ford resumed drinking his milkshake and turned in place, as if he was still in the spinning desk chair.

"When I rounded up wild horses for the government," Lily said to Beau, "we only took the younger horses. To help control the population. An older horse like Solomon would be left to run free." The more she thought about it, the more she wondered if this wasn't something she should tell Zane about.

Ford came to a halt, jaw dropping open. "Are you saying there's a baby Solomon out there? That's even better!"

"I feel it needs to be said," Beau began in his fatherly, no-fun voice. "But I have qualms about Ford riding out with you looking for Solomon."

"Son of Solomon, Dad. *Lightning*," Ford corrected, resting his head on Beau's desk. "I'm a good roper. Auntie says so. And if we catch our horse before Christmas, I can ride him in the Santapalooza Parade!"

"Do you see what you've started?" Beau frowned at Lily, who was smiling at Ford's enthusiasm, almost having forgotten about Zane.

"If Santa brings Ford a horse for Christmas, Ford won't need to track down Son of Solomon." Lily got to her feet and took her nephew by the hand. "Have you written a letter to Santa, Ford?"

"Yep." Ford's head bobbed. "Several. But I can write another." He towed Lily toward the door. "Let's get home and write a letter to Santa in case we don't catch Lightning."

"No one's ever seen a herd of horses with Solomon," Beau, the fun-killer, said sourly.

"Doesn't mean they don't exist." Lily set Ford's cowboy hat at a jaunty angle. "Ford needs a new horse for Christmas. One way or another."

"Yup," Ford said, all smiles.

"Oh, that's just not fair," Beau cried as they left his office.

"THANKS FOR LETTING me ride your land," Zane told Tate as he tightened his horse's girth strap at the Rowland Ranch.

"If I didn't have chores to do around here, I'd ride out with you," Tate said, opening the gate to a dirt road that dissected his pastures. "Nice weather. The wind isn't too strong and it's not too cold."

Zane swung into the saddle. "Anything I should be on the lookout for on your back acreage? Things you're worried about?"

"As a rancher, when don't I worry?" Tate grinned. "But you can look to see that each water trough is working. Note any fences or shelters in need of repair. Or if you find any animals in distress." Tate tipped his hat back. "You know. Just the usual."

"Got it." Zane shifted his weight from side to side, making sure the saddle and stirrups felt secure. "And you've seen Solomon out at the end of this lane?"

"Last week." Tate nodded. "Enjoy your wild-goose chase."

Zane didn't justify the ribbing with a response. He cued Arthur forward, muttering to himself about foster brothers giving him grief.

Behind him, Tate closed the gate.

Arthur's brown ears swiveled backward and he tried to break into a trot, his hindquarters swinging around until they were practically dancing down the lane.

Zane used his hands and feet to cue the gelding into a straighter gait. Then he patted Arthur's neck. "Don't get all skittish on me. We're just out for a ride." Just because Zane had a length of coiled rope didn't mean he was going to use it.

Just because I told people Lily's going to be my date on Friday doesn't mean I'm wooing her.

They were friends. She'd said so at the party last night and again this afternoon. Friends helped friends out of binds. Plus, when he'd said she was his date, she hadn't denied it.

Although... She hadn't looked happy, either.

But Zane could fix that. This. Their friendship. He'd apologize for putting her on the spot and they'd continue on as they had been.

He smiled to himself.

Arthur tested Zane's control, walking faster and trying to break into a trot. He knew open roads were meant for running.

Zane eased up on the reins and the gelding shot forward.

Sheep and alpaca in pastures on either side of the dirt road hurried away from them as they passed.

Tate was right. It was a good day for a ride.

As for finding the white stallion...

That was another story.

"I CAN'T DO IT," Ford griped, dropping the lariat and riding Mouse past the practice steer. "I could rope it if I was riding Jet."

"Let's not get carried away, Ford." Lily picked up the stiff rope her nephew had discarded and coiled it back up. "You have to walk before you run."

"I can run." Ford heeled Mouse into a trot. "See?"

Jet bumped Lily's shoulder with his nose. He wasn't saddled and he wanted to be part of the action. Smart horses were never slouches.

"Yes, Jet." Lily turned to give him some loving strokes on the neck. "I know Ford isn't trying very hard and I know you want to have a go. But this is his time."

Ford reached the far end of the pasture and turned Mouse around, either cuing him into a gallop or Mouse decided running back to Lily and Jet was the quickest way to end the ride. Ponies were notorious slackers, and Mouse much preferred to be treated like a house pet, receiving affection and snacks, than a working animal.

"You've got a good seat," Lily praised the boy. "I can tell you practice riding a lot. But to be a good roper, you need to practice just as much."

Ford slid off Mouse's hindquarters instead of doing a proper dismount.

"Bad habits, Ford," Lily gently chastised, reaching for the pony's reins. "You're responsible for the behavior and safety of your animal."

"I have to be a big brother to Mouse, too?" Ford came to stand next to Lily, leaning heavily into her. "Nobody told me that."

"I doubt that very much." Lily sighed. "But because you practiced roping on the ground and in the saddle, I suppose you deserve a cookie."

"Yay!" Ford turned and would have run for the

gate, but Lily stopped him with a hand on his shoulder.

"Not so fast, cowboy. You need to take care of your mount first."

"Yes, Auntie." But despite being excited about cookies, Ford dragged his feet, removing Mouse's tack with the slowest of movements.

"It doesn't matter how slow you go, Ford." Lily brushed Jet with a currycomb. "I'm not going to do it for you."

Ford pouted. "You know what, Auntie?"

"What?"

"Sometimes, you're no fun."

ZANE ARRIVED BACK at the Done Roamin' Ranch after dark, not having found a trace of Solomon.

Lily had been right. Riding out alone was inefficient. The ranch owned a drone. He might be able to borrow it. He'd have to ask ranch foreman Chandler, though.

Zane put his horse away, gave him an extra cup of oats, wiped down his tack and then entered the bunkhouse, tired and hungry.

All eyes—nine pairs—turned toward him in silent disapproval.

"What?" Zane tugged off his cowboy boots, then hung his hat on a hook with his jacket. "Is something wrong?"

"Yes." Bart crossed his arms over his chest. "You. You're all wrong."

"You need to tell your mother to stop putting

ideas in our foster mother's head." That was Jack, hopping off his top bunk and looking just as unhappy as Stewart.

"Or pretty soon we're all going to be targeted for love." Bart nodded his head. "There won't be a place in town where we Done Roamin' Ranch bachelors have peace."

"You're blowing this out of proportion." Zane leaned over and attempted to find a spot for his boots beneath the bench just as someone entered the bunkhouse, most likely Chandler. One of his boots was stuck and he stayed bent over, moving it this way and that, trying to line it up with the others. "Mama Mary isn't going to pull the same malarkey on you that she's been pulling on me. She's not like that. She's sensible most times, except when my mama rolls into town. My mama is a bad influence."

The bunkhouse was still.

A bad feeling filled Zane's chest. But he ignored it because his boot wasn't fitting where it belonged and that was because…there was something jammed behind it. Zane stretched his arm farther back. "My mama has never gotten the better of me. She'll get tired of this dating game she's playing and leave before Christmas. And then Mama Mary will realize the spell she's been under and return to normal."

Someone sat down on the bench next to where Zane was looking. "Glad to know what you think of me, son."

Zane's hand closed on a dirt-encrusted tennis ball, most likely Rusty's. "Mom?"

"And Mama Mary," a staid voice said. "Or should I say No-Backbone Mama Mary?"

"And Bad Influence Mama Duvall," Mom added.

Zane stood up slowly, trying to smile after having put his foot in his mouth. "Why, if it isn't my two rays of sunshine."

"Flattery won't work," Mom said. She had a box of Christmas ornaments in her lap.

"Apologies might," Mama Mary said. She carried wreaths the likes of which she usually put in the windows of the bunkhouse.

"Might take more than apologies." Mom wasn't as forgiving.

The cowboys in the bunkhouse gave him dirty looks.

"Let's take this outside." Zane put his boots, jacket and hat back on. And once they were on the other side of the bunkhouse door, he asked, "Why are you making me miserable? Encouraging women to approach me as if I need help in the dating department."

"Well, you do." Mom's tense expression loosened. "You're nearly thirty. Thirty is old."

"Rita, just tell him." Mama Mary joined the fray as the voice of reason. "Zane, the fact is your mother's clock is ticking down."

"You're sick? Why didn't you say something?"

Zane was aghast. His chest instantly full of worry. "What's wrong?"

"Nothing! I just want to have more grandkids before…" Mom shrugged deeper in her jacket. "Before I'm too old to crawl around on the floor with them."

"Tell him the rest, Rita." That was Mama Mary. Sounding like her usual self.

Mom said not a word.

Mama Mary faced Zane. "She doesn't want you to be alone."

"I live in a bunkhouse. I'm never alone when I'm in Clementine." Zane may have protested, but he understood what his mother meant. There was something about having your person that implied you'd never be alone. No matter where you went. It was why he'd started dating with purpose last summer, because many of his foster brothers were finding their perfect match. But he wasn't going to let his mother know that. "If anyone's alone, Mom, it's you."

"I'm not alone." Mom turned a plain gold band on her left ring finger, revealing a large, sparkly diamond. "I'm getting married again. To a fine man. He's a doctor."

"And you thought that would bother me?" Zane asked, fighting an unusual feeling of envy.

I'm going to be the only one alone in my family.

"Yes. I can see it in your eyes. You looked at me that same way when you were a teenager and I asked you to come back and live with Eileen and me in Tulsa. It was as if you felt you were the odd man out and you preferred foster care to the two of us."

"I…" Zane took a step back, a deep breath, a look at the past. "Yes. I used to feel that way. And maybe I still feel that way…a little. But I'm an adult now. I have a way I want to live my life."

"If you feel alone, it's hard to find love if you don't go looking for it," Mom pointed out.

"We both agree that you don't look," Mama Mary said. "Except when you did all those speed dating things last summer."

"It was more than speed dating." Zane swallowed a groan of frustration. "Now, thanks to you both, I've met and talked to plenty over the past few weeks. You can stop now."

"Because you're sweet on the tall girl?" Mom asked. "Lily, isn't it?"

"You're always together," Mama Mary added. "Meeting at Clementine Coffee Roasters in town. Or so I hear."

Zane opened his mouth to deny it before realizing this was his chance to put an end to their meddling. If he was willing to go all in on this dating ruse with Lily. "Yes. I'm sweet on Lily." How easily the words came to his lips. "Granted, we've been dancing around the idea of dating but she's my date for the party on Friday night."

Mom clapped her hands. "I love this. And I love you, Zane."

"Congratulations," Mama Mary said, her expression all but glowing.

"You're acting like I proposed to Lily." Zane tried to calm their enthusiasm. "We haven't even agreed to date on the regular."

"Oh, but it'll come. I can see it now." Mama Mary nodded. "She's just your type."

What type is that? he wondered.

"Engaged by Christmas," Mom murmured. "So romantic."

Zane left them to their daydreams to walk next door to Chandler's house and ask about borrowing the ranch drone. He needed more of a plan if he was going to capture Solomon.

Not to mention, he had to figure out how to ask Lily not just to fake date him tomorrow night, but to go steady through Christmas Day.

CHAPTER ELEVEN

Second Party of Christmas:
Adults Only, Ornament Exchange
Hosted by: Black Rock Ranch

It was Friday night, and Lily was nervous.

Rationally, she had no cause to be. It was just a holiday party.

And a date.

That was Ms. Irrational, whispering romantic nonsense in Lily's head. If this was a date, they would be going Dutch on the ornament. That's what folks did when they went on first dates with someone they barely knew.

Beau and his family were sitting out the second of twelve parties since kids, including babies, were not invited. Lily had wanted to stay at home, too. She'd spent the past twenty-four hours telling herself that Zane hadn't asked her on a date. He'd only said they had a date to deter single women. And most of the time, Lily was rational about that fact. She could have shut him down the moment he'd announced she was his date for tonight. But like a good friend, she'd backed Zane up. She had to show up and pretend to be Zane's date.

Pretend.

She wasn't nervous when she clung to that reality.

But then Ava showed up around 5:00 p.m., gussied up and eager to help Lily get ready for her *date*.

And that's when the nerves kicked in, along with the comments from her family.

"You're so lucky, Lily," Ava said, romantic stars in her eyes as she repositioned an ornament on the Christmas tree.

"I think Auntie should marry Zane." Ford held up a chicken drumstick for emphasis. And then he took a big bite.

"Just don't marry him today," Nora teased, sitting in a dining room chair next to a bassinet with Cady.

"Marriage? This is moving way too fast." Beau stopped eating dinner to fix Lily with a firm stare, the kind their dad had wielded all too swiftly when he thought Lily was getting out of line.

Lily stared at her family—all five blond-hair-framed faces. She'd never felt so out of step with them as she did in this moment.

"Cat got your tongue?" Beau asked, still looking intimidating.

"It's less of a date and more of a meetup," Lily mumbled. "Marriage isn't in the cards." Like, ever.

Of course, no one believed her.

Lily retreated to her bedroom, only to have Ava follow her.

The teen touched the coil of white ribbon with a bell attached, the one Lily had taken from Zane's white holiday sweater. Then Ava picked up a framed photo of Lily and Beau riding horses when they were kids. "Are you going to change clothes?"

Lily glanced down at her gray jeans and red blouse, then at Ava's fancy blue cocktail dress. No cowboy hat for the teen this evening. Her blond hair flowed in smooth locks over her shoulders.

Lily refused to be cowed. "Yes, I'm wearing this, Ava." To meet up with her *friend*.

"Okay." Ava set the photograph back on the dresser and fixed Lily with an assessing stare. "I have tweezers in my bag."

Lily thought she knew where Ava was going with this. "My brows are fine." Lily smoothed them with her fingers.

"I have tweezers for your upper lip," Ava clarified, running a finger over hers.

"My upper lip is fine." Stiff and without whiskers.

"That's a choice." Ava studied Lily's hair next. "Can I do your hair?"

"Nope." Lily ran a pick through her thick, wavy hair. The ends barely touched her shoulders. "I like my natural curls."

A sliver of uncertainty pierced her thoughts... Maybe Zane would take a look at her wild locks and decide she wasn't his type. Not even for a fake date. Because that's the vibe Ava was sending her.

"Can I put a little makeup on your face?" Ava dug into her bedazzled clutch bag. "Maybe tone down those freckles?"

"No." Lily rolled her shoulders back and checked her appearance in the mirror, satisfied that she looked like herself.

Like Zane's friend.

"I'm not going to hide my freckles. They're a part of me."

"How about perfume, then?" Ava produced a small vial and then a smaller metal tube. "Or lipstick? Lipstick will highlight those nice teeth of yours."

"No." *Ugh.* "Listen, Ava. I'm going like this." Lily gestured at herself in the mirror, taking inventory of frank brown eyes, floofy brown hair and big, brown freckles clustered like a map across her face. "This is me. Feel free to do whatever you'd like to, though."

"Okay. Sure. What time is Zane picking us—" Ava noticed Lily's frown "—*you* up?"

"I'm assuming I'm meeting him there." What a poor excuse for a date this was.

Ava frowned, as if she knew it, too. "Then, is it okay if I catch a ride with you?"

"I guess so." Lily didn't plan on drinking or staying at the party long. Besides, these weeknight parties were only supposed to last two hours to help out ranchers and other early risers. "I just need to pick up an ornament for the exchange." She planned to stop at the feedstore on the way over, buy one and drop it into one of those cute gift bags.

"I have an ornament for you." Nora popped into Lily's bedroom. She held a small box wrapped in dark green Christmas paper and was smiling mischievously.

"Nora…" Lily kept her distance. "It's supposed to be a nice Christmas ornament, but your expression tells me you've wrapped a gag gift." Like something Zane's mamas would have provided to ensure she had an excuse to talk to Zane.

"It's not a joke. It's a nice ornament." Nora fussed with the red bow. "If you must know, it's a white horse ornament. There are prizes for the ornaments brought tonight. And I thought with Solomon a topic of conversation in town that it would go over well. It was in the bag of supplies I preordered and you picked up from the drugstore today."

"Well, I… Thank you. That's very thoughtful." Lily took the wrapped box. "Ava, what kind of ornament did you bring?"

"A fairy princess." Ava glowed, looking her age. "It's an adorable ornament, kind of like me."

"I think Stu considers you adorable," Lily floated that out there.

Ava adopted her old-soul, sour expression. "Old souls aren't adorable."

"O-kay." Lily thought Ava could be charming when she acted her age.

But what do I know? I'm fake dating a man I practically just met.

Lily headed toward the front door. "Let's get this night over with."

"For someone who has a date with Zane Duvall, you sure are grouchy." Ava followed her down the hall. "If I was in your shoes, I'd be smiling nonstop and telling everyone I'm Zane Duvall's girl."

"Ava, maybe you should date Zane." Beau was still in overprotective older-brother mode. But he was also in good-husband-and-daddy mode, loading the dishwasher. "You'd make a cute couple."

"I'd love to," Ava gushed, beamed and generally looked like a teenage fan girl who'd just won a date with a beloved member of a popular boy band.

Inexplicably gutted, Lily sighed. "I'm leaving now." She put on her boots, coat and cowboy hat with practiced efficiency, and then she was out the door.

"Wait for me." Ava trotted along behind her on her high heels.

The sun was setting and it was nippy out. Ava's bare toes were going to be icicles before the night was through.

Lily drove them to the party venue—the community center on the other side of town. The invitation noted the evening's sponsors were Clem and Maggie Coogan. Appetizers and drinks would be served.

She and Ava stepped up to the check-in tables. Lily smiled like a good friend's happiness depended upon her looking innocent.

"Merry Christmas, ladies." Lily told them her name, pretending not to recognize the older women she'd met briefly at Wednesday's party. "Where am I sitting?"

She was given a table and chair assignment and instructed to place her wrapped ornament in a basket in the center of her assigned table. A quick peek at the guest list for her table and it became clear that at each table had four seats assigned to men and four to women.

Was matchmaking afoot? She assumed so.

"Now I know how Zane feels," Lily muttered as she entered the large hall and took in the gold and silver holiday decorations and setup.

Round tables covered in black linen tablecloths filled the community center in neat rows. Candles glowed in short sparkling pots on each table. Small bowls of candied nuts and various kinds of bite-size crackers were available. Christmas trees flanked the small stage and offered a true holiday scent. Small colorful lights and paper garland were the trees' only decorations. A choir version of "O Tannenbaum" played softly through speakers on the stage.

All in all, it was really sweet.

Lily found her seat.

A moment later, Ava sat down next to her. "You forgot to tell Rita and Mary when you checked in that you had a date with Zane. I told them because I know you didn't want him to sit at another table. They had him sitting between a rodeo queen and a pharmacist."

"Thanks," Lily mumbled.

Zane dropped into a chair on Lily's right. He looked handsome in a fancy-yoked, black button-down, a black cowboy hat and black boots—a cowboy's night-on-the-town attire.

It is a date.

Lily mustered a smile, almost wishing that she'd taken some of Ava's advice about how she looked.

"Evening, ladies." Zane placed a lumpy package in the basket in the center of the table. He smiled, not specifically at Lily but in her and Ava's direction. He didn't press a kiss to Lily's cheek or apologize for not picking her—*his date*—up.

It's not a date. This proves it.

Lily shouldn't be disappointed.

But she was.

"I MISSED YOU at Clementine Coffee Roasters this afternoon." Had Zane made a mistake thinking Lily was fine with the dating ruse? He was getting the cold shoulder.

"I'm sorry. Did we have a *date* earlier?" Lily turned to face Zane.

He felt as if he knew every distinctive angle of

her pretty face. Those intelligent brown eyes. That hint of a dimple on one cheek before both blossomed when she set her smile free. Those bold freckles that formed a pattern he knew he couldn't identify without closer inspection.

It was the chill in Lily's tone that was unfamiliar.

Uh-oh.

Zane had the strangest feeling that he'd stepped into a proverbial cow pie while wearing his "going out" cowboy boots.

"We did not have a coffee date, per se," Zane said slowly, trying to carefully navigate the thorny terrain between them. "Every afternoon that I've come into town this week, though, you've been at Clementine Coffee Roasters. But you weren't today."

"I didn't get an afternoon coffee today," Lily put her nose in the air, which was very unlike her. "I was busy. Had no time."

"She had no time to exfoliate, either." Ava ran a finger over her upper lip as the music changed to "Carol of the Bells." "I always take care of my skin before a date. My skin glows, doesn't it?" She framed her face with her hands.

"It glows." Stu plopped into a chair next to Ava and tossed a wrapped ornament into the basket in the center. "Ava always looks beautiful."

"Stu and I crushed on each other when we were *children*," Ava said with stilted composure, although there was a tic in her cheek.

"It was love," Stu said simply, grabbing a handful of candied nuts from a bowl and crunching away.

"Past tense," Ava was quick to say. Her ticking cheek was turning red. She angled toward Stu to say, "Lily and Zane are on a date."

Lily didn't roll her eyes but Zane got the feeling she wanted to by the way she stared at the ceiling. "Ava, I've told you. Zane and I *aren't* on a date." She drew a deep breath and shifted her gaze to her lap, where her hands were clasped.

White-knuckled.

Double uh-oh.

Zane hadn't just stepped into cow pie. He'd fallen in it on his backside.

"I'm here." Lily's cheeks pinkened. "Zane is here. You could even say that we're here together. On a meetup. But *we. Are not. On a date.*"

Zane had the strongest urge to cover Lily's clasped hands with one of his own, to give those white knuckles a gentle caress, to reassure her that this was definitely a meetup of sorts. And to smooth the way to asking her to meet up through Christmas.

Of course, if he did any of that, he imagined Lily would bunch up the fingers of one hand and slug him.

Oh, the mamas would really go to town then.

"Lily, we both heard Zane yesterday," Ava pressed, having become Lily's staunchest supporter. "He said that you were his date tonight. Don't be a doormat."

"Don't be rude, babe." Stu rested his arm on Ava's chair back.

"Don't call me *babe*, Stuart," Ava snapped back.

Lily's eyes widened and she looked at Zane the way she used to—*before he'd said she was his date*—as if they were friends who had ringside seats to a good show. "*Babe?*" she whispered.

Zane bit back a grin.

"Hey, b… *Ava*," Stu said softly, leaning closer to her. "I thought we got things straightened out after the party the other night when you—"

"Zip it," Ava commanded, pushing her ex-boyfriend out of her space.

Lily's mouth formed a small O.

Zane smiled and moved his arm over the back of Lily's metal folding chair.

But before he made contact with the chair back, a woman stepped between Lily's and Zane's chairs. She had on a pretty little cocktail dress—black—and a pretty big smile—accented by sparkly red lipstick. "Zane, I was hoping I'd be sitting with you, despite all those dating rumors." She gave Lily a dismissive glance that hit the Rile Button on Zane's temper. "I heard you want to take a run for Solomon, so I got you a white horse ornament. For luck."

Lily groaned, not that Zane knew why.

"That's…" Zane gave Lily an apologetic look. "That's very thoughtful, Missy."

"*Wishful*," Ava said in her most self-righteous tone. And when Zane and Missy both gave her perplexed looks, Ava tossed her long blond hair over one shoulder and clarified, "It's a Pirate Bingo Gift Exchange. You can't *give* a certain someone anything. You have to hope—*to wish*— that Zane still has the white horse ornament at the end of the game. That's why it's *wishful*, not thoughtful."

"That's exactly what an old soul would say," Lily murmured, lips turning up slightly at the corners.

Stu smoothed Ava's hair over her shoulder. "I wish—"

"Shush," Ava cut him off, cheeks heating again.

"Are you Zane's date?" Missy asked Ava, brow clouding.

"No." Ava pointed at Lily.

There was a moment of silence, filled only by the rousing *ring-ding-a-ling* chorus of "Carol of the Bells."

During which time, Lily looked as if she *wished* the floor might swallow her up.

Zane did cover Lily's clasped hands then, gave them a gentle squeeze and bent his head until Lily glanced at him. "Sorry," he whispered. "I handled this all wrong."

The pink in her cheeks deepened. She nodded once, as if to say she understood. But she didn't move—not to ease her hands away, not even to turn either hand so their palms touched the way dating couples did.

Triple uh-oh.

Except this time, instead of worrying that he'd done something wrong, Zane was concerned that his mistakes to do with this ruse—*his presumption and oversight*—were making Lily think less of him.

"Will you excuse me?" Zane got up and headed toward the exit.

LILY WOULDN'T FAULT Zane if he walked out the door and just kept going. This was more awkward than she'd ever imagined it could be.

And I have a vivid, worst-case-scenario imagination.

She'd spent the last few nights pacing the halls with fussy Cady, while having imaginary conversations between herself and her deceased parents and trying to understand why she'd been blindsided by Rowdy. None of which ended with anyone feeling good about themselves. She needed a dose of the positives where her parentage was concerned.

Without Zane around, Missy drifted off, clutching her wrapped ornament to her chest like an unwanted consolation prize.

"You need to stake your claim on Zane." Clearly offended for Lily, Ava was prepared to go to war on her behalf. But then she paused and peered at Lily's face. "If you want him, that is."

Although Lily's impulse was to shrug to indicate she didn't care, she didn't move. Not a muscle. She feared she'd look pathetic if she admitted to anyone that she wanted to date Zane when some folks clearly thought she was punching above her weight class. And if she accepted this so-called date as real, she feared she'd look pathetic when Zane finally confirmed it was just for show.

Either way, I'll feel pathetic.

"Lily, I'd like you to meet my mamas." Zane appeared next to her. His mamas stood behind him, hanging back. "They don't believe we're dating."

No one does.

Lily blushed. "Zane—"

"Sometimes Lily doesn't believe we're involved, either. It's all happening so fast." Zane drew Lily to her feet and bussed her lips.

His lips...touched my lips and...

Lily felt lightheaded. Weak-kneed.

Though Zane had only lip-bombed her the way a nervous seventh grader might have—*without an ounce of romance*—it made no sense that she felt as swoony as if he'd told her he was falling in love with her, or had taken her into his arms and kissed her for all he was worth to prove that fact.

Zane looped his arm around Lily's waist and turned to face his mamas. "Lily's new to town. We're newly together. I thought this might be a good time to let my mamas know they don't need to send more women my way."

All the excited feelings Zane's kiss had engendered evaporated like water boiled out of a pan left on the stove too long.

"Zane's not very romantic, is he?" Ava sniffed her disdain. "I'm a little disappointed."

Everyone stared at Lily, as if expecting her to defend Zane.

Or agree with Ava.

Frankly, Lily was leaning toward agreeing with Ava.

"Lily's shy," Zane said when Lily remained speechless. "Who could blame her? She's meeting two mamas, not one." He snuggled Lily closer to his side. "*And* she knows how devious you two are."

Way to put me on the spot, Zane.

"Hi." Lily tried to smile at the pair of older women. "I've witnessed your matchmaking creativity." Not deviousness. "Not only are you both brilliant but you care a lot about your son."

"I wouldn't go so far as to praise them for their antics." Zane shifted awkwardly.

"They made me laugh," Lily said cautiously.

"*I* didn't laugh." Even now, Zane wasn't smiling.

"I agree to disagree," Lily said, frowning at him, smelling his woodsy cologne and trying not to get lost in his dark brown gaze. "We had quite a good laugh over the Christmas cards the night we met. And the ugly Christmas sweater shedding bells like breadcrumbs was magnificent."

Zane made a sound much like an unhappy growl.

"She's a keeper," the more feminine of the mamas proclaimed. She wore a long blue dress under a fuzzy gray vest with a wreath pinned on the collar. "I'm Zane's first mama. You can call me Rita, dear."

"Lily wins by a mile in my eyes," the gray-haired cowgirl agreed. She wore an oatmeal sweater set over her blue jeans and had fashioned a necklace of Zane's white ribbons and jingle bells. "You can call me Mary, honey."

Zane relaxed, his hold on Lily easing, as well. "So, you'll pull back on your ridiculousness?"

"We'll see how your relationship with Lily goes." Rita smiled sweetly. "There are still ten parties to go. No offense, Lily."

"None taken," Lily said.

"I have…" Mary started over, exchanging a smile with Rita. "*We* have baby gifts for Nora. We've been too busy to drop them by."

"No rush," Lily assured her.

"Oh, and since we're covering details, there's mistletoe over by the entrance." Rita pointed to the doors where they'd checked in. "You'll want to stop there for another kiss before you leave."

Another kiss?

Lily didn't know whether to be happy or wary.

Zane shooed his mamas away before she could decide.

His mothers whispered to each other as they walked back toward the entrance, glancing over their shoulders.

"That could have gone better." Zane faced Lily, hands on his hips. "They're now suspicious of this being a ruse."

"Or they're curious. The whole town is curious." Lily's hand fluttered about, indicating the folks in the rest of the room. "Everyone is looking at us."

Zane scanned the hall. "Not everyone."

But, as far as Lily could see, a lot of the women who'd sought him out because of his mothers' efforts were staring.

"They just need convincing that you and I fell in love at first sight." Zane smiled at Lily but it wasn't an endearing smile. It was more like an I-have-to-pretend-I-like-you smile.

Lily much preferred his open grin and hearty laughter.

"I assumed you fell in love at first sight." Ava had been shamelessly eavesdropping. She considered Zane. "But now, I'm not sure you're the type to tumble head over heels, Zane."

Agreed.

"Of course I am." Without warning, Zane drew Lily close and right before their lips met, he whispered, "Will you kiss me?"

Lily rolled her eyes. "This is why you're single. You talk too much." And then she gave in to temptation and kissed Zane the way a couple their age and their supposed whirlwind romance were supposed to kiss. With passion and heat.

The venue erupted in applause.

Take that, world. Lily Smith has a date with Zane Duvall. A real date.

Mission accomplished, Lily began to ease back, prepared to lose Zane's friendship forever.

But Zane drew Lily closer, kissed her deeper, as if he'd forgotten this was all for show.

"You are so lucky," Ava whispered behind Lily.

Lily wasn't feeling very lucky.

She was feeling in danger—*at risk of falling for Zane for real.*

Whoa.

Kissing Lily is...

Wow.

Zane eased back, head spinning. He hadn't expected shooting stars and fireworks when they kissed.

Lily hadn't, either. She stood woodenly in his arms, a flush to her cheeks that highlighted her many freckles, brown eyes wide and bright, watching him.

She's waiting for me to define what just happened.

That would be a tall order.

I don't know how to define what just happened.

Zane was too worried about the flush he felt in his face and the rapid beat of his pulse. Because...

That was some kiss.

A doozy, his grandmother would have said.

Knocked the sense right out of him.

A cowboy with a white ten-gallon hat sat in the chair next to Lily's, the one Zane had occupied earlier.

It was a welcome distraction. Zane glanced over to tell the cowboy politely that the seat was taken, only to freeze, his smile not quite reaching his lips.

Rowdy Brown sat beside Lily.

"Brown, what are you doing?" Zane asked in a low voice.

"Don't make a scene," Lily said quietly to Zane before facing the old man. "I didn't expect to see you here."

"I didn't expect to come," the old grouch admitted. "Lot of fuss and nonsense at these parties. *Merry Christmas.*" Only Rowdy uttered the greeting in the same sarcastic way Scrooge would have said, "*Bah, humbug.*"

"But somehow you've managed to finagle a seat at our table." Zane put his hand on the back of Rowdy's chair. "I think you should find a table elsewhere."

Rowdy didn't acknowledge Zane. He stared at Lily. "That's not up to you, son."

"We have nothing to talk about," Lily said in a wobbly voice. "Especially not like this."

"Don't we?" Rowdy made a throwaway gesture toward Zane. "Didn't I tell you to stay away from the Duvall boy? I've watched him most of his life. He's either finding trouble or attracting it. Bad luck, he is. Can't hold down a job. Bears grudges for decades."

Zane clenched his jaw. "That's the pot calling the kettle black."

Rowdy harrumphed. "It's either him or me, Lily."

"Lily will always pick me because we're dating." Zane drew Lily to her feet and started moving them away from the table as a unit. "You stay here, old man. We'll be sitting elsewhere."

"Isn't Lily a bit young for you to woo, sir?" Ava asked Rowdy.

Zane could have kissed Ava for her snark. But he didn't. He kept walking.

"*Merry Christmas*," Rowdy said sourly, getting up and leaving the table. He headed off, his posture ramrod straight, at odds with the pitch and roll of his stride.

Lily stopped and watched him go, shaking her head. "That man…"

That man walked out the front door and got in the truck he'd left at the curb.

Good riddance.

"How did you say you knew Rowdy?" Zane waited until he saw Rowdy drive off before returning to their seats, only realizing when they'd sat in their chairs that Lily hadn't answered him. "You can't want to work for the man."

"I might have considered it at one point. But now..." Lily's expression faltered. "He was my mother's... He knew my mother. He's pretty gruff, isn't he?"

"He's rude," Ava said flatly.

"He's just some lonely old dude," Stu said. The teenage cowboy had sat back in his folding chair, stretched his legs beneath the table and tucked his thumbs into his jeans pockets. He looked right at home. "Being alone... It changes a fella."

Lily turned to Zane, a quirk to her brows. "That's deep."

"Cowboy wisdom," Zane murmured, for her ears only. "Sometimes they get it early." He thought Chandler would probably say that Zane was still waiting for his wisdom to come in.

"And sometimes early is when an old soul appears." Whatever Lily meant by those words was lost on Zane.

Ava got it, though. She beamed at Lily. "That's exactly right."

Their table filled up. Conversation turned to more neutral topics with their tablemates, the kiss between Zane and Lily all but forgotten.

By Lily, Zane assumed.

Because Zane...

Zane wanted another kiss. Just to make sure the first one hadn't been a fluke.

But he was afraid if he seemed too eager to kiss her again, Lily would call the whole dating thing off.

CHAPTER TWELVE

"I CAN'T DECIDE if you're a stranger or a familiar face." Coronet Blankenship, the owner of the Buffalo Diner, greeted Rowdy at the door. "Either way, I need to seat you in a place of honor." And then she led him to a booth in the back. "Or in other words, a place where you won't be disturbed."

"Thanks." Rowdy sat in the booth, tipped his white cowboy hat back and gave the diner a quick look-see. Not much had changed since he'd last been inside a year or so ago and there were few customers tonight. Rowdy gave the woman he'd gone to school with a rarely used smile. "Always liked coming here, Coronet, even before you took over."

"You've got a funny way of showing your loyalty." Coronet had white hair and a way of looking at Rowdy that was different from most folks in Clementine. She showed no fear or prejudice against him, nothing like that Duvall lad Lily was hanging around with. "You could stop by for a meal every once in a while, Rowdy. Folks our age shouldn't be eating meals out of a can or a box."

Feeling caught, Rowdy grumbled, "You'll have to prove your vittles are still better than food out of a can or a box, then."

"Everything here is homemade," Coronet said defensively. "Or have you forgotten?"

"I remember," Rowdy said in a conciliatory tone. "I sure would like a slice of your meat loaf, if you've got it. And if you still make it with your grandmother's recipe."

"Yes to both." Coronet gave a brisk nod. But before she left him, she laid her hand on his shoulder. "It's good to see you out and about, Rowdy. You should come in more often."

"Maybe I will." If he and Lily could work something out.

Coronet headed toward the order window, leaving Rowdy to his thoughts. His thoughts often followed a circular path since he'd met Lily.

What would the DNA results reveal?

How could they not reveal Lily was his daughter?

Had she taken the test yet?

How long did he have to wait?

And... What would happen afterward, either way?

Rowdy was used to giving a command and having it obeyed. Waiting wasn't his forte. Granted, his impatience and stubbornness might have added to the list of detrimental things Lucas had considered before he left Clementine with his family. But at his age, Rowdy wasn't likely to change his personality much.

Speaking of personalities, Lily's reminded him of Dawnice, who hadn't let Rowdy be grouchy or impatient. Which begged the question: *Can Lily ever accept me as her father?*

If only he had those DNA results.

CHAPTER THIRTEEN

WHILE THE EMCEE explained the rules of Pirate Bingo for the ornament exchange and servers passed out drinks and small plates of appetizers, Lily's mind drifted back to the kiss she and Zane had shared.

She hadn't been able to process her feelings afterward because Rowdy had shown up, squashing the wonder she'd felt when Zane had returned the fervor of her kiss. At the older man's appearance, she'd tensed, fearing Rowdy was going to tell everyone he was her father.

But now, she could relive those all-too-brief moments in Zane's arms...

He kissed me as if we're dating for real.

And he'd told Rowdy they were dating, too.

"Zane gets to choose an ornament first," Ava said, interrupting Lily's thoughts.

The order of gift selection was made by drawing straws that had been passed out by organizers. Zane had number one. Lily number eight.

Zane chose the ornament Nora had bought and wrapped for Lily, making quick work of the red ribbon and green paper. "A white horse." He chuckled. "This explains your groan when Missy told me she brought the same ornament. You were worried about duplicates."

"Yeah." Lily scrunched her nose. "I didn't think or hope or *wish* that *you'd* get the ornament. It's a random game, right? *Ha ha*." But Lily was afraid in all her earnestness that she looked exactly like Nora—seeking out a romance with Zane. She waved a hand as if the ornament and her confessions were no big deal. "Anyway…"

"It's my turn next." Stu extended his hand toward Zane. "I'd like the white horse ornament, please. Someday, I plan on catching Solomon. This will serve as a good reminder of my dream."

Zane handed it over, not looking pleased.

Ava tsked. "Zane, if you really want that horse ornament, you can steal it back after we've all had a turn. Those are the rules." And the way the old soul stated them let everyone at the table know that the rules would be abided by in this game. "Now, Zane gets to open another package and then player three can decide whether to steal or try their luck with a wrapped ornament."

Zane chose a bright yellow package with a shiny gold bow.

"That's mine." Teen excitement was back in Ava's voice. She grasped Lily's arm and whispered, "I hope he likes it."

Zane lifted the silver fairy princess from the box by its gold cord. "Very cute. Next." He dropped it back in its box, clearly not as entranced as Ava had been.

Ava's hand slipped off Lily's arm and she pouted.

Lily elbowed Zane and urged him to "Gush a little more," before nodding her head in Ava's direction.

"Ava should steal my ornament since it reminds me of her," Zane said dutifully. "Delicate and pretty."

"Good job," Lily whispered to him when Ava's expression lightened.

"You always want everyone to be happy," Zane noted.

Lily smirked. "Don't say you consider that a bad thing."

His gaze grazed her lips, making her pulse increase. "Sometimes, you have to follow your heart, even if it hurts someone else."

"We're speaking of this ornament game...*aren't we*?" Not that kiss? Lily's voice was low and thick. She cleared her throat. "Of course we are. Ha ha." Zane wasn't sending some kind of romantic message to her.

But her pulse refused to slow.

I'm such a dork when it comes to relationships.

The round of ornament opening proceeded. Someone stole the fairy ornament from Zane. It was stolen again by a woman sitting next to him. Then Ava stole it on her turn.

Lily was the last to have a turn. She considered

her choices. A pinecone snowman. A gold snowflake. An angel. The fairy princess. A snow globe of the North Pole. The white horse. Or one as-yet-unwrapped ornament. "I'm stealing the white horse from Stu. My nephew, Ford, will love it."

"I made it through so many rounds that I thought I was safe with my Solomon." Stu huffed but dutifully unwrapped the last ornament. It was a large cowboy snowman. "Oh, but I'm happy with this. It's my vibe."

"Too bad, Stu. Since I have the last choice, I'm going to steal that cowboy snowman from you." Zane initiated the trade. "And that means you get to take home the snow globe, buddy."

Stu took the steal gracefully, half-heartedly pointing out, as Zane had earlier, that a snow globe wasn't a tree ornament. But he gave it a good shake and smiled at the results when Ava told him how lovely it was.

Gifting game over, they dug into their appetizers—egg rolls, mini-pups in blankets and a selection of meat, cheese and fruit.

"That was fun, wasn't it?" Rita, Zane's biological mother, came to stand in the narrow space between Zane and Lily's chairs. Her gaze took in the prizes displayed on the table. "Everyone did a good job selecting ornaments. Except Zane, of course." She patted his shoulder. "I bought the angel for him to contribute tonight."

"Hoping I'd find my own angel, no doubt."

Zane reached for Lily's hand and pressed a chaste kiss to the back of it. "Be at peace, Mom."

Lily's heart thudded in her chest as Rita moved to the next table.

It's just for show. It's just for—

Zane caressed the back of her hand with his thumb.

He wouldn't touch me like that if it was just for show.

A bit of Lily's guard fell away. She stared at Zane but he'd turned as someone at the stage called for everyone's attention. She had a great view of his black cowboy hat, of every gentle bend and crisp crease.

But nothing inside her was clear.

"Thank you all for coming." The emcee of the ornament exchange tipped his tan cowboy hat back, grinning at the crowd. "I hope you had fun. My name is Clem. My wife, Maggie, and I are your hosts." That met with a round of applause. "Our judges have been circulating through the room and have chosen a few ornaments to receive prizes—most unusual, sweetest homemade and best Christmas ornament. The prize goes to the one who *brought* the ornament, not the final recipient."

The crowd let out a collective, "*Aw.*"

Lily had forgotten there would be prizes for the ornaments.

"Although white horse ornaments appear to be

a popular choice," Clem went on, "I can tell you that none of them were chosen for a prize."

Several people seemed disappointed. Glancing around the room, Lily noted at least five white horse ornaments like hers. Solomon was a popular figure in Clementine.

The winners were announced, none of which were at Lily's table. A woman named Willa won the best homemade ornament prize, a delicate, crocheted cloth star with sparkly sequins, unexpectedly receiving cheers from attendees. She thanked the judges profusely for a fifty-dollar gift card to the feedstore.

"She needed that," Zane told Lily. "She's going through a tough divorce. I'm glad she won."

"Thank you again for coming," Clem said when all the prizes had been handed out. "See you Saturday for the pancake family breakfast and games at the Done Roamin' Ranch. Merry Christmas!"

People applauded and got to their feet, gathering their coats and ornaments, wishing folks a Merry Christmas. A crew of teens descended upon the tables, clearing dishes and crumpled wrapping paper.

"That's our cue to leave." Zane drew Lily to her feet. "I'll walk you out but first I want to ask Clem if he's seen Solomon."

Ava and Stu seemed to know the teen cleanup crew and pitched in to help them, leaving Lily standing alone. She couldn't leave without Ava.

And she didn't want to leave without Zane walking her out in case…

Well, in case Zane wanted to kiss her goodnight.

A girl can dream, can't she?

"This isn't going to end well," she murmured.

Rowdy appeared beside Lily and leaned heavily on Zane's chair back. He was winded and had a ruddy complexion.

"You need to bring your cane when you go out," Lily told him, friendly concern beating out worry that Rowdy would say something to Zane about her and Rowdy's potential family tie, given the bad blood between the two men. "And slow down, Rowdy. The last thing you need to do is fall. If you break a hip, you'll never be able to get up or down your front steps. And I know you value your independence."

The old man blinked at her blankly for a moment, as if no one ever encouraged him to care for himself.

"Sorry. Just some things I've thought about since we met." Lily's gaze sought Zane's. But he was still talking to Clem, his back to Lily. "I should be going." Not that she moved toward the exit.

"Did you do as I instructed with the…you know what?" Rowdy demanded in a low voice, having regained his grouchiness. "Did you take the test?"

"Were you waiting outside this whole time just to find out?" Lily asked instead of answering him, partly to see if she could throw him off again. Partly because Lily was curious…and slightly concerned for his well-being. "Did you sit in your truck for an hour? That had to be cold. Did you have a blanket?"

"I went to the Buffalo Diner for a hot meal," Rowdy muttered in a tone less barbed than she'd heard him use in the past. "Coronet makes a decent meat loaf."

Lily was unaccountably relieved that he hadn't been out in the elements. "I've never mastered meat loaf. Mine is either too wet or too dry. I've tried homemade bread crumbs, prepackaged bread crumbs and oats. It's a disaster every time." Lily was babbling now, sounding more like Ford than herself.

She blamed it on nerves. The longer she talked to Rowdy, the more likely it was that Zane would notice. She glanced toward Zane but he wasn't paying attention to them. His back was still to her. "And yes. I put *that test* in the mail."

"Good." Rowdy smiled, which only minimally made him look less grumpy.

"But you know how I feel," Lily continued in a soft voice. "No matter the result, I—"

"You'll change your tune. I'm a wealthy man." Rowdy's chest puffed out.

"I don't care about that." She frowned. "I make my own way in the world."

"Everybody cares about money." Rowdy gave her a disdainful look. "Especially that Duvall lad you're seeing. You know he used to live on that ranch that's the grand prize of all these shindigs."

"No... I..." She hadn't known, perhaps because in a small town everyone knew. Perhaps because everyone assumed Lily had known, even Beau and Nora.

Ava appeared at Lily's shoulder and introduced herself to Rowdy.

"I know who you are," Rowdy mumbled, frowning at Ava.

"Knowing who I am and knowing me are two separate things," Ava said smoothly. Lily got the impression that Ava believed she'd come to Lily's aid with Rowdy, and maybe she had. "How do you know Lily?"

The crotchety old man scrunched his face and looked like he was going to snap.

"Be nice," Lily said to him, almost without thinking.

"We...have mutual *friends*," Rowdy said by way of explanation to Ava after a moment's pause. And then he fixed Lily with a hard stare. "Bring me the documents as soon as they come in."

"Aye-aye, Captain." Lily tipped her cowboy hat, trying to make light of the situation, one her parents had left her in by not telling her the name on her birth certificate, the one on the line labeled "father," might not be fact.

Rowdy frowned and picked up the white horse ornament. "You have a lot to learn about respect and decorum." And then he tottered off, taking the horse ornament with him.

"I figured you needed rescuing." Ava's gaze drifted toward Stu, who was helping one of the cleanup crew—a giggly, young brunette—fold chairs and stack them in a corner.

"I didn't need saving. But I appreciate the solidarity." Lily decided she didn't want Zane to walk them out for fear of another messy run-in with Rowdy. "Are you ready to go?"

"Aye-aye, Captain." Ava repeated Lily's farewell to Rowdy, then gestured toward Zane. "Aren't you going to say goodbye?"

"Naw. He's busy and it's nearly Ford's bath time." After which, she always read him a bedtime story.

They walked toward the clogged exit and Zane's mamas, who were saying farewell to each departing guest, handing out candy canes and wishing folks a Merry Christmas.

"I can't decide if it's you who isn't romantic or if it's Zane." Ava glanced back at Zane before inching closer to the doors.

"Maybe it's a little bit of both." Lily nodded to Rita and Mary as the way cleared for them to leave.

"Hang on." Rita blocked their exit with arms extended. "Lily, you haven't taken advantage of the mistletoe with Zane." She pointed to the scrappy cluster of green leaves above the double doors.

"I like you, Rita," Ava said, earning a disapproving frown from Lily, an expression the teen ignored. "We're both romantics with Lily's best interest at heart." She turned and waved madly toward the date Lily was leaving behind. "Zane! Zane! We're leaving." She pointed at the mistletoe and then at Lily.

Those still inside laughed.

Zane strode over to them, capturing Lily's gaze and making her feel self-conscious because he certainly looked eager to kiss her again.

"Where are your manners, son?" Rita demanded, pointing at the mistletoe. "You don't let your date just walk away, especially when there is holiday magic left to be used."

"Not his fault, Rita. I've got baby duty tonight and needed to rush." Lily leaped at Zane, if only to buss his lips. "Good night. Merry Christmas." She tried to run off.

But Zane caught her hand. "I'll see you to your truck."

"Atta, boy," Ava said, earning an odd look from Zane, probably causing the nineteen-year-old to explain. "We were just discussing how your relationship lacks an element of romance."

"The way yours and Stu's did, no doubt," Lily muttered, feeling ornery. "And that's not what we were discussing, Zane. We've made enough public displays of affection as a couple for one day. We don't need to be hanging all over each other the way your mamas and Ava seem to think we should."

"Right..." Zane said slowly, brow furrowed. "Are you going to the pancake breakfast tomorrow?"

"Gosh, yes," Ava gushed. "I'm so excited. The Done Roamin' Ranch puts on the most terrific Fourth of July parties. And last year's drive-through holiday display was just the best. I can help if you need me, Zane."

Lily was beginning to think Ava was better qualified to be Zane's fake date than she was.

Zane looked at Lily expectantly.

"My family will be there," Lily admitted. "So I'll be going. Honestly, I wanted to go when I saw all-you-can-eat pancakes."

"Great." Zane pushed a lock of Lily's hair around her ear. "Want to go riding on Sunday?"

"Of course we do," Ava blurted. "I'm not the best rider and I don't have a horse but—"

"Ava," Zane gently cut her off. "I was asking Lily."

"Oh." For the first time Lily could remember, Ava seemed at a loss for words.

"Is this about Solomon?" Lily asked.

Zane nodded. "I could use your help. Only experienced riders will do."

Definitely not a date.

It was time Lily hitched up her jeans and stepped back into the friend zone. "You could use the help of a *team*." Lily struck upon an idea.

"I could bring Ava, Stu and Ford if you've got a drone."

"Oh, I love that idea." Ava was back to her perky self, which was at odds with her old-soul self.

Honestly, the teen had to figure out who she was—old soul or starry-eyed teenage romantic.

"Experienced riders only," Zane repeated.

From behind them, Stu called to Ava. She stopped to wait for him while Zane and Lily continued on to her truck.

It was dark outside. The stars were coming out and homes nearby had colorful lights outlining their eaves. Lily had to admit that Clementine had a certain charm.

Zane opened Lily's truck door for her. "We need to talk about what happened in there."

The kiss, she thought he meant, not the fact that Rowdy had singled her out. And she had no intention of talking about either one.

Lily climbed into her seat and fixed a smile on her face. "I know where I stand with you. We're friends. You needed me to run blocker to your mamas tonight and it turned out okay."

"Yeah, about that…" Zane stared deep into Lily's eyes, making her glad she had a seat because nerves made her feel like an ungrounded live wire.

Had she been standing, she might have swooned.

He continued to stare at her, looking as confused as she felt.

Is Zane going to say he felt that kiss had been real? That they should date for real?

It was a foolish wish. She'd never had a man she began a friendship with fall for her, even though she had a painful history of falling for them herself.

It was a history she vowed not to repeat.

Zane cleared his throat. "I need you to pretend to be my girlfriend through the entire Christmas party scene. Ten more parties, like my mom said."

Air left Lily's lungs in a whoosh.

She'd wanted to know where they stood relationship-wise. Now, she had her answer.

She was fake date material to him. Nothing more.

Therefore, Lily had to draw a line in the friend zone sand and stay on her side. "As long as we're clear about personal boundaries. There will be no more kisses, no more holding hands, no whispering between us." No more chances for Lily to lose her heart and make a fool of herself.

If she hadn't already.

Does he know I've already fallen a little for him?

Oh, she hoped not!

"I'm… I'm…" Zane might not have been able to put how he was feeling into words, but he looked and sounded flabbergasted. "How can we pretend to be involved if we don't—"

"We'll tell folks that I'm shy about public displays of affection." Lily was proud of her businesslike tone. "Trust me. It's easier this way."

"How so?" Zane still didn't look convinced.

"We're *Friends*." With a capital F. "When I first sat down next to you at the Buckboard, you didn't look at me and think, *Wow, I wonder what it would be like to date her.*"

He scoffed. "You have no idea what I was thinking."

Oh, but she did. "You looked at me like I was the enemy at first, checking to see if I carried one of those red Christmas card envelopes. And then, you commiserated with me about your mamas' plots. Don't deny it. There were no sparks when we met." At least, on his part, she bet. "Once you saw I didn't have a Christmas card, you labeled me as friend material."

"That was… There were…" Zane frowned, then pointed toward the community center, lowering his voice. "*There were sparks in there.* Everyone saw. Even my mamas. *Especially* my mamas. If I'm not allowed to so much as hold your hand, folks—*my mamas*—are going to suspect we're faking it."

"We are faking it." Lily clung to the words, trying to believe them, for her heart's sake. "This can't be real. That kiss was an accident, a mirage, a…mistake. I don't believe you can fall for someone if there's no spark upon a first meet."

Zane's jaw dropped.

"That's right. I'm right. Case closed." Lily shut

the door just as Ava climbed into the passenger seat. Lily refused to look at Zane.

"I heard raised voices. Were you guys fighting? Having a lovers' tiff?" Ava looked hopeful.

"Shut up, Ava."

And surprisingly, the young woman did.

CHAPTER FOURTEEN

Third Party of Christmas:
Pancake Breakfast & Games
Hosted by: Done Roamin' Ranch

"ZANE, YOU'RE SUPPOSED to pour the pancake batter in the shape of a stocking or a star." Mama Mary came into the kitchen of the main house and elbowed Zane away from the griddle, where he was standing. "Round cakes won't cut it today. Why don't you help at the cornhole or horseshoe tournaments?"

"I'd prefer to work the griddle." Where he couldn't be targeted by the single ladies in attendance, without Lily by his side. Never had he kissed a woman so well and thoroughly only to have her reject him afterward.

He'd lain awake for hours last night wondering how he could make this right, and then wondering what right was—*friend or girlfriend*. At daybreak, Zane still wasn't sure.

"You're hiding? All right then. I won't ask from who." His foster mother gave him several large cookie cutters in the shape of a star. "Here. Put these on the griddle and pour the pancake batter in. When the sides bubble, remove the form and then flip your cakes."

Zane gave her a displeased look. "I've already filled two warming trays with round flapjacks." The rest of the breakfast was being cooked in other kitchens in other houses on the ranch, including the bunkhouse, which was going to smell like bacon for days. "Why didn't you give me the cookie cutters before?"

"Because I forgot. Is that what you want to hear? Or do you want me to say, *thank you for pitching in*?" She placed her palms on Zane's cheeks and brought his face down low enough that she could kiss his forehead. "Just because we got off to a bumpy start this morning doesn't mean we aren't going to get the hang of it by the end of the party."

Bumpy start...

"Speed bumps could mean slow down. Or stop." Zane poured batter into the star forms on the griddle. The batter sizzled and rose, responding the way it was supposed to. It was a reminder of Lily and her expectations for a "true" romance. He hadn't responded the way she believed he was supposed to. "I should be grateful that you're not asking me to press Pause the way Lily did." Zane wiped a hand across his forehead, already regretting the overshare.

"Is that what's bothering you? Is Lily asking

you to pump the brakes on your relationship?" Mama Mary scoffed, busy pouring batter into Christmas-stocking-shaped cookie cutters on a different griddle. "Did you come on too strong with that kiss last night? It seemed like a doozy."

Yes, it was.

Zane recalled the glowing memory of Lily's kiss and realized how much his foster mother seemed to have gleaned from what was supposed to have been a fake date. The last thing he wanted was to diagnose his rocky relationship with Lily in the company of Mama Mary. But he did admit, "Lily believes sparks need to fly on a first meet. She didn't see my sparks." He'd been enamored with her during a Christmas card onslaught and had kept his cards to himself.

"Lily's throwing up a red flag." When Zane would have preferred a checkered one. Or at least, to have checked Lily's boxes enough that she'd be comfortable hanging out with him, fake dating or otherwise. "I like her but…"

"I don't believe you need to be attracted at a first meet." Mama Mary peered at her pancakes. "Is Lily having second thoughts about dating you completely or…?"

"I guess she needs a bit of space." It was the kiss that had spooked her. But Zane was confused by it, too. "Lily did agree to go riding with me tomorrow."

"Please don't tell me you're using your search for Solomon as a date." Mama Mary poured more pancake mix into a bowl. "That's not very romantic. And that's what early dates are about—*romance*."

"Okay. I won't tell you that I'm killing two birds with one stone." Zane shrugged, turning the star pancakes over. "Maybe me and Lily have a different type of courtship than normal."

Maybe he'd accept her offer of a compromise, of no more kisses if Lily continued to fake date him.

The thought caused him to scrunch the pancake he was trying to flip. Now it was inedible.

The more he dwelled on it, the more he wanted more kisses from Lily.

Mama Mary tsked. "You should be in the stage of getting to know her, or each other, not hunting down uncatchable stallions."

"You can get to know a person on a trail ride. Have you ever considered that I'm not a traditional sort of romantic guy?" Although he'd never thought of himself in those terms before, he supposed it was true.

Ava would certainly agree.

"Women like romantic gestures," his foster mother continued to make her case. "Do you know that my Frank has never once bought me a vacuum or dishwasher for Christmas or my birthday? He's always bought me something meaningful, even if it's only flowers. Now, *that's* romantic."

Good man, his foster dad. "What are you suggesting?"

"If you insist upon taking Lily horse hunting, at least bring her something to show your regard for her. It can be as simple as a single flower."

Zane pondered that for as long as it took to remove three stars from the griddle. "Any other ideas?" Because flowers didn't feel imaginative enough.

"Well, it can't be anything that Lily could use to help you catch Solomon. That would just look self-serving. It needs to be something you know Lily enjoys and something she wouldn't buy for herself."

"This courting business isn't for the faint of heart."

"Zane is inside making pancakes." Nora had baby Cady in a sling beneath her jacket. "You should go inside and help him."

"Nice toss, Ford." Lily clapped, although Ford's beanbag toss had missed the cornhole board by several feet.

"Are you ignoring me?" Nora nudged Lily's shoulder with her own.

"Yes." Lily clapped some more. "Here you go, Beau."

Her brother's toss was long, overshooting the target.

Nora made all the right commiserative noises, then said, "If Chandler or his son sink a beanbag next, this game is over for Ford and Beau."

Lily nodded. The male Smiths were competing in the cornhole tournament and looked to be knocked out in the first round. "Maybe they'd have better luck playing horseshoes."

"I don't think Ford could toss a horseshoe far enough to hit the stake." Nora uncovered Cady's face long enough that a passerby could take a peek.

"Adorable," the cowgirl said before continuing on toward the horseshoe pits.

A lot of people had turned out for the pancake breakfast, which was being served in shifts. There were kids of all ages running around. Christmas music was piped into the ranch yard from speakers on the front porch of the grandest house on the property. Inventive homemade decorations were everywhere. The oak tree Lily and Nora stood under was wrapped in holiday lights with glittery ornaments the size of basketballs hanging from their branches. There were wreaths on fence posts and snowmen made of tires painted white.

All this Christmas cheer made Lily stressed about the shopping she hadn't done yet, which was preferable, though, to stressing over seeing Zane again or wrestling with her feelings regarding her parents keeping Rowdy a secret.

Movement on the main house's front porch caught Lily's eye. Zane carried a serving tray of pancakes down the front steps.

"Nora…" Lily put her arm around her sister-in-law's shoulders. "I need some baby time to bond with my niece." If only as an excuse *not* to seek out Zane. Heaven only knew what he'd say to her after the way they'd left things last night.

Nora grinned. The ends of her blond hair lifted in the brisk winter breeze as she showed Cady's blissful little face. "I heard you and Zane kissed last night at the ornament exchange. I'm surprised you're wasting time here with me at all."

"The gossip network in Clementine is better than the CIA." Lily was struck in the leg by a beanbag thrown by a young cornhole competitor. She tossed it back to the boy, who barely caught it before his exuberant brown dog tried to. "We won't be repeating that kiss anytime soon."

Nora drew Lily closer, whispering, "Was Zane's kiss so bad you needed to hide from him this morning?"

"No!" The word popped out and immediately, Lily knew she was in trouble.

"So, it's the opposite." Nora's expression turned sly. "The kiss was five stars and it scared you."

"Something like that," Lily grumbled, shifting her feet. "It just wasn't expected, since I picked up no signs that he was attracted to me before we lip-locked."

Nora chuckled, patting Cady. "Zane asked you to the party. That's a sign he's attracted to you. Maybe your attraction radar needs adjusting."

"Maybe," Lily allowed, not convinced.

Nora studied Lily's face. "Have I ever told you about the first time your brother kissed me?"

"No. And I don't think I want to hear this."

Lily held up her hands in the international gesture for Stop.

"It was marvelous," Nora continued anyway, speaking in a wistful voice as she rocked from side to side. "Or so I thought. Beau said he felt no spark. And yet, he gave it another chance because he liked spending time with me. So, before we left my dorm room for our second date, he kissed me. He kissed me *good*. And the rest is history." She fussed with Cady's baby sling. "Isn't it, baby girl?"

"Your experience was the exact opposite of mine."

"Not the *exact* opposite." Nora huffed. "I said your brother didn't have the hots for me at first."

"At first kiss. Still…" Lily thrust her hands in her jacket pockets. She felt restless.

"Fine. We'll talk about something else." Nora shifted the baby in the sling. "We've only talked a little about the letter Rowdy sent you." Beau had told her after that first party. "How are you feeling about that situation?"

"Confused," Lily admitted. "If it's true, I don't know whether to be annoyed with my parents for not telling me or be hurt because they didn't think they could tell me." Lily's throat began closing, choked up with emotion because she'd imagined much worse reasons for the secret to be kept.

"Oh, honey." Nora drew Lily as close as she could given the baby slung across her torso, rubbing her back consolingly. "If you're looking for answers that went to the grave, you'll drive yourself over the edge. Your parents were good people. You have to trust they made the choices they thought were in your best interest. You have to forgive them for inadvertently hurting you or you'll never be at peace."

Lily nodded. She'd been avoiding judgment, waiting for the facts the DNA test would bring. But Nora's words reminded her of something. "Rowdy told me last night that Zane has held a grudge against him for decades." Something Zane had implied in his own conversation with Lily.

"Holding grudges... That's a red flag, hon." Nora eased back, nose scrunched. "A bigger obstacle than no sparks detected at your meet-cute."

"Ha ha." Lily rolled her eyes.

"Hey." Nora nudged Lily with her shoulder once more, looking serious. "Relationships are hard enough when you're with someone who gets along with most people. Let's set aside Zane for a minute. Imagine yourself a decade from now if you don't forgive your parents for the way they handled this thing with Rowdy. Your face will be pinched. Your attitude sour. Your hair might even fall out."

Although Lily mostly agreed, she nudged Nora away. "Don't you dare use that scare tactic on your children. And for your information, my hair will never thin or fall out. It's thick and ornery and here to stay."

Nora chuckled. "Fine. But how will a grudge

impact Zane as the years go on, especially if Rowdy turns out to be…who he claims to be."

"It would be great if we could all get along." Not that Lily believed that plea would work with Zane and Rowdy.

"And what about Rowdy? He gave you dirt on Zane because…"

That was easy. "He's like Zane—a man who doesn't know how or want to forgive or compromise." Lily shrugged deeper into her jacket as a chilly wind rushed past. "Unlike Zane, Rowdy is exhausting to be around, not to mention, an accident waiting to happen. He only uses his cane at home and he's as unsteady as a newborn colt. I see a fall in his future, sadly."

Cady mewed loud enough to be heard from beneath her blanket.

Nora uncovered her sweet face and bent to kiss her forehead before picking up their conversation once more. "If you aren't related to Rowdy, what does it matter how he chooses to live? I know you. You're here today and gone someplace more interesting tomorrow. Even we don't hear from you on the regular."

Lily frowned. "When you put it like that, I sound…unfeeling."

"You're anything but," Nora assured her, jiggling the fussy baby.

"Hey, Lily." Zane approached, holding two plates loaded with food like a peace offering.

"Have you eaten? I thought we could eat together. I put extra pancakes on your plate."

He remembered.

"She'd love to," Nora said before Lily could decide if she wanted to accept or reject Zane's offer.

Ford ran up to Zane. "Is that for me? I'm starving. Losing at cornhole has made me hungry."

"Is that so?" Zane smiled benevolently at Ford. "Let's go find a seat and get you some food. Come on, Lily."

The two traipsed off.

"Yes, go on, Lily." Nora gave Lily a stronger shove. "We're right behind you, supporting you all the way."

Lily frowned at her sister-in-law. "Why does that not reassure me?"

"Probably because we're on Zane's side," Nora whispered just as Beau joined them.

Beau kissed Nora's cheek. "Speak for yourself."

"I should have stayed home in bed." But Lily's stomach growled and she headed off after Zane and Ford.

With a quick step.

"I HEARD THERE'S gonna be musical ponies later. I'm so-o-o excited." Ford ate a star pancake like a cookie, without butter or syrup, trying to stuff it into his mouth whole before his mother took charge.

"Too much." Nora held her hand beneath Ford's mouth.

Ford dutifully spit the pancake into her palm.

Nora wrapped it up in a paper napkin, then transferred a stocking pancake from her plate to Ford's. And then, she went back to rocking her baby side to side.

In Zane's eyes, Nora was up for Mom of the Year.

Zane loaded his fork with eggs.

"Ford, you're too young for musical ponies." That was Lily's brother, Beau. The blond accountant hadn't stopped giving Zane dark looks since they'd sat down to eat. "I don't want you to hurt yourself."

"Aw." Ford took a bite of sausage, talking with his mouth full. "If you had your way, Dad, I wouldn't go riding with Auntie tomorrow on the hunt for Solomon."

Zane set his fork down. He'd thought he'd discouraged anyone but Lily from riding with him tomorrow.

A thundercloud formed on Beau's face. "Little boys have no place on scouting rides for wild horses. You should have asked me."

"She asked me," Nora said. "I think it'll be good for him."

"Chances are we won't see a thing," Lily reassured her brother, scratching one of the freckles near a yet-to-fully-blossom dimple. "And Ford is an experienced rider," she told Zane, letting her smile and those dimples blossom.

That was the intriguing thing about Lily, Zane

realized. There were so many facets to her appearance and personality, from those dimpled freckles to her matter-of-fact approach to chasing down wild horses.

"Auntie?" Ford swallowed, staring at Lily incredulously. "You told me we'd catch Lightning."

"I said we'd look," Lily said, smiling indulgently. Her patience with her nephew seemed to know no bounds.

She'd be a good mom, too.

"Be prepared for a long ride," Lily continued, turning toward her brother. "A long, *safe* ride."

"I'll take plenty of cookies, Auntie," Ford reassured her. "And we'll find Lightning, too, lickety-split."

"Hang on." Zane caught Lily's eye. "Who or what is Lightning?"

"The son of Solomon," Ford answered for Lily in a tone suggesting Zane should have known this.

"Obviously," Lily added, smiling at Zane for the first time that day. "Horses have babies, you know."

"At first, I wanted to rename Solomon when we catch him," Ford went on. "But then I thought about all of us and how having a member of his family would be even better, right, Auntie?"

"Yep." Lily kept on smiling.

Lily's smile… The knots of tension in Zane's chest eased.

"Zane, honey. You are one hard man to track down." A young, attractive brunette appeared at

Zane's side, digging in her large, red leather tote. "I know I'm late but...your mom wanted me to give you this." She handed him a small box of chocolates. "And then this came in the mail." She handed him a red felt heart. "And I heard that I owe you a cup of coffee, so here." She handed him a can of espresso.

"Her purse is like Santa's sack," Ford breathed reverently. "You never know what she'll pull out next."

Laughter arose from the table next to them where Evie, who continued to play his mamas' matchmaking games, sat with some of her single friends. From the way they were looking at Zane, he didn't think they were laughing at Ford's wit.

The tightness in Zane's chest returned. He'd thought there'd be no more mama-induced ambushes.

Yet, here we are.

Lily placed a hand on Zane's arm. She nodded when their gazes met, as if she had his back, as if she always would. "It's a nice gesture."

Zane breathed easier. He smiled at his gift-giver. "Thank you. I didn't catch your name..."

"I'm Francine." She smiled at him, and then at Lily's family when she made introductions. "I thought these things for Zane were integral to the Twelve Parties of Christmas?"

"No." Lily got up and gathered her breakfast plate and utensils. "Why don't you have a seat? I'll get you something to eat."

"That is so sweet." Francine sat next to Zane, hopefully not noticing him frown at Lily's retreating back.

"You must be new to town," Nora said kindly, still rocking that baby, not making a dent in the food on her plate. "I haven't seen you before."

"I'm a friend of Ava's. We went to dental tech school together. I work part-time in Clementine and part-time in Friar's Creek." Francine smiled at Nora. "You have great teeth, by the way. It's a dental geek thing." And then she glanced at Zane. "Yours are nice, too."

Had he smiled to show her his pearly whites? He didn't think so. But that reminded him. "Where is Ava?" Zane hadn't seen her all morning.

"She and Stu are in the horseshoe competition." Francine gestured over her shoulder. "Can someone explain to me what my deliveries to Zane mean? Ava told me not to bother but I gave Rita my word I'd seek you out."

"Zane's looking for a Mrs. Zane," Ford piped up. "And my mom says his mamas want to pick his wife for him. So they have girls give him stuff." Ford shrugged. "Seems weird to me."

Beau choked on his orange juice. Nora hid a smile behind her hand.

"You should take those things back, Francine," the boy continued. "Out of all the women in the world, Zane's gonna marry my auntie."

Lily chose that moment to return to the table with a plate of food for Francine. Lily gave Zane a chilly look, contrasted by the heated look her brother gave Zane, both underscored by Nora's laughter.

"Hey, I didn't say it," Zane told Lily. But he wasn't as averse to the idea as he might have been just days before.

Zane blamed it on that darn kiss.

"How old do you have to be to compete in musical ponies?" Lily asked Zane.

As announced, the game appeared to be played the same way musical chairs was played, except that the ponies were the chairs. And unsaddled. And free to move around the arena.

"We set the age at eight," Zane told her, sitting next to her on the metal arena railing. "Just like they do in junior rodeo."

Since Ford's announcement that Zane was going to marry her, things had been strained between them.

A cowboy stopped on the other side of Zane. "Are you still in town? What's it been? Six months? Are you home for good this time? Or is the itch to move on increasing?"

"I'm happy here." Zane glanced at Lily.

The cowboy continued along, leaving Lily wondering...

"I can see the questions in your eyes," Zane told her. "We both mentioned working other jobs in other places."

Lily nodded. "But you seem to always return to Clementine, whereas I...just keep moving."

"We're alike, yet different." Zane nodded. "Our résumés could probably fill a page. But unlike you, I've followed my interests beyond ranch work."

"Because..."

"Your work is supposed to be your passion." Zane eased his shoulders back but didn't take his gaze from Lily's. "I've often thought something I was enamored with would turn into something I was passionate about but... When it didn't, I'd come back here."

"That's brave."

He tilted his head from side to side. "Some might say a waste of time."

"And if they did, it'd be because they play life safe." Lily leaned closer, feeling a connection she'd never felt with Zane before. "It's easy to stay in one place, to find the right partner, buy a house in the right school district. But for people like us, there's always something appealing about what might be on the next horizon."

Zane nodded, dark eyes intense in their regard of her. "Or that there's something missing in where you currently are."

Lily sucked in an unexpected breath.

He could be what's missing.

In the center of the ring, the tall, lanky ranch foreman, Chandler, called for everyone's attention. "We're about to start musical ponies. In my experience, some kids are going to fall. But rest assured, the loamy soil in the arena creates a soft landing."

Ford climbed up on the other side of Lily. "If I was playing, I wouldn't fall off. Good cowboys don't fall off horses."

Lily refrained from reminding Ford that he'd taken a tumble the other day just by leaning on Jet.

"We have Doc Nabidian here in case there are tears." Chandler pointed the older man out. "But we've yet to have a broken bone."

"Knock on wood." Zane and several other cowboys rapped their knuckles on the metal arena railings.

"That's not wood," Lily pointed out.

"It's the thought that counts," Zane told her just as his mamas walked past. He placed a hand over Lily's on the rail, his raised brows as if asking Lily if it was okay.

Outwardly, Lily did nothing but say evenly, "You're becoming a problem."

But inside...

Inside, Lily was in turmoil.

Zane's hand was warm. His touch invigorating. And those cocked brows accenting his confident male attitude?

This. This is what was missing before. Him.

Lily smiled, even though she knew she shouldn't. "And you don't care that you're a problem for me, do you?"

Zane shook his head. "I'd rather be your problem this holiday season than anyone else's."

Lily frowned. "My Christmas Cowboy? Who'd believe that?"

"Just my mamas." Zane turned toward the cluster of ponies in the arena as the familiar notes of "It's Beginning to Look a Lot Like Christmas" filled the air.

The small cowboys and cowgirls walked in a circle around the ponies, each slowing before passing one in case the music stopped.

Zane's mamas stared their way, exchanging words, making Lily feel as if she was under a microscope.

"I could do this," Ford murmured.

"Me, too," Zane murmured.

Lily didn't dare glance his way. Emotionally, this was new territory for her. She had to tread carefully. She had to be sure.

"Ford, I bet you'll win musical ponies when you're eight." Lily gave her nephew a side hug, careful not to shift her hand from underneath Zane's.

CHAPTER FIFTEEN

"Are we there yet?" Ford asked from the back seat of Zane's truck on Sunday afternoon, clutching the drone's remote like it was the key to unlocking the universe and if he let it go, someone would steal it from him. "I'm ready to ride."

"You just asked three minutes ago," Lily said from the front seat. She wore faded blue jeans, a gray hoodie and her brown cowboy hat. She'd tossed her shearling jacket in the back seat before they'd left an hour or so ago. "And the answer is the same, Ford. No. We're not there yet. We won't be riding until we spot Solomon, silly."

Zane chuckled.

He'd imagined this trip for him would be laden with verbal landmines. Each getting him in deeper with Lily. But since she'd brought her nephew along, it was as if that kiss and subsequent argument on Friday night had never happened, as if Ford had never proclaimed they were going to marry each other.

No. They were back to Lily's beloved friend zone, which suited Zane just fine since he was beginning to think it was in the friend zone that he could establish a more solid relationship with her. Sparks or no sparks.

Zane glanced in the rearview mirror, catching his chaperone's eye. "Have you spotted a white horse, Ford?"

"No, sir. And I've been looking. Can't we ride horses until we see him?"

"Nope," Lily said.

Smiling, Zane drove down a seldom-used road, heading toward a ridge where they could look over the valley and launch the drone. They jostled over the bumpy gravel, dust kicking up behind Zane's truck and the large horse trailer hitched to it.

"I don't see Solomon. Or Lightning. Or any horse," Ford lamented. "There isn't even a cow out here."

"Well, let's hope the drone can locate him," Lily said, lowering a pair of binoculars she'd brought and then applying a layer of peppermint lip balm, from the tube he'd gifted her this morning. "If we don't find Solomon, we're just chasing ghosts out here."

They pulled the trailer to a stop near an open patch of land on a rise dotted with scrub grass and more scattered gravel. It was their second stop that morning.

"I call dibs on flying the drone." Ford struggled to unbuckle his seat belt, hindered by his thick blue jacket.

Lily hopped out and then helped him get free. "Zane said no drone flying for you, cowboy."

"It's not my drone," Zane said, gently taking the controller from Ford. "Or I'd let you try it, big guy."

"Auntie…" Ford pouted and ran to her. "I can fly the drone. It's just like my video game at home."

"The one where we race cars and crash into rainbows and waterfalls for fun?" Lily was trying to make light of things or at least help Ford see the light—that he was too young and inexperienced for the equipment.

"I crash on purpose." Ford crossed his arms over his chest, a mulish expression on his little face. "At least, we should ride horses. All we've been doing is driving around."

"We aren't getting the horses out until we find Solomon." Zane sent the drone into the air, watching the controller screen instead of the drone itself. It was dizzying to follow the ground as it sailed past. He sent the drone higher up and slowed its forward progress.

"And there it goes." Ford kicked a rock with his cowboy boot. "No fun for me."

"You can look through my binoculars." Lily handed them to Ford.

Out of the corner of his eye, Zane saw Ford point the binoculars at his feet. "Whoa. That beetle is humongous."

Lily laughed, moving closer to Zane but keeping herself a friendly distance from him. "Anything?"

"Nothing." Zane sent the drone even higher, increasing the amount of land in the viewfinder.

"There's another bug!" Ford announced triumphantly.

"Which is great," Lily told Ford. "But we're looking for horses. Check on the pasture, Ford."

The boy straightened. "Whoa." He lost his balance and fell onto his butt, nearly losing his straw cowboy hat. "Head rush."

Lily hurried over to help him to his feet. "You've got to move slowly."

"I don't do slow," Ford complained, patting his straw cowboy hat down on his head. "That's why I wanted to fly the drone. It goes fast."

"There's nothing here," Zane proclaimed after several minutes of sending the drone in a grid across the fields below. He guided the drone back toward them, setting it down carefully on the road.

Lily chuckled. "That's better than your last landing." Where the drone had skittered and bounced before flipping upside down.

"I could do a good landing," Ford muttered. And then louder, "A perfect landing."

"Before I let you do any landings," Zane said mildly, "you have to learn to fly without crashing."

"I could do that, too," Ford assured him.

Lily cleared her throat, drawing Zane's gaze. She shook her head.

"Let's see how things go at the next stop." Zane collected the drone and returned it to the back seat of his truck.

They all got back into the truck.

"On to the next lookout." Zane set the truck in gear and pulled forward.

"I'm bored." Ford kicked the back of Lily's seat.

Good aunt that she was, Lily had a ready response for that. "Here. You can play on my phone. I've got the alligator game on there."

"Crunch-crunch," Ford said gleefully, accepting Lily's phone and tapping the screen like a pro.

Lily touched Zane's arm. "We should get out and ride at the next stop if only to tire him out."

"That doesn't sound very efficient," Zane countered. "And you were the one who said we have to approach this search in a productive manner."

"That was before I imagined Ford riding along." Lily angled herself toward him. "Five-year-old boys need adventure, not methodology."

"And we have a tiny chaperone with us because…" Zane knew but he wanted to hear her say it. He had to wait about a quarter mile first.

"Because this isn't a date." Lily pursed her lips. It looked like she was considering whether to ask him to turn around and head back.

"I never said it was a date." But the idea appealed, the same as it had after their big kiss on Friday night. He reached for the tube of lip balm she'd left in the cup holder and applied it to his lips, deliberately easing across the boundary of her friend zone by doing so. "Why didn't you go to college?"

Lily drew back. "Who said I didn't?"

"But you didn't." Zane wasn't certain how he knew. He just did. "Neither did I."

"You're right. I didn't go. I set out to see the world, as my father used to say." She dipped her head, so that her face and those freckles were hidden by her brown hat brim. "I liked the social aspect of school and some subjects were interesting. Not math."

We're so alike, it's funny.

Zane told her a bit about some of the unusual occupations he'd tried—stock car driver, short-order cook, circus animal wrangler. "My tenures were shortest in jobs that involved math."

"I enjoy working on ranches." Here, she raised her head so that Zane could see her light smile and her glowing brown eyes. "And I like establishing a rapport with horses."

"But not with people," he surmised.

Her smile dimmed a bit. "I like people just fine."

"At a distance," he guessed. "After all, you don't date."

"Doesn't sound like you do, either, if your mamas are to be believed." Lily leaned on the center console, as if needing to be close to read his reaction to her next words. "Why don't you date more?"

This felt like an important question. His answer would make Lily clam up, or alternatively, open up.

Zane proceeded slowly, piecing together an answer on the fly. "Well, since I... I'm not sure what I want to be or do when I grow up. Until then, it doesn't seem fair to those dates." The statement reminded Zane about Chandler telling him it was time to choose a career path and stick to it.

He rubbed at his suddenly tight chest.

"That's fair." Lily eased back into her space, tipping her cowboy hat up a little. "I've never really planned my life or factored in dating, or not. But I know plenty of people who do."

"Ava comes to mind," Zane said in a teasing tone.

"That's true." Lily peered at Zane's face once more. "She thinks you're the kind of cowboy who'd make her happy."

Zane scoffed.

"Regardless of how many times she calls herself an old soul, she's still too young to be with me. My money is on Stu." But he didn't want to talk about Ava or Stu. He circled back around to a topic that interested him—Lily. "So tell me. How do you approach dating? Other than what you told me about there needing to be sparks at that first meet." Just saying that out loud riled him. She'd set off sparks in him when they first met, and every meeting since. But they'd been a gentle flame until their lips touched.

"I... I'm not sure what you mean." Lily glanced away.

"Come on. You know exactly what I mean." Zane kept his tone light, kept his frustration at bay. "Do you date to have fun? To break up the monotony? To feel like you aren't the odd man out?" He'd dated for those very reasons. "Or are you dating to find the man you'll spend the rest of your life with?"

"First off..." Lily drew a long breath, releasing it slowly before facing him once more. "I can count on one hand the number of dates I've had in the past decade. Sad, I know. But I haven't been looking at my life as if a partner is necessary to make me happy. Frankly, it was freeing just to be out on my own. My father was something of a Debbie Downer when it came to me."

Zane smiled. "No offense to the Debbie's of the world."

"Agreed. Perhaps in this case, the phrase should be Davie Downer. No offense to the Davies of the world." She chuckled. "My dad just didn't *get me*, you know. He doted on Beau and my mother. But me... He looked at me sometimes the way you look at a mangy cat who's strayed into your yard. Like I didn't belong."

Ouch. "That's rough. Poor you."

"You're not going to defend my dad?" Lily gave

a wry laugh. "Most people are quick to come to his defense and make excuses for him."

He bet her brother, Beau, fell into that camp.

"Most people aren't former foster kids," Zane pointed out. "As a foster, I've heard every kind of story imaginable about family dynamics. If you say your father's love was withheld, I believe you."

And that might just explain, in part, why Lily was so touchy about dating and relationships in general.

They drove over a small rise, revealing another field that seemed to stretch on forever.

"Look!" Lily pointed.

On the other side of the fence, perhaps one hundred yards out, Solomon stood watching them, as still as the white horse ornaments brought to the Coogans' party.

"It's him!" Ford cried. "Stop the truck. Mount up. Chase him down and *find me Lightning*." This last bit came out in a commanding growl.

Zane parked and they hurried to take the horses out. Arthur, his raw-boned, bay gelding. Jet, Lily's black gelding. And Mouse, Ford's brown pony.

Ford ran around the trailer, his hat slightly crooked on his head. "Can I fly the drone *now*?"

"No need for the drone." Zane tightened his horse's girth strap. "We have Solomon in our sights."

Ford groaned dramatically but stood beside Mouse, rubbing the pony's nose while Zane and

Lily checked their tack was secure and offered their mounts water from a bucket.

But when they were ready to ride…

"Where's Ford?" Lily looked around, a panicked note in her voice. "Ford? Where are you?"

"*WHEEEE!*" Ford exclaimed over the sound of the drone's sudden propellers.

"Ford!" Zane barked, running around the horse trailer and lunging to grab the remote before the low-flying drone crashed into something. He managed to land the thing with only the briefest of skids and no tumbles. "What are you doing?"

"Duh." Ford crossed his arms. "I'm *practicing*."

While Zane inspected the drone, Lily ran over to her nephew. "You need permission, Ford, it's not your drone. If it's damaged or if you broke it, you'll have to pay to replace it."

"I could just write a letter to Santa and ask him to replace it." There was a hint of hesitation in Ford's voice, a loosening of his crossed arms at the consequences of his actions. "*If* it's broken. Is it okay, Zane?"

"It seems fine." If the kid hadn't reminded Zane of himself at that age and there had been damage to the drone, Zane might have been angry, more so with himself than Ford. He knew better than to leave temptation within a curious boy's reach. But no harm, no foul. "We don't need the drone when Solomon is right there." But when Zane looked up, the white horse was gone. Zane was tempted to launch the drone, after all. "Mount up. Let's see if we can catch him."

Zane stowed the drone in the truck bed and then they rode out. The horses were eager to run but Zane knew no matter how eager he was to catch up to Solomon that the horses needed to warm up first.

They reined them in at a fast walk until they reached the place where they'd last seen Solomon.

"He's not here," Ford moaned, slouching in the saddle.

"Circle around. Let's see if he left tracks." Zane thought that unlikely given the lack of recent rain, but he was taking Lily's advice to heart—act on solid leads.

"There are tracks here." Lily pointed at the ground near her. "Looks like he ran that way."

They set off at a trot but soon transitioned to a ground-eating gallop that quickly left Ford and his pony behind. Lily signaled Zane to stop and trotted back to her nephew.

"I don't like being forgotten." Ford was teary.

Lily dismounted, gave him a hug and then sent the boy off ahead of them. "You set the pace, Ford. We'll follow you."

Once Ford had Mouse moving at a modest tempo, he began singing "Frosty the Snowman." It was the first time that day that Zane and Lily were truly alone. And Zane couldn't think of anything to say, even though he wanted to say so much—about himself, about the quail he saw scuttling between scrub brush, and to ask her questions about herself. More questions than he could count right now.

"Lovely weather we're having," Zane finally said. "Cold but dry."

Lily glanced at him, brows raised.

"Come on," he prodded. "I'm trying over here."

Ahead of them, Ford sang louder.

Lily sighed. "I suppose anytime the sun is out, it's a beautiful day for a ride."

"That's better." Zane patted Arthur's neck. "I used to live over the hill there. That's where the ranch is located. The one Rowdy Brown is giving away as a grand prize."

"If you win it back, will it make you happy?" Lily spoke slowly, as if unsure about asking. "Would you forgive Rowdy and move on with your life?"

The poor taste in Zane's mouth indicated his answer was no.

And Lily seemed to know it. "I suppose asking if you'll forgive him if your name *isn't* drawn on Christmas Day is a moot point, as well."

Zane shifted in his saddle. "Why should I forgive Rowdy? Do you want me to? You don't even like him."

"Rowdy said you bore grudges. He said..." Lily trailed off.

That I couldn't hold down a job.

Zane pressed his lips together.

"It's important to forgive, Zane. I've been

thinking about that a lot lately, wrestling with my own capability to shed hard feelings and blame. And I... I wish you felt the same way." Lily cued her horse into a trot and left Zane in her dust. She caught up to Ford and began singing "The Twelve Days of Christmas" with him.

Lily wanted him to forgive the man responsible for the breakup of his family?

Never.

Zane held Arthur back, letting Lily and Ford sing together, not even weighing in on whether it was nine ladies dancing or nine drummers drumming when they got confused.

But he didn't like the distance between them. Not the physical and not the emotional.

And he couldn't think of why.

CHAPTER SIXTEEN

"Stop singing, Auntie." Ford tipped his cowboy hat back and looked up at her on the much taller Jet.

"Is it because I didn't think nine was drummers drumming?" Lily asked.

Ford nodded. "Sometimes a cowboy just has to sing the way he thinks is right."

"Understood. You've got to go your own way." Lily tried to fill herself with cheer, tried to project that veneer to Ford and hoped Zane would...

She didn't know what she wanted Zane to do or how she wanted him to feel.

Oh, yes, I do.

She wanted Zane to consider her a romantic possibility, not a friend who helped him pull off a fake dating ruse. But the only time she'd felt his interest in her to be more elemental had been during that kiss. She didn't want their relationship to be based solely on that...on the chemical reaction of lips touching for a matter of seconds. Maybe minutes? Nonetheless, Lily wanted Zane to appreciate the beauty of who she was—inside and out.

It's my hang-up more than it is his.

As if summoned by her thoughts, Zane came alongside her on his big-boned bay, settling in at a walk next to her. "Ford, there's a copse of trees ahead. Why don't you ride over and see if Solomon is hiding in there?"

"Okay!" With a whoop, Ford cued Mouse into a trot. It was a slow trot.

Jet watched the pair leave, muscles bunching as if he wanted to catch up to them.

"I hope you don't mind," Zane began. "I wanted us to be alone again for a minute."

Lily may have taken a page from his book and grunted an acknowledgment. She wasn't feeling particularly generous with him at the moment.

"Who is it you've forgiven? Or are trying to forgive?" The prairie wind gusted. Zane settled his cowboy hat more firmly on his head. "Or should I ask why forgiveness is so important to you? Have you never received forgiveness you wanted from someone? From a boyfriend or…or family?"

Lily glanced toward Ford but he was out of hearing range and approaching the scrub oak trees. And then her gaze returned to Zane. To the lines defining his handsome face. To the eyes that regarded her with compassion.

Slowly… Lily began to tell Zane about how she'd received a letter from a man claiming to be her father, carefully leaving out any mention of Rowdy or when she'd received the letter.

"You were an outcast in your own family," Zane

said slowly. "I'm sorry. I guess that explains why you've never set down roots."

"What do you mean?" Lily was taken aback. "I have roots. I have Beau and his family."

"But Clementine isn't your home. You have no *home*. No place of your own that holds special memories."

Lily felt a cold, empty space in her chest.

He's right.

"Not that you can't decide to have one. A home, I mean." Zane's gaze softened. "What is it they say? Home is where the heart is."

Stay in one place? Year after year?

Lily was filled with trepidation and she wasn't entirely sure why. She tried to puzzle it out loud with Zane. "Every feeling I've had toward the people I thought were my parents has been called into question. Did my father's resentment about my mother's liaison get transferred to me? Was my mother trying to protect me or herself with this secret? But in the end, I won't have answers. I just have to try and make my peace with it, or I know I'll never be able to move forward. I'll always have a bitter thought in my head whenever someone mentions my mother."

"You think that's what's holding me back?" Zane sat up in the saddle, looking surprised. "The fact that I hold grudges?"

She kept herself from nodding because she said, "Only you can answer that."

Zane's expression turned thoughtful. And then he glanced at her. "Who was it that was your friend but didn't pan out as anything more? Was it a while ago, or someone more recent?"

Lily rolled her eyes, not inclined to tell him. "Why do you want to know?"

"I'd like to give him a good thumping because he made you extra cautious."

"Meaning he ruined your chances to successfully fake date me?" Lily smirked.

Jet had lengthened his stride, doing his best to catch up to Ford and Mouse when Lily held him on a tighter rein.

"I've changed my mind," Zane said. "It's punishment enough that this guy has probably realized what a mistake he made when he let you go."

Be still my heart.

Lily's mouth went dry.

"Hey, come over here!" Ford shouted. He'd gotten off his pony and was standing between some trees. "I found something."

Zane and Lily galloped over. Jet didn't need more than the lightest of cues.

When they got closer, Ford held up a horseshoe. It had a nail stuck in one hole.

"A horse threw a shoe out here?" Zane glanced around.

"Maybe that shoe belongs to a horse that was being used to track down Solomon?" Although

Lily couldn't explain why the horseshoe would be in a small cluster of trees.

"Makes sense, I suppose." Zane scanned the horizon. "Let's follow the trail some more."

After a few miles, they reached another wire fence. On either side, there were hoofprints. Signs of a takeoff and landing.

"That is a special horse." Lily was a bit in awe. "I bet he'd be good at the steeple chase." Horse jumping competitions.

"Was he alone, Auntie?" Ford hopped off Mouse and pressed his fingers into a hoofprint. The dirt crumbled and lost its form at his touch. "Where's Lightning?" Ford's eyes lit up and a smile flashed across his sweet face. "Can we jump the fence, too?"

"We're not jumping that." Zane quickly rained on Ford's parade. "I don't think Arthur has ever jumped anything higher than a fallen log."

"Same as Jet," Lily admitted.

"Well, Mouse can do it." Ford climbed back in the pony's saddle, then stood in the stirrups and pointed toward the fence. "We can do anything!"

"There will be no jumping today, Ford." Lily studied the empty grazing land on the other side of the fence. "Is that someone's property? Or is that still government land?"

"I believe it's government land." Zane resettled his cowboy hat on his head. "But... The closest properties to this would be my family's former ranch and Rowdy's spread."

The last thing Lily wanted to do was encounter Rowdy. "We should head back."

"Back-back? Or back to the truck?" Zane scanned the area ahead. "I'd like to drive out a bit further and use the drone again."

"Can I fly it?" Ford asked. "Please. You said I need practice."

Zane nodded.

Ford crowed his pleasure.

The ride back to the truck was uneventful, as inconsequential as their conversation.

They loaded the horses into the trailer. Watered the livestock. Ate cookies and drank water. Then they drove farther out, past miles of empty pasture. Nothing moved other than scrub brush bending to the will of the prairie wind. There was no Solomon. No horses. No cattle.

Zane brought the rig to a halt on a rise. "This seems like a good place to get out the drone again."

"That's me. I'll do it." Ford was overly excited whereas moments earlier he'd looked about ready to doze off.

Lily helped Ford out of the truck while Zane set the drone in the middle of the dirt lane they'd been driving on.

"Let me have the controller." Ford darted around Zane, trying to grab it. "Please-please-please."

"Wait." Zane was calm in the face of all Ford's

boyish excitement. "I'm going to launch it in the air and then you can fly it around."

Ford looked crestfallen. "But takeoffs and landings are the best part."

"That's fair, Ford." Lily came over and placed her hands on her nephew's shoulders, drawing him to her.

Filling the air with the buzz of small propellers, Zane launched the drone. Then he brought the controller near Ford. "The only toggle I want you to touch is the one that goes side to side. Here. Not this one. It controls the up and down." Zane showed Ford the difference. "We don't want any crashes."

"I won't crash it. I promise." Ford accepted the controller, and scurried a few feet away. "I can see everything on the screen. This is so cool."

Lily agreed. "Can you slow down, Ford?" She was getting queasy peering at the ground rushing past on the display.

"Was that a horse?" Ford tried turning the controller like a steering wheel but the drone kept speeding forward. "It *was* a horse. How do I make it go back?"

"Toggle around in a circle." Zane moved Ford's finger on the horizontal control knob.

They were all leaning over the controller, squinting at the screen. Lily had left her binoculars in the truck.

"That's him!" Ford cried, trying to direct the

drone with an imaginary steering wheel once more. "Go back! Go back! Go back!"

"I didn't see anything. Did you?" Lily asked Zane.

"A flash of white." Zane tipped his cowboy hat back and leaned in closer. "It could be anything. A rock. A reflection off a pond."

"Solomon," Ford said firmly. "It's him. I saw him."

Working together was a challenge, but Ford and Zane managed to bring the drone back around and slow it down.

"It's Solomon! Let's say hello." Ford forgot every bit of instruction and caution he'd been told. He pushed the vertical toggle down...down...down...

It was indeed a white horse, grazing and growing larger on the screen as the drone careened toward it.

Lily glanced up, searching for the horse and drone with her own eyes.

In the far distance, a white horse lifted its head, turned tail and ran as the drone dive-bombed him.

"Ford, *stop*!" Zane shouted, but it was too late. The drone veered wildly and then plummeted to the ground.

The visual feed stopped. The screen went dark.

"Shoot," Ford whispered, frowning. He glanced up at Zane. "How do I get another life?"

"This isn't a video game." Zane had the controller and was trying to launch the drone once more. "It's not responding."

"I'll get it!" Ford offered, already running toward the fence. "We need to find Solomon again."

"Hold up, cowboy," Lily called, hurrying after him. "You're not going out there alone. Zane, should we take the horses?"

"No. There's no gate nearby. We'll hop the fence and walk over." Zane joined them at the fence and helped them get to the other side. "Maybe we'll find out what Solomon likes about this place."

When they reached the crash site, the drone was miraculously intact, tilted on its side in a bush, which Zane said was why it wouldn't fly.

But all thoughts of the drone disappeared as a majestic white horse stood just beyond it, his head high, his eyes alert.

"*It's him*," Ford whispered, frozen in awe.

Lily didn't dare move, either.

"Stay back," Zane warned. "He's wild. Don't spook him. Let him make the first move."

But it wasn't Solomon who made the first move—it was Ford. He took a cautious step forward, his wide eyes shining with excitement.

"Ford, no!" Lily whispered, grabbing his shoulder.

"Look," Ford murmured. "He's not scared of me."

To their amazement, Solomon didn't bolt. Instead, he stood his ground, watching them with calm, intelligent eyes. He didn't move when Ford took another step toward him.

"Well, I'll be," Zane said in a quiet tone. "Solomon's got a soft spot for troublemakers."

Ford sneezed.

The spell was broken.

Solomon raced off, head and tail high, gliding toward the fence nearest Rowdy's ranch.

"FORD IS NEVER going to get over this," Lily predicted. "And neither are you."

She sat in the passenger seat of Zane's truck. Ford was asleep in the back.

They were just a mile or so from Clementine proper, still bouncing across the government dirt road. Lily was right. The day had been thrilling. And not just because they'd found Solomon. The more Zane learned about Lily, the more he wanted to learn.

He was still on cloud nine over getting so close to the stallion. It probably helped that the drone hadn't been damaged. But Zane knew he had to proceed carefully. "It was a good day. A good memory."

Lily reached for the lip balm they'd been sharing all day. "Frankly... Solomon looked younger than I'd thought he'd be. I'd guess nine, or ten years old. How long has this legend been around?"

"Longer than that. Maybe this actually is the son of Solomon." Zane grinned.

"More likely *grandson* of Solomon." Lily

dropped the tube back into the cup holder. "Did you ever see Solomon when you lived on your old ranch?"

Zane hadn't thought that far back. "I guess... I remember my dad talking about him, but I don't remember ever seeing the horse. No. Occasionally, I'd see a herd of horses over by Rowdy's."

Lily was quiet.

Zane glanced at her. "What's wrong?"

Lily was frowning and staring off into the distance.

"You don't think I should capture him, do you? Is that why you've gone quiet all of a sudden?"

"No." Lily's expression turned apologetic. "My mind wandered. But... No. I'm not sure you should capture him."

Zane felt a sliver of betrayal but he pushed harder, trying to understand her point of view. "Did you feel the same way when you chased down mustangs?"

"No. But those horses were destined for good homes, not the rodeo roughstock corral." Lily's voice lowered. "When we were talking earlier and you said I had no roots, no home base... Then I saw Solomon and I feel this kinship. His home is wherever he is. He's a nomad. Like me."

"Like me, too." Zane didn't want her to present an argument he'd agree with. "This is a deep, philosophical conversation when it should be about economics and that horse's future." Zane slowed as he came up to the highway leading into Clementine. "Without inoculations, without dewormers, hoof trimming, proper nutrition and so on, that horse won't live as long as a domesticated animal."

"But will he be happy fenced in? Tied down? Spirit broken?" Lily's cheeks pinkened. "Change is hard, whether you're a horse or a human."

"Are you trying to say you'll always be a rolling stone?" Zane didn't like that idea. Lily was good with Ford, good with people, good with...*for* him. "I wouldn't mind seeing you stay in town."

"As your permanent fake girlfriend until you find the next job that interests you?" Lily stared out her side window. "No, thanks. A few weeks of pretending is more than enough."

He was quickly talking himself out of the pretending part and disappointed she wasn't on the same page.

"Does that mean you'll still be my girlfriend for the rest of the Christmas parties?" He held his breath, waiting for her to answer.

"Zane... It goes against my better judgment but—"

"That's a yes?" He reached for her hand, entwining their fingers together.

"Yes."

They spent the rest of the drive back to her brother's house making arrangements for the next party.

It was all rather…domestic. Comfortably so.

As long as Zane chose to believe he could change Lily's mind about the pretend part of their relationship.

CHAPTER SEVENTEEN

"You just met Zane. And now you're officially dating?" Beau stopped in the midst of changing Cady's diaper to stare at Lily on Monday morning a week after Lily had gone riding with Zane. "And I had to hear about it from one of my clients in an email this morning? This doesn't sound like my down-to-earth sister."

"You mean the woman who never dates?" Nora asked, seemingly on Lily's side. She moved a bright gold Christmas ball to another branch. "Are you saying you'd prefer if she *never* dated anyone?"

"You want me to be a spinster?" Lily smiled. She didn't feel like spinsterhood was in the cards anymore. She'd spent a week dating Zane and even though they'd kept things low-key in terms of public displays of affection, she was beginning to trust the growing feelings between them.

"What's wrong with Zane?" Ford popped up in Lily's defense, having finished his cereal. "I like him. He let me fly his drone."

"He let you *crash* his drone," Lily teased.

"But I found Solomon." Ford was still extremely proud of that. Had been for a week.

"You found Solomon," Lily agreed. "And this dating thing between Zane and I isn't serious." They'd only held hands on Saturday night at the Sixth Party of Christmas, a holiday trivia contest that had been hosted by the Pierce Ranch.

"It's not serious? Then why are you dating him?" Beau demanded, finishing Cady's diaper change and lifting the good-natured baby into Nora's arms, halting any more ornament adjustments. "At your age, you should only be dating men who you feel are serious about a commitment."

"At her age?" Nora's brows shot up.

"At my age?" Lily's brows shot up.

"Sorry." Beau went into the kitchen to wash his hands. "But you know what I mean. Half the people your age have already been to the altar at least once."

"And half again to divorce court." Lily shook her head. "Your problem is that you want to protect me from heartbreak but in order to do so, you'd have me never risk my heart."

"Sorry." Beau looked sheepish. "Thus is the conundrum of every older brother. I'll go back to minding my own business now."

"Why aren't you having more dates with Lily?" Zane's mother demanded on Thursday morning. Christmas tree earrings dangled from her ears.

"We have a date on Friday night." Zane sat at

the kitchen table in the main house at the Done Roamin' Ranch poring over a local map with Chandler, trying to pinpoint locations of Solomon sightings in the last few weeks. "This is where Ryan and Jo live, right? They mentioned they saw Solomon yesterday, while the next ranch over is Dix and Allison's. They saw him a week ago."

"That's a long way from where you saw him on Sunday." Chandler studied the map. "It's like he's moving back and forth, north to south."

"Is this the nonsense keeping you from spending time with Lily?" Mom peered at the map.

"Life is keeping me from spending time with Lily every day," Zane countered. "She's helping her family and I'm working."

And for now, Zane was happy with the way things were. He and Lily had had a nice time in the past week. Granted, they hadn't kissed. But they regularly held hands and Lily had seemed comfortable with that.

"Obsessed over a horse," Mom scoffed. "And the Bad Luck Ranch. You should spend more time on your love life."

"Everything in good time." Zane rolled up the map. "We're going to look at these in the bunkhouse. Talk to you later, Mom."

"Bye-bye for now, son." She headed the other direction toward the living room.

Zane and Chandler grabbed their coats and cowboy hats and crossed the ranch yard.

"You should listen to your mother," Chandler said in a low voice.

"Why?"

Rusty ran up to Chandler, dirty tennis ball in his mouth.

Chandler took the ball from him and gave it a hard throw, sending his dog racing past a trio of inflatable reindeer. "Because she was looking at you like she had something in mind."

"More matchmaking?" Zane sighed.

He and Lily needed to up their dating game.

"THIS IS A MISTAKE." Lily was driving toward Rowdy's place and talking to herself.

Nora and the baby were at the doctor for a wellcheck. Ford was at school. Beau was at work. It was the first chance Lily had to sneak off to Rowdy's. The first chance since she'd gotten close to Solomon, that is. And she felt guilty about it.

Hence her speed.

Lily drove too fast and took the slight rollercoaster rise at a speed that dropped her stomach. "He'll probably complain about that." But when she pulled into the ranch yard, no one came out to meet her.

Immediately, she thought the worst—that Rowdy had fallen and couldn't get up.

Lily ran up the porch steps and pounded on the front door, taking note of the lack of Christmas wreath, strings of lights or other holiday decorations outside. "Rowdy? Rowdy, are you there?"

No answer. No sounds of uneven footsteps approaching the door, either.

But there were sounds at the ranch.

The steady ring of a blacksmith's hammer on metal.

Lily turned, hurrying down the stairs and heading for the outbuildings. There was a van parked between a large garage and the larger barn. Its back doors were open like metal wings, which blocked her view of the smithy and the source of all that banging.

Lily came around the back door and stopped. Shocked.

Rowdy straightened, setting down the hoof of a white horse. "What are you doing here?"

"Solomon?"

Rowdy wore smithy chaps, a baseball cap and his characteristic frown. "Did the DNA results come in?"

"No." Lily approached the white horse he was shoeing. "I want to know why—"

"Why I think you're related to me?" Rowdy took the horseshoe he'd been fitting back to the forge at the other end of the van. "It may have been a short romance between your mother and me, but it's the truth. And if you didn't believe it, you wouldn't have taken that DNA test."

"No. I don't..." Lily stopped and started again. "I came to ask you about Solomon." She came over and examined the white horse. It was a mare. A young mare. "A week ago I saw a horse

I thought was Solomon hop a fence and head this way." That wasn't exactly true. She hadn't seen the stallion jump the fence, only that there were hoofprints. "Where did you get this horse?"

Silence.

Lily turned her attention back to Rowdy. "Do you own Solomon?"

"No." The old man used tongs to turn the horseshoe back and forth in the fire.

"Do you ride Solomon?"

"Nobody rides Solomon." Oh, that snap to his voice. Rowdy removed the shoe from the fire and moved it to the anvil, where he pounded it with his hammer.

Lily waited until he was done hammering to speak again. "Why don't you make it easy on me and tell me what's going on with Solomon? Because white horses are rare and I'm having a hard time believing the one roaming around Clementine is as old as local legend claims or as wild."

Rowdy took the hoof in his gloved hand. But instead of moving to fit the shoe on the mare, he stopped to stare at Lily, a rare smile on his face. "You're my daughter, all right. Sharp as a tack."

Lily bit back a comment about her heritage not being proved. Yet.

"You should learn a trade," he said. "When times are tough, a having a special skill can keep food on the table."

"I have a trade." Feathers ruffled, Lily placed a hand on the mare's neck, drawing on the animal's calm the way she might have reached for Zane had he been here.

"Ranch hand isn't a trade." Rowdy strode over, leaned a shoulder into the mare's shoulder opposite Lily, then lifted her hoof and placed the shoe on it, testing the fit. "Any fool can hop on a horse and herd cattle from one pasture to the next. Just ask that Duvall boy."

"Be nice."

"Don't hitch your wagon to that fella. He's—"

"Bad news. Yes, I heard you the first time." Not that she was going to argue with him about it. "Tell me about Solomon."

"It's a long story and I have work to do." He set down the hoof and straightened, staring at Lily over the mare's withers. "There's plenty of things to do around the place—stalls to muck, fences to fix, trees to trim. If you're foolish enough to reject my offer of learning a trade, make yourself useful."

"But—"

"I've said my piece. Now git!"

Not wanting to extend the bickering, Lily wandered back to the ranch yard, not intending to do anything for the old grouch. But a horse's whinny had her turning and walking to the far side of the barn.

Stalls opened to small paddocks. Beyond them, a broad pasture covered the hillside. There was no scrub brush here. The ground was covered with ankle-high yellow grass. And on that grass? A small herd of horses. Most of them white.

"Wait until I tell Zane," Lily murmured.

"You're not telling a soul." Rowdy stomped over to her, nearly losing his balance on the uneven soil. His tone was as rough as his stride. "Never. Tell. Anyone. In fact, forget you've seen them."

Lily faced him square-on, hands on hips, head held high. "Forget? Even if the DNA proves I'm related to you?"

Rowdy huffed and puffed and grabbed onto a wooden fence post near her, leaning on it for support. "I don't like your attitude."

"I'm not too keen on yours, either."

They stared at each other until Lily realized the horses in the pasture were approaching. There were eight horses in total. Three brown. Four white. One a muddy mixture of the two. They came to greet Rowdy, only approaching Lily once he'd given them some love—a scratch behind the ear or cheek, a pat on the neck, fingers combing through a lock of hair over their eyes.

They love him. And he loves them back.

Lily's heart squeezed. It was the same bittersweet pain Lily had experienced when she witnessed the man she called Dad shower affection on Beau.

Rowdy will never love me like that.

"It's a shame." Lily blinked back unexpected tears.

A white horse approached her, reaching his head over the fence to nuzzle her shoulder.

Showing her affection the way a sibling would. The way Beau had done all her life when Sonny Smith snubbed her.

Lily's breath hitched. She rubbed the horse's white ears and murmured, "Thank you." For making her feel as if she belonged. She sniffed and wiped away a tear from her cheek. "Which one is Solomon?"

"Solomon is dead," Rowdy said gruffly, accenting his words with a lusty sniff as if he, too, was nearly overcome with emotion. "Buried him on top of that hill."

Lily patted the neck of the next horse to greet her. "You started the legend of Solomon?"

Rowdy nodded. "Didn't mean to. Just happened. After your mother left me."

The next horse in the line inched closer, extending her nose to try and nibble Lily's hair.

Lily gently eased the filly's nose away. "That's not food, you little stinker."

Rowdy chuckled.

He'd laughed in front of her before. But it had always been a harsh sound, released at someone else's expense. Mostly hers. But this. His laughter was unfettered. Free.

This is the man my mother fell in love with.

This is the man I wouldn't mind calling father.

Lily drew a deep breath. "I think I'd like to learn more about the blacksmith trade." In the hopes that she could learn more about Rowdy and how the legend of Solomon began.

Rowdy nodded. "Best get a move on. Pearl will be getting antsy." He led Lily back to the mare he'd been shoeing.

For the first time, it felt as if they'd found common ground.

CHAPTER EIGHTEEN

Lily was a quick study.

And she had no hesitation about setting a hammer to a heated horseshoe. She was a hard worker.

Hadn't taken Rowdy longer than thirty minutes to be fairly bursting with pride.

Lily lifted Pearl's hoof and tested the fit of the horseshoe she'd shaped on the anvil. "What made you fall in love with my mother?"

Rowdy's spine went rigid. He wanted to say, "*That's none of your business.*" But before he said a word, Pearl whinnied.

"I'm sure he doesn't want to tell me the tale, either, Pearl." Lily straightened, holding the shoe with a leather-gloved hand. Holding Rowdy's gaze with a tentative smile. "But no matter what those test results say, I don't doubt you loved her."

All the emotions Rowdy normally locked away—heartbreak, grief, regret—seemed to claw their way out, making it hard to hold on to his resolve.

"No one asks me about Dawnice," Rowdy rasped.

"Not even your son? Lucas?" Lily cocked her head. Rowdy shook his head. It was easier than trying to speak. He blinked, realizing his eyes were watery, his composure tenuous. "Give me that." He took the horseshoe from Lily and went to pick up nails and a hammer.

"You aren't going to answer, are you?" Lily stayed by Pearl's side, stroking the filly's neck.

"Would you answer me if I asked why you thought Sonny was a bad father?" There. He had a bargaining chip. Rowdy felt better able to face his daughter. He turned and sat on the edge of his blacksmith van, waiting for her to answer.

Lily's face was pinched. The breeze teased the ends of her hair beneath her cowboy hat. "This isn't a fatherhood competition. My dad is dead."

Your dad is sitting right here!

With effort, Rowdy held back the words. His need to know about Sonny wasn't for self-worth. It was because Lily had told him the first day they met in person that she didn't need another bad dad.

Rowdy nodded slowly, considering his words the way he did with Lucas sometimes. The way he'd done with Dawnice. "I know Sonny wasn't a total loss as a father or you wouldn't have turned out so well."

Lily bit her lower lip. There was a shadow of hurt in her eyes that told Rowdy a lot. Again, regret at losing Dawnice overwhelmed his senses.

If I'd only known...

"My dad was...fair." That assessment seemed hard-won from Lily. "He was never outright mean or had a harsh word. It was just…" Her eyes filled with tears. She blinked rapidly. "It always felt as if he…didn't want to show me love."

"I'm sorry," Rowdy said softly, heart aching because his child hadn't been loved as well as she could have been. "You can blame me." He didn't want her blaming Dawnice.

"That's…kind of you to say but…" Lily sniffed, still blinking as if she had a bit of dust in her eyes. "I won't let you take the blame for my childhood."

"I suppose I should thank you for that."

Pearl tossed her pretty white head. She was getting impatient and had every right to be. She'd been waiting a long time for this last horseshoe.

Rowdy brought the shoe, nails and hammer over to the filly's side, and bent to his work. "You can probably guess why I fell in love with your mother. My reasons are probably some of the same reasons you loved her. Her sense of humor. Her big heart. The way she saw the best in everyone." While he often saw the worst. "She made me want to be a better man."

Surprisingly, he wanted to be a better man now. If only so his daughter could be proud of him.

CHAPTER NINETEEN

"Zane? Can I have a word?"

Zane was in the barn, trying to replace a broken hinge on a stall door when Mama Mary approached him wearing a bright green sweater with a snowman on the front. "Is this a conversation I'm going to want to be sitting down for?"

His foster mother slipped her arm around his waist. "I'll be kind, I promise."

Zane smiled and finished unscrewing the broken hinge and set it on the ground, before examining the state of the wood it had been fastened to. "What's up?"

"It's your mother."

"She doesn't think I'm moving fast enough when it comes to Lily," he surmised.

"Yes. She hoped you'd be engaged by Christmas." She picked up the broken hinge and tucked it in her pocket. "I'll take care of this for you. I told your mother that Lily doesn't want to move that fast but…"

"My mother wants me to focus on other women, then," he guessed, deciding the wood was in good enough shape to install a new hinge. He chose one from the toolbox at his feet. "Women who are eager to find a man and settle down." Like Evie, who'd told him the night he met Lily that getting married and having a baby by next Christmas wouldn't be so bad. "Can't you politely tell her she's overstayed her welcome? After all, she's got a fiancé to get home to. A man I haven't even met, by the way."

"You'll meet him soon. He sounds wonderful."

Refraining from commenting more, Zane worked the hinge back and forth, making sure it was lubricated.

"As for your relationship with your mother… Remember, it's not that easy for her." Mama Mary moved to greet the horse who'd poked his head over the door of the next stall. "There's a lot of guilt about the past that your mother still carries in her heart."

"She shouldn't. I turned out fine." He tested the fit of the new hinge to the existing holes.

"Are you?" His foster mother moved closer to Zane. "Fine, I mean. If I told you I couldn't stand Chandler's parents because of the situation they put him in as a boy twenty years ago, would you think I was fine?"

Zane finally looked Mama Mary in the eye. "I'm confused. Is this about Rowdy Brown and the ranch? Or about me and Lily?"

"Can't it be about both?" She laid a hand on

his shoulder and gave him a little shake. "Your mother thinks the two are related."

Pressure bore down on his chest. "And you think…"

"You're looking for something. Something you haven't found. Not with all those jobs you've tried. And maybe not with any of the women you've dated, including Lily." Her hand returned to her side. "Do I know for certain this restlessness is tied to this idea in your head that all your troubles start and end with Rowdy Brown and the Bad Luck Ranch?" She shook her head. "That's something only you can puzzle out." She patted his arm as she walked by, heading toward the door she'd come through. "But it's our past and the way we frame it in our hearts that limit or expand our chances at happiness."

After she'd gone, Zane was left wondering if Mama Mary was right about what had created his inability to settle down. Even Lily had pressed him about forgiveness, asking him more directly if his happiness was tied to Rowdy buying out the Duvall family.

He wasn't prepared to answer those questions. But he was afraid if he didn't, he'd lose this chance with Lily.

"THIS IS SOLOMON." Rowdy set a thick album on his dusty, cluttered desk and opened to a page filled with photos of a pair of white horses. In one picture, Rowdy stood between the animals, holding their lead ropes and grinning from ear to ear. "And Buttercup."

"You bought two white horses?" Lily had shed her jacket and her cowboy hat, having worked up a sweat toiling over the blacksmith forge. All the while she was hoping for Rowdy to tell her about Solomon. But he'd made her wait. "Why?"

"Bought a matched set for me and your mother. Thought we could ride in the Santapalooza Parade on Christmas Day." His voice had that same gruff quality from earlier, when they'd spoken at the pasture out back.

"What did she think of your gift?" Lily flipped the page, expecting to see a picture of her mother with the horses. All she saw were more photos of Solomon and Buttercup.

"She left before I told her." Rowdy sat down heavily in his desk chair, looking older than ever. Pale. Shriveled. "It was a blow."

Lily sat in the chair opposite him. Waiting.

"Met your mother at church. Wasn't looking for romance," Rowdy said in a strained voice. His eyes shone with unshed tears. "I was looking for solace. My wife and your mother were friends before Linda left me. Dawnice brought me a casserole. Your mother saw I needed someone to talk to and asked me to meet her for coffee. We became friends first, commiserating over our sometimes-difficult marriages. Money was important to Sonny. Dawnice thought money was more important to him than love. As for me…

Linda left me for much the same reason. Learned a lot about love talking to your mother."

"There were no sparks between you?" Lily asked, curious for two reasons—to put the past in perspective and to have a benchmark for her and Zane. "Not during all the casserole and coffee talk?"

Rowdy shook his head. "It wasn't until your father moved out that we leaned more heavily on each other and allowed our feelings to grow into love."

A love that hadn't lasted.

That wasn't the answer Lily wanted to hear when she had her own doubts about love with Zane.

"I bought the horses before your father came to ask Dawnice to come home." Rowdy's voice broke. "It was going to be a surprise. But then... She was gone the day before they were delivered. And I... After a week, I set them free on government land behind my property."

Lily couldn't imagine investing in a pair of good horses and just releasing them into the wild.

"Best thing I ever did." Rowdy tapped the photo album, still looking fragile. "They found their way to the herd of wild horses that run on my back fifty acres sometimes. And Solomon..." He emitted a weak laugh. "I'd go into town and hear he'd been sighted. Might have created a story about him a time or two."

"So you've kept the legend going ever since." Honestly? That was pretty cool.

"And built upon it." Rowdy nodded, finally looking at Lily. "Buttermilk returned to me. Pregnant. And in the winter, Solomon always showed up, sometimes when I left the gate open, often when I didn't." He chuckled, more to himself than to share mirth with Lily. "Annoyed my son, Lucas, at first, letting that pair go. He was only ten. But he came to appreciate being in the know about Solomon's legend."

Somewhere in the house, a grandfather clock chimed, reminding Lily that she'd have to leave soon to pick up Ford from school.

She leaned forward in her chair. "But that was nearly thirty years ago and… All those horses. That's a lot of inbreeding."

"*Inbreeding?*" Rowdy's voice practically shook the rafters. "I brought in other stock. Always white. Got some Thoroughbred blood in the mix."

That explained the fence jumping.

"And… You just turn them loose? So none of those horses have been ridden? Why shoe them, then?"

"Every one of my horses is saddle broke. I keep the foals in the pasture to tame, train and gentle them." Rowdy's voice rang with pride. "In the end, that's one thing Lucas and I didn't agree on. My son sees it as a waste of resources. He doesn't realize…" Rowdy's face became pinched, and his voice coarsened "...how much those horses and that legend mean to me."

"Love," Lily whispered. "You did it out of love for my mother."

"Yes." Rowdy's eyes filled with tears once more. "I always held out hope that she'd come back to me."

"But all you got was me." Lily imagined she'd been a disappointment. "Or, you'd have a piece of her if the DNA results say what you're hoping for."

Rowdy wiped at his nose.

"I don't want anything from you, apart from you knowing the truth about me." That seemed like it needed to be said.

Rowdy sniffed again. "I just want the truth to come out."

Lily fell back in her seat. "I'm not going to change my name or get a T-shirt that says I'm Rowdy Brown's daughter." Zane would end things. Their friendship. Their...their...whatever it was between them.

"You'll be a Brown, I'm sure of it. It's a name to be proud of."

"Is it? I'm the product of an affair you had with a married woman." Lily was unable to keep her voice low. Her emotions were running high and fast, like a strong current that was sweeping her along. "I know you've told me I happened during a separation, but people will think differently."

"People?" Rowdy scoffed, recovering his gruff

nature. "What other people think doesn't matter! What's inside you matters."

"You're wrong. I think my father felt shame. That's why he... That's why *he couldn't love me*." Unable to say more, Lily stormed out of the house, got into her truck and drove away.

CHAPTER TWENTY

"I'M SURPRISED YOU agreed to ride out with me again," Zane told Lily on Saturday morning. "Given you think Solomon should be left to roam free."

He drove his truck and horse trailer along a different road that bisected two plots of government grazing land. It was another region but the view was much the same. Miles and miles of scrub brush glowed under a bright winter sun.

"Maybe I'm not entirely convinced," Lily said enigmatically. She'd brought candy canes for them all. They sat in Zane's cup holder.

"We have to find Lightning, son of Solomon," Ford said from the back seat. "Course, we'd come with you on your horse hunt." He held the drone's remote. He'd been more effusive in his greeting of Zane this morning than Lily had been.

"Ford likes the idea of a free horse just as much as you do," Lily said, hardly smiling. She hadn't brought her binoculars today and yet she kept looking out and across the fields as if she was hopeful of a sighting.

There was something off about her mood, but Zane was determined to be patient and hopeful that she'd confide in him when she was ready. "It's not exactly a free horse if you consider all the labor involved, plus gas."

"Wear and tear on your vehicle." Lily gave him a measured smile. "Good argument."

"Can't take credit. I was watching a documentary about pirates hunting for treasure and that's what the expedition leader said." It had made sense to him, though.

"I'd like to be a pirate someday," Ford said.

"You'd make a good pirate." Zane slid Lily a sly smile.

She returned it. "Avast and shiver me timbers."

"I just want a cool sword and a chest with lots of sparkly stuff," Ford told them. "When do we find our horse? I bet when we find him today, he'll recognize me and come right up to us."

"Maybe," Lily said, unexpectedly promoting the boy's fantasy. "Solomon could surprise you."

"Solomon isn't tame." Zane was sure of that. "We got close the other day because we surprised him is all."

"I've heard lots of cowboys have tried to catch him." Lily was staring out the window again. And she sounded almost…jaded.

"Lots of cowboys have tried to catch him," Zane repeated.

Lily turned that frank brown gaze his way.

"Cowboys you know? Or is this just talk? More of the legend and less of the truth?"

"I..." He wasn't sure. "I've seen cowboys at the Done Roamin' Ranch chase after him."

"Right. But did they have their own posse like you do?"

"*Posse.*" Ford repeated the word as if he liked the sound of it.

"Do you know something I don't?" Zane asked Lily.

She shrugged, avoiding his gaze. "It just feels like there's not a lot of facts to back up this story and without facts... Maybe the legend needs to stay a legend."

"Stay a legend?" Zane tipped his hat back and slowed the truck as they approached a pothole. "I'll give you a fact. We saw Solomon."

"With our own eyes," Ford said, giggling. "Come on, Auntie."

"Yeah," Zane said. "Come on, Auntie. The next thing you'll be telling me is there's no Santa Claus."

While Ford gasped, Lily drilled Zane with a narrow-eyed stare. Her cheeks were flushed with color, practically rivaling the dark brown of her smattering of freckles.

She's the prettiest gal I've ever seen.

But he wanted to buy his own place right here in Clementine. A ranch, big or small. Somewhere he could call home.

Somewhere Lily could call home, too. Maybe.

Lily was hoping they'd have no "Solomon" sightings today. But in her experience, hoping had never amounted to much.

And about an hour into their journey, Ford cried out, "Over there! *I see Solomon!*" This last was uttered in his growly voice.

"Lucky us." Zane pulled over. "We're near a gate into that pasture."

"Lucky us," Lily murmured, peering out the window. Sure enough, a white horse was grazing far out on the horizon.

Run!

The horse raised its head.

Run!

"He's gonna make a break for it," Zane predicted, jamming the truck into Park and hopping out.

"Oh, man. I'm bummed, Auntie."

Lily got out of the truck slowly, then opened Ford's door. "Are you bummed because we found the horse without using the drone?" She helped him unbuckle his seat belt.

"Yep." Ford leaped to the ground like he was a superhero. "But we're going to catch him today. I can feel it."

Zane had the trailer open and was backing Mouse out. "Open the gate, Lily."

"Slow down, cowboy." Lily entered the trailer, moving up to Jet's tie-down.

The gelding fidgeted, anxious to get out and stretch his legs.

"Do you have eyes on him, Ford?" Zane came into the trailer to get Arthur.

"I don't see him anymore." Ford jumped up and down. Beneath his jacket, he had on a red T-shirt that featured Old Saint Nick making out his nice list. "Let's. Get out. The *drone*."

"Good idea." Zane fastened his horse to a trailer ring. "Lily, can you check the tack while we put the drone in the air?"

"Sure." Again, Lily hoped for no sightings. Again, she was disappointed.

"He's over the rise," Zane announced when they had the drone safely back on the ground. "Mount up."

"I got to fly the drone." Ford leaped into the saddle. "Zane said I'm getting better. I think I want a drone for Christmas."

"You'll have to write another letter to Santa." Lily led Jet through the pasture gate and then swung into the saddle.

"I have a good feeling about this," Zane told her when he'd come through the gate and shut it behind them.

Ford rode Mouse up next to her.

Jet and Mouse touched noses, their equivalent of a high five.

Great. Even the livestock are hyped up and positive.

Lily considered dropping her rope when Zane and Ford weren't looking.

Wouldn't that be hard to explain.

"Ford, you set the pace." Zane came up beside Lily, staring at her for too long. He knew something wasn't right.

Things hadn't been right inside Lily regarding the Solomon hunt ever since she'd listened to the origin story that Rowdy had told her. Those horses were free because Rowdy loved her mother.

Ford set out, cuing Mouse into a trot. His riding tune today was "Jingle Bells," most likely because it was as choppy as the pony's gait.

Lily eased up on the reins, letting Jet fast walk forward.

"Can I ask you a question?" Zane was still looking at her, matching Arthur's speed to Jet's.

"I thought we were past the part of our…" *friendship* "…relationship where we had to ask if we could ask something." Did his eyes flicker when she said *relationship*? Lily couldn't be sure.

"I want to get you a Christmas gift."

Lily's jaw dropped.

A Christmas gift between a man and a woman defined their relationship.

"You don't want me to." Zane shifted his gaze forward, sliding on a pair of sunglasses.

"I didn't say that." It was kind of wonderful.

"You haven't said a lot today." He still didn't look at her.

But she looked at him. His profile highlighted his chiseled features, a reflection of his stubbornness. And his pride. His form in the saddle was perfect. His hold on the reins light but firm. He was a master horseman. Zane didn't do things by half measure.

But at relationships… He was just as bad as she was.

"I've hurt you," Lily said, fighting the press of the truth at the back of her throat. She had no right to share Solomon's story with him. No matter how much she wanted to.

Zane shook his head. "I was wondering if I'd hurt you." Those dark brown eyes swung her way, probed her face. He leaned over and touched her arm, a brief, gentle squeeze. "We only see each other at the Christmas parties. And although that's great, I learned a lot more about you on our last ride. Are we good?"

She nodded, struggling to swallow around the emotion suddenly stuck in her throat. "It's been a hard week for me. I…" She couldn't tell him she'd met with Rowdy. "I think getting up with a newborn every night is taking its toll on me." She wasn't napping when Nora and the baby did. There was just too much to do around the house, plus the shopping—they had to eat—and Ford to be shuttled here and there. Yesterday afternoon, he'd gone to the library for a kids' Christmas craft session with his friends.

"Do you want to skip out on the party tonight?"

"Are you sure you want to take me?" Lily chuckled. "Line dancing to carols? I'll be a menace on the dance floor and not in a good way."

"I've got your back," he assured her, smiling gently.

He was being so authentic and open with her, while Lily was doing the opposite. It was gutting because she didn't want any secrets between them, whether they were friends or something more.

"About that Christmas gift..." Zane continued to regard her warmly. "Shall we exchange gifts?"

"I'd like that."

Ford stopped Mouse and turned toward them in the saddle. "Hey, can we go faster now? Before Solomon gets away?"

"Yes, sir." Zane cued Arthur into a slow lope.

Lily let Jet do the same.

The horses' slow pace matched Mouse's fastest gallop.

Several minutes later, they reached a fence.

"I always thought government lands had fewer fences than this." Lily looked around but didn't see any horses. Stress she hadn't known she'd been carrying between her shoulder blades suddenly disappeared.

"I was told some politician got funding to divide the land into smaller parcels so the government could rent to more ranchers." Zane stood in the saddle, scanning the horizon.

"We missed him again." Ford lay forward on Mouse's neck.

"There's a gate north of us." Zane turned Arthur

in that direction. "Let's ride the fence line and look for tracks."

"Are you okay, Ford?" Lily asked, wanting an excuse to head back. "Good to keep going?"

"I'm so good, Auntie, that I think we're gonna catch Solomon. Just you see." Ford sat up and patted Mouse's brown neck. "Let's do this." He kicked Mouse onward.

"Let's do this," Lily repeated under her breath, bringing up the rear.

"No tracks," Zane said a few minutes later. "There's a rise and some trees. Maybe he went over there." He galloped ahead.

Ford and Lily followed at a slower pace.

Stress returned, putting a kink in Lily's neck. How could she protect whatever white horse was out there? If Zane caught one, someone would just spot another later on. Would that put Clementine into a frenzy to find all the sons and daughters of Solomon?

"I could use a cookie," Ford said. "And a hot chocolate."

"Double whip, double marshmallows." Lily smiled. Trust Ford to lift her spirits. These horses had dodged cowboys for two decades. Surely, they could evade Zane and dodge would-be captors for another couple of weeks, or until her pretend boyfriend gave up the chase.

Zane wheeled Arthur around, took off his cowboy hat and waved it like mad.

Lily's spirits sank.

"What's wrong with Zane, Auntie?"
"I think he found Solomon."

ZANE COULDN'T BELIEVE his luck.

Solomon stood within the small grove of trees, looking completely relaxed.

Lily and Ford couldn't catch up to him fast enough.

"Listen," he said in a low voice. "Lily, you ride to the right. I'll ride to the left. Ford, you stay here."

"In case he runs this way?" Ford asked, using his outdoor voice. "You want Mouse and me to stop him?"

Solomon's head came up. His white ears swiveled forward.

"No, Ford," Lily said none too quietly. "You need to stay still here so he doesn't get spooked. Remember how much he liked you last time. Stay still."

"And don't sneeze," Zane whispered, freeing his lasso. Then he jerked his head to indicate Lily should move.

Solomon was fifty feet ahead.

Lily and Zane walked their horses to either flank. Lily had her rope in hand, sliding the loop into a larger circle as Zane did the same. As one, they twirled their ropes to the side of their mounts. Having gained enough momentum, they raised the loops over their heads.

She must be a good cowhand.

But Zane had no more time to admire Lily's work. Solomon was on the move, walking slowly out of the trees and toward Ford.

Lily leaned forward in the saddle, as if preparing to throw.

"Wait," Zane said, loud enough for Lily to hear. Solomon took off.

"Now!" Zane shouted, cueing Arthur into a small turn.

"Now!" Lily shouted, spurring Jet forward.

He and Lily threw at the same time. But because Lily had moved, Solomon pivoted, galloping toward Zane. Their lariats collided midair where Solomon would have been if Lily and her horse hadn't moved.

And then the white horse galloped away, bolting past Ford and racing toward the fence. He didn't even break stride when he jumped it.

"I'M SORRY," LILY SAID for what felt like the hundredth time. "I miscued Jet before my throw."

Actually, she'd sent her horse lurching forward on purpose. To the desired effect. Solomon was still free.

"It's okay, Auntie." Ford brought Mouse closer to Lily and patted her cowboy boot. "You just need more practice."

Zane made a noise that might have been a form of agreement. He hadn't said much since Solomon's getaway.

"I'm sorry," Lily said again.

Zane nodded.

He remained silent until they had the horses loaded and were in the truck heading back to Clementine. It might have been that he waited until Ford had stuffed himself with snickerdoodles and fallen asleep in the back.

Or it might have been that Lily finally mentioned something that resonated with him. "Are you okay?"

"I... I think I had what my foster father would call an epiphany." He removed his straw cowboy hat and tossed it on the dashboard, then ran a hand through his hair. "I watched Solomon run away and..."

Lily waited.

"The way he ran. It was like he had wings, you know?" Zane glanced at her.

"He was beautiful. Graceful."

"Wild," Zane breathed.

Lily laid her palm on his arm. "That was your epiphany?"

"No." His sigh was heavy. "It feels as if everyone around me has been telling me I need to find a path that leads to my future. A job with a future. A woman with a future." He took his eyes off the road for a moment to look at her. "Even you."

"Me?"

He faced forward, flexing his fingers on the steering wheel. "You told me to consider forgiving Rowdy in order to have peace with myself.

You told me to think about how catching Solomon would change his future, too."

Lily nodded.

"I watched Solomon run away and I realized he's like the stars to me." Zane's expression hardened. "At some point in a person's life, you have to realize you're not going to be an astronaut or a professional athlete. That dream is realized by only a very few. And I... I realized catching Solomon... Well, he's not a bucking bronc. He'd be a swan among ducklings. Like you said, his spirit would be broken and I..." Zane reached for her hand.

Lily took his hand, gladly.

"In the midst of all that, I realized that I've been Solomon. Running toward anything that interests me. Running in the opposite direction when things don't seem to fit. Leaping over fences to head back where I feel safe. My mothers. My foster family. You." He gave Lily's hand a gentle squeeze. "You're all correct. I need to find something to do with my life, to forgive and move forward to create a place and a family to spend the rest of my life with."

"Oh, Zane." His words touched her heart. His words could have described her, too. "That's so brave."

"Sounds sappy to say out loud." His hold on her hand increased. "I missed roping a legendary horse and somehow, my path forward became clear." He spared her a glance, a significant glance.

And oh, how Lily's heart pounded.

Because there were sparks in that glance. Gentle, loving sparks.

But Lily wasn't as brave as Zane. She didn't trust that what she was finally seeing would last.

Come spring, she still planned to move on.

CHAPTER TWENTY-ONE

The Ninth Party of Christmas:
Christmas Carol Line Dancing
Hosted by: Sunny Y'all Ranch at the Buckboard Bar & Grill

"OH, GOODY. LINE DANCING." Lily frowned and walked between Zane and Ava toward the Buckboard's entrance on Saturday night, still harboring a guilty conscience for sabotaging the capture of Solomon. The sun had set and strings of red, green and gold blinking lights outlined the Buckboard. "How many more parties are there?"

"Three." Ava wore a full-skirted black velvet minidress with white cowboy boots and a stylish yellow cowboy hat. "I don't want these parties to end."

Since the ornament exchange, Ava had chosen to show up at the Smith house an hour before every party began, inviting herself to ride along when Zane picked Lily up. Ava had quit encouraging Lily to try various kinds of makeup or to change her clothes; otherwise, Lily would have put a stop to her cousin being a third wheel.

Sad to say, the Glamberry lipstick Lily had purchased when this whole fake dating thing started still sat in its package on her dresser.

"I might be too tired to line dance." Lily slowed as they neared the door and the line of folks waiting to enter. They were all dressed in their Saturday night finery whereas Lily wore a sparkly silver sweater she'd borrowed from Nora over her gray jeans. "Long ride today. And Cady had trouble sleeping last night."

"There's no getting out of it." Zane placed his hand on the small of Lily's back, sending an unexpected thrill through her. "I'm your ride and we're here now."

Lily stared up at Zane, smiling a little, not quite ready to give in. "If you're making me stay and dance, I should wear a placard that says *Warning! Bony Elbow Zone*." More likely, she'd stomp on some toes but that just seemed cliché.

Zane stared at Lily, amusement in his dark brown eyes.

More trucks pulled into the Buckboard's parking lot. The wind pushed at their backs. The entry line inched ahead. And Lily paid little heed to any of it. Because—*hello, personal insight*—she liked being near him.

It's going to be hard to leave come March.

Or it would be if she and Zane kept up like

this—half pretending, half not that they were falling in love.

"You can't be that bad of a dancer." Zane took Lily's hand as they reached the end of the line. "You two-step like a dream."

A dream.

Lily held those words close. She'd never been anybody's dream anything before. "I'm a worse line dancer than you can imagine. Just you wait and see."

"He won't have to wait long." Ava rose up on her toes, craning her neck to see past the people ahead of them in line. She had her arms wrapped around her waist since, unlike Zane and Lily, she hadn't brought a jacket. "I see folks on the dance floor already."

"Ava!" Stu slid out the door. The tall, young cowboy hurried to Ava's side.

Not that Ava allowed herself to look happy about it.

This, too, had become routine—Stu doting on Ava, Ava pretending disinterest, and then by the end of the night, Stu would finagle a good-night kiss.

Lily smiled to herself. Stu was good at breaking down Ava's old-soul facade.

The wind pushed past.

Zane drew Lily close, pressed a kiss to her cheek—*A kiss? I haven't had one in almost two weeks!*—and then he whispered, "How much do you want to bet that Stu steals a kiss from Ava on the dance floor tonight?" He drew back, giving Lily that smile that they often shared when their thoughts wandered along the same lines.

"That's an easy bet. Ava won't let that happen," Lily whispered back, leaning against Zane's sturdy chest and staring up at a face that had become dear to her.

"It's a bet, then." Zane nodded briskly. "If Stu kisses Ava on the dance floor, I'll kiss you on the dance floor."

"Wait? What?" Lily pushed back. "I didn't agree to those terms."

The line in front of them surged forward.

"You said it's an easy bet." Zane strutted through the Buckboard's door to the check-in desk. "I gave you easy terms."

Behind them, Ava and Stu laughed. But when Lily glanced at them to see what was so funny, they simply smiled at her.

"Zane's more of a romantic than I originally thought." Ava gave Lily a thumbs-up.

Before Lily could reply, Zane reached from inside the Buckboard and drew Lily in.

"Hello, Lily, my love." Rita came around the check-in table and gave Lily a businesslike hug, a quick catch and release, followed by her hands landing on Lily's shoulders. She peered at Lily's face, long black skirt practically tangling around Lily's legs. "How are things going? Is my son treating you right? You know you can come to me to talk about anything. He was such a happy baby. Never caused me any stress. And then the teenage years descended and he flipped the script on me. Hasn't completely flipped back yet."

"Oh?" Lily managed a smile.

"Take it down a notch, Mom." Zane bent over the table to fill out his ticket for the grand-prize drawing for his former home. He'd mentioned trying to forgive Rowdy during their excursion this morning. Could he?

Would he try harder if he knew Rowdy might be my father?

"Is there something on your mind, Lily?" Rita asked, her hands still resting on Lily's shoulders, her gaze alight with something hard-edged. "Something you want to discuss?"

Does she know how I sabotaged Zane's capture of Solomon?

"No?" Lily couldn't quite bring herself to remove Rita's hands from her shoulders.

"Mom." Zane drew his mother away and guided her back to her place behind the table. "Take a breath. Don't scare Lily away."

"Wouldn't dream of it." But Rita's gaze on Lily was still sharp, giving off the impression that she'd found fault in Lily and wanted her to admit it.

Lily silently vowed to admit nothing.

"There are prizes for the best line dancers tonight." Mary nodded and hugged Lily next. Her blue jeans and snowman holiday sweater made

Lily feel less underdressed. "Watch out. Zane is very competitive."

"He shouldn't dance next to me, then." Lily chuckled. "I'll trip him up for sure."

"Doom and gloom." Zane dropped his ticket for the grand prize into the jar. "Don't believe her. Lily is twinkle-toes doing the two-step. Her line dancing caveats are getting old."

Lily chuckled once more. "Come along, Fred Astaire. I'll show you my two left feet."

The Buckboard had embraced Christmas inside as well as out. White lights were strung above the bar and draped along the far wall. There were decorated fir trees glowing with lights and shiny ornaments on stage and a row of various stockings hung from the edge of the stage, each with someone's name written in red glitter. Lily presumed there was one stocking for each employee.

They found a table, removed their jackets and headed for the dance floor. Again, Lily was between Ava and Zane. Again, she cautioned them to keep their distance.

"Hi, everyone." A broad-shouldered cowboy stood on stage. "I'm Keith. Welcome to Christmas Carol Line Dancing!"

The crowd applauded.

"Even though folks are still coming in, we're going to get started with the dancing." Keith grinned. "Because we've only rented the Buckboard for two hours and nobody wants to waste time listening to me speak when you could be kicking up their heels."

The crowd roared their approval as Keith waved and left the stage.

The music began with guitar notes. "Jingle Bell Rock."

"I know this one," Lily murmured to herself. And it was slow, thank goodness. Clapping to the beat, she repeated the upcoming steps to herself, "Right-right. Left-left. Heel brush. Toe tap. Turn."

And then the verse began, a cue for dancers to begin.

"Oh." Lily went left instead of right, bumping into Zane. "Sorry." She brushed her heel on the ground, tapped her toe and turned the wrong direction, getting in Ava's way. "Sorry." She backed up and bumped into Zane.

"Zane, I don't think Lily was kidding when she said she can't dance." Ava laughed and twirled about.

Stu laughed along with Ava. He danced next to her, a huge grin on his face.

"Breathe." Zane took hold of Lily's hand, swaying back and forth instead of doing the steps. "When everyone turns this time, follow my lead."

Lily felt the heat of embarrassment and the pressure to exit the dance floor. But there was Zane's hand around hers, so she smiled. "Oh, you are a brave man, Zane Duvall."

But by the time the song was over, with his help, Lily hadn't bowled into anyone else.

"Success!" Without thinking, she launched herself into Zane's arms, barely noting that beside them, Stu swept Ava into his and kissed her.

"A bet's a bet," Zane murmured. He lowered his head and kissed her.

And it wasn't a seventh-grade sort of kiss.

"Take that romantic business off the dance floor!"

Zane didn't know who interrupted their kiss but he did as asked. He stopped kissing Lily—*reluctantly*—and towed her off the dance floor—*less for the safety of others and more to give himself a chance to kiss her again.*

But they were immediately swarmed by his mamas.

"Just when I doubt the sincerity of your relationship, you go and surprise me." Mom hugged him and Lily.

"You two look so sweet together." Mama Mary's hug lasted as long as his mom's. "Lily, I feel as if we should get to know each other better."

"Oh." Lily's face pale, making those freckles, the ones he was so enamored with, stand out. And she had that deer-caught-in-the-headlights look. As if she didn't know whether to stay or make a run for it.

Zane firmed up his grip on her hand. "I'm going to tell you two what I've been saying since before Thanksgiving. *With respect, leave me and my love life alone, please.*"

"Oh, but if Lily's the one, she'll feel so much more at ease with you if she gets to know us." That was Mama Mary, reaching for Lily's free hand.

"We're not as scary as you believe, Zane." That was his mom, trying to edge between him and Lily.

"Go on, Zane." Lily eased her hand free of his. "You can dance while I talk to your mamas."

"Yes, son. Go win a prize for your boogie-woogie skills." Mom nudged him out of the way.

She and Mama Mary wasted no time leading Lily off.

"Don't be fooled by their words," Zane called after Lily when she glanced at him over her shoulder.

"Come on, Zane." Ava appeared by his side. She took his arm and gave it a tug. "Let's dance."

He didn't want to dance. He wanted to kiss Lily again.

But he was left with a gal too young to be wanting his attention.

And, of course, the opportunity to win something.

So he headed back out on the dance floor.

"WHAT AREN'T YOU telling us?" Rita asked Lily when they arrived at the buffet.

"I'm sorry?" Lily moved to the end of the table. "You think I'm hiding something?"

"Yes. You keep your distance from our boy to

the point where we have doubts about you as a couple."

"And then you kiss like that." Rita scoffed. "Give us the skinny, now that it's just us girls."

"I'm...*shy*?" That had been what Zane had told his mamas at the ornament exchange party.

Both women studied her intently. Doubted her openly.

The only way Lily was getting out of this interrogation was to stick as close to the truth as possible. And if that didn't work, throw herself on their mercy. "I don't have much experience dating. Am I doing it wrong?" And then, without meaning to... Lily's eyes welled with tears.

Of course I'm doing it wrong.

"Oh, honey." Rita gave her a side hug.

"You dear, sweet girl." Mary hugged her from the other side.

"Everything is happening so fast." Words tumbled out of Lily's mouth. She only hoped they were the right ones. "I came to Clementine expecting to spend most of my time helping Nora with the baby. And then I met Zane—*completely by chance*—and we kept bumping into each other, about as gracefully as we did on the dance floor just now. And the next thing I know, we have standing dates for this holiday season." Lily drew a pained breath. "I like Zane. He's smart and witty and..."

He kisses like a dream.

She couldn't say that.

"You feel like you're in over your head." Rita nodded.

"You aren't sure if Zane's interest will last into the new year." Mary nodded.

Lily nodded along with them. "I feel like I'm whining. Like I should have more confidence in myself. Or Zane. Or us." This was very close to the truth. Her eyes welled with tears once more.

"Baby girl." Rita tried to smooth Lily's unruly curls beneath the brim of her cowboy hat. "We're here to support you."

"You were right to confide in us." Mary patted Lily's shoulder but gave Rita a significant stare. "You need folks in your corner."

"This is just supposed to be fun." But Lily was very much afraid that she'd passed fun and moved into serious territory because…because…

She was falling in love with Zane.

How had that happened?

"YOU'RE A REALLY good dancer, Zane." Ava beamed up at him with more than friendly interest in her eyes. Her hand on his arm stopped him from leaving the dance floor at the end of "Rudolph the Red-Nosed Reindeer."

They'd been line dancing for three Christmas songs. And yeah. It was fun. But it wasn't the same fun without Lily by his side, her hand tucked into his.

"You're a good dancer, too, Ava." Zane removed her hand from his arm and scanned the Buckboard for Lily. "What happened to Stu?"

"He's hungry. He got some food and went to our table." Ava smiled at Zane. "Have I told you that you have good teeth?"

"Many times. Excuse me." Zane left Ava and the dance floor and went in search of Lily. He should never have left her with his mamas in the first place. He spotted her tall frame by the check-in table and headed that way.

Something had happened. There were murmurs going round folks not on the dance floor. Phone screens were being passed from one person to another. Zane hurried to join Lily, who was looking a bit shell-shocked. "What happened?"

"Alex Sylvester got in a wreck driving back from a stock auction." Mama Mary showed Zane her phone screen.

There was a picture of a rig's front end wrapped around the base of an oak tree. Steam rose from the truck. The driver's door looked to have been cut open with the Jaws of Life.

"Is Alex okay?" Zane asked, slipping his hand around Lily's.

"He's got a broken leg and…" Mama Mary closed her phone screen. "We'll know more soon. A couple of us are going over to the hospital later."

Zane nodded. "Let me know if there's anything I can do." He didn't know Alex well but there was always something to be done on a ranch.

"Me, too," Lily said quickly. "I can help."

"He'll appreciate that." Mama Mary managed to smile. "There is one thing the party committee needs to decide quickly because of this."

"Alex was hosting the last party of Christmas." Mom frowned. "On the twenty-third."

Mama Mary's frown was deeper, if that was possible. "I don't feel right asking someone to host again. Seems anticlimactic to stop at eleven parties, doesn't it?"

"It's not cheap to be a host." Mom glanced at the sea of people at the current party. "That's why we recruited successful ranchers."

"I'm sure everyone will understand." Zane looped his arm around Lily's waist. "Are you hungry?"

Lily stared at him blankly. "What about Rowdy Brown? Did you ask him if he could host?"

"Rowdy Brown?" Zane felt sucker punched. "Why would you think of him?"

"He donated the grand prize." Lily patted Zane's chest. "He might do it."

"It's a thought." Mama Mary searched Zane's expression. "How do you feel about it?"

His mother was more blunt. "Would you go if the last party was held at Rowdy's?"

No.

"I..." Zane glanced down at Lily.

She was worrying her lower lip. "I think you should say yes. If Rowdy agrees, that is."

"He won't agree," Zane predicted, feeling certain.

"But if he does... Would you come? Would

you…talk to him?" There was an unreadable expression in Lily's eyes that worried Zane.

And his mamas…

They were hanging on every nuance of expression and tone between him and Lily.

"If Rowdy agrees…" Zane drew Lily closer, fitting her against his side as if she belonged there. "And that's a big *if*… I'll talk to you about striking some kind of truce with the old geezer."

"That's a start," Lily told him, brown eyes bright. And her smile…

Her smile said without words that she was proud of him.

CHAPTER TWENTY-TWO

THE DNA RESULTS arrived in Lily's email inbox the following Monday during breakfast with a subject line in all caps that said: *YOUR DNA QUESTIONS ANSWERED*.

Staring at her phone, Lily was hesitant to scroll down. Would they be the answers she wanted?

"Bad news?" Beau asked, putting eggs on Ford's plate.

"You tell me." She handed him her phone. "I can't look. It's the DNA results."

"What's DNA?" Ford asked.

"*Do. Not. Ask*," Beau said in a firm voice.

Ford repeated the phrase, moving his scrambled eggs around his plate, a confused expression on his face. He stared at his father. "If I don't ask, how am I going to learn anything?"

"He was kidding, Ford," Nora said, holding the baby and rocking from side to side. "You should always ask about things you don't know."

Like when I asked about Zane's past.

Beau finished looking at Lily's phone and laid it face down on the table. His face turned pale.

Rowdy is my father.

Lily swallowed the lump in her throat. "It doesn't change anything for us, Beau. You're still my brother."

"But..." Beau seemed to swallow a similar lump in his throat. "It means Mom isn't who I thought she was."

"Human?" Lily rubbed her brother's shoulder. "We're all human, Beau. And Rowdy said Mom and Dad were separated when it... *I* happened."

"Who are we talking about?" Ford asked.

"A cartoon your dad and auntie used to watch as kids," Nora said without looking up.

"Was Rowdy the bad guy?" Ford wasn't letting this go.

"Yes," Beau said, while Lily shook her head.

"I'm not sure if I should root for Rowdy or not," Ford admitted.

"How about eat your eggs while you decide?" Using his fork, Beau moved the eggs Ford had separated on his plate back into a neat pile.

"It'll take longer than that to figure this out," Nora said softly.

"It takes Ford forever to eat his breakfast," Beau countered. "He's got five minutes to finish and get out the door or he'll be late for school."

Ford laid his head sideways on the table. "I want pancakes for breakfast. Stars and Christmas stocking ones."

Like Zane had made.

Lily tousled Ford's blond hair. "That sounds nice."

The way Zane was offering a truce to Rowdy sounded nice, especially now that she knew for certain Rowdy was her dad and her dad was hosting the last of the Twelve Parties of Christmas.

"WHAT'S HE LIKE?" Nora asked later that morning. "Rowdy, I mean. I've seen him around town but..."

"He's..." Lily searched for a word. "*Sad.*" Yes, that was it. "The ranch seems...lonely." Until she'd gone out back and discovered all those descendants of Solomon. "And his house isn't cluttered but it feels...neglected." Overlooked, like the man who lives there.

"You know I'm a cashier at the grocery store," Nora said. "Rowdy has a weekly order he picks up every Friday morning. Lunch meat, canned soup, canned fruit, canned vegetables. It's the same every week. The store manager brings it out to his truck. I asked Izzy about him once. She works at the feedstore. He picks up his order there, too, without coming inside."

"That also sounds sad." Lily thought about the hitch and roll Rowdy had to his walk, as if it pained him. And she recalled the pride and warmth in his voice when he talked about her mother and those white horses.

"It is sad. I think we should do something about

it." Nora handed Lily the baby. "He's your daddy. I'll get dressed while you change Cady's diaper."

"Nora…"

"Humor me, Lily. I haven't been out of the house often enough since Cady was born. Let's take a drive over to Rowdy's."

"This is a bad idea."

"Sometimes bad ideas produce the best outcomes."

Thirty minutes later, the two women parked in front of Rowdy's ranch house.

The man whose DNA she shared came out onto the porch, frowning and leaning heavily on his cane. "What's the meaning of this? I don't like surprises."

"My sister-in-law wanted to show you her baby." Lily ascended the porch steps carrying Cady's loaded diaper bag and a tin of macadamia nut cookies she'd made. "And since it's a little cold outside, we're coming in."

Nora carried the baby up the steps after her. "Hi, Mr. Brown. I'm Nora. We've never been introduced. I'm Lily's sister-in-law and I work at the grocery store."

Rowdy grunted, turned on his heel and ambled into the house, leaving the door open for them to follow. He moved to the right, heading into the office where he and Lily had talked before.

"Hey…um… This is a social call?" Lily turned the opposite direction, entering the living room. "Sitting in your office reminds me of being called to the principal's office when I did something wrong."

There was another grumble from Rowdy. "Did you get into scrapes often?"

"Hardly ever."

"Oh," Nora said from behind Lily. "I see what you mean now." She ran a finger over the coffee table, leaving a trail in her wake. She smiled at Lily, then drew a heart in the dust.

"*Nora*," Lily whispered, shaking her head.

"Did whispering in class get you sent to the office?" Rowdy rolled on past Lily, making a beeline for a well-worn, blue wingback chair. He sat down, yet looked highly uncomfortable. "Don't use this room much anymore. No one makes a social call."

"Not even when you were asked to host the last Christmas party?" Lily was curious about that.

"Got a phone call," Rowdy said matter-of-factly.

Lily sighed. "Excuse me for a minute." She went down the hall in search of the kitchen.

It was in the same state as the rest of the house—uncluttered but it felt as if it hadn't been wiped down in more than a decade. There was a single plate, fork and clear glass in the sink. A clean saucepan sat on the stove, no doubt waiting to be filled with a can of soup.

Lily dug around underneath the sink, where she found a spray can of furniture polish and an old, dirty rag. Too dirty of a rag. She grabbed a roll of paper towels. "Beggars can't be choosers, I suppose."

Lily returned to the living room and proceeded to dust.

"What are you doing?" Rowdy demanded.

"Taking care of you." Lily proceeded to wipe down the coffee table. "Isn't that what family does for each other?"

Rowdy scowled. "As I recall, you only wanted to know the truth. You didn't want to be family." He made a shooing motion with his hand. "I don't need coddling."

Lily and Nora ignored him.

Lily moved to a display cabinet with a collection of white horse figurines, including the horse ornament he'd swiped from her weeks ago. "Why did you decide to give away that ranch as a grand prize?"

"Tax break, obviously."

"You're in financial trouble?" Lily faced him. "Why didn't you just put it up for sale?"

"I'm *not* in financial trouble."

Something wasn't adding up. "You do realize that if someone wins that ranch, they'll be your closest neighbor? Might even see Solomon a time or two." Or a whole herd of horses.

Rowdy glanced at Nora, working his mouth as if he had a lot to say but didn't want a word of it to be heard by her.

It felt as if she was facing a dead end. Lily

switched tactics. "What made you agree to host the last Christmas party?"

"You did." Rowdy's chin thrust out. "I was told you suggested I step in."

That surprised Lily into silence.

Cady began to fuss. Nora dug out a rattle from the diaper bag.

Lily shook the can of furniture polish and then pressed the nozzle. The spray can sputtered and ran out of juice. "Let's hope your vacuum cleaner is in better shape than your other cleaning supplies." Lily went in search of the appliance.

"I don't need you poking around in my business," Rowdy shouted after her.

"Didn't stop you from poking into mine," Lily shouted back.

"Do you want to hold the baby?" Nora asked.

Lily hesitated in the hallway.

"Why?" Rowdy grumbled.

"Because babies love everybody." Nora, gem that she was, sounded chipper and confident. "Even lonely old men like you. And besides, we're family now. Meet your great-niece, Cadence Smith."

"IF I COMMIT to stay in Clementine and at the Done Roamin' Ranch, what are my options?" Zane asked Chandler when he found him Monday morning in his office. He stood in front of his desk, having removed his hat.

The ranch foreman had been peering at his

computer screen in an office that was decorated with a small wreath hung in the window. He removed his reading glasses. "Your options? Like a career path?"

Rusty walked from behind the desk toward Zane, squeezing his favorite tennis ball in his mouth.

"Yes." Zane reached for the ball but Rusty leaped out of reach, wagging his tail. "Why does that dog only let you throw his ball?"

"Because I feed him." Chandler studied Zane, snapping his fingers to call Rusty back to him. "What brought this on?"

"I made a decision last night with my future in mind, like you told me I should." But it all started here. "If I stay, can I be a location manager when we supply stock to rodeos? Or someday be the ranch foreman?"

Chandler rocked back in his office chair. "You want to replace me?"

Rusty stood on his hind legs and placed his front paws on the arm of Chandler's chair, further rocking the boat. He dropped the tennis ball in Chandler's lap.

Zane thought it best to keep quiet.

Chandler threw the ball out the open door into his living room, setting Rusty on a merry chase. "My question still stands. Do you want to replace me?"

"Someday. Yeah. I'm almost a decade younger than you, remember?" Zane's hold on his hat increased, his nails digging into straw. "And I bring a varied skill set to the job." He didn't mention his aversion to math.

Chandler rubbed his eyes. "How about we start with one year at a time?"

"A year?" Zane came closer and rested his hands on Chandler's desk, dropping his cowboy hat in the process. "What can you possibly want me to do for a year that I haven't already done?"

"Be patient."

Zane scoffed.

The sound was echoed at his feet by Rusty huffing. The dog had Zane's hat brim in his mouth and his mischievous brown eyes on Zane.

"Give me that." Zane made a grab for his hat but Rusty was quicker, lurching sideways and then scrambling behind Chandler's desk. "Tell your dog to give me my hat."

"Patience," Chandler said again, giving the dog a pat on the head.

Zane rolled his eyes and held his tongue. "I can be patient. I can be steady."

"Even when things get rough?" Chandler continued to pet his dog.

He's just toying with me now.

"Give me my hat." Zane held out his hand.

Chandler didn't even break a smile. There was something going on here that Zane wasn't getting. "Rusty, drop the hat."

The dog seemed to spit Zane's hat onto the

floor, creating a trail of slobber. And then Rusty pawed Zane's hat like he did his dirty tennis balls.

"Great. Give it to me." Zane made the gimme gesture with his hand.

Chandler picked up his hat and passed it over, not smiling or apologizing for the drool on the hat brim.

Zane slapped the hat against his pants leg and turned to go.

"That's what I mean," Chandler said.

Zane paused, glancing back over his shoulder.

"When things go south, you can't just bolt." Chandler looked grim.

No. That wasn't it. He looked disappointed. Like Zane had failed a test.

"You have to be committed to stay, Zane, to hear what needs work or improvement on your part. You have to take a breath when times are tough and hang in there."

"You think I can't take teasing from a dog?" Zane plopped the damp hat on his head. "You're wrong. I hear the hay truck. I'm in charge of getting that stored, remember?"

And then Zane marched out, feeling annoyingly out of sorts.

When a man made a decision and put himself on the line, he should feel good about himself.

Lily sneezed.

Rowdy's house was large and full of things to dust. But even though she'd vacuumed and dusted with a damp rag, dust motes still danced in the streams of sunlight coming through the paned windows.

Nora was a trooper. She'd tackled the kitchen, which left Lily and Rowdy mostly alone when they were in the same room together. Sad to say, Lily was eager to clean spaces the older man wasn't in.

There was a sunroom in the back that had a wrought iron table and sole chair. There was a framed picture sitting on the table. Lily picked it up, wiping off the dust to see the people in the photograph clearer.

A blond-haired woman with big, round sunglasses stood in the crook of Rowdy's arm in front of his barn.

Mom.

Lily sank down on the iron chair. It wasn't a soft landing.

How young they both looked. Her mother smiled broadly, head resting on Rowdy's chest. There was no doubt they were in love. Mom hadn't been as openly affectionate with Sonny. But, had she returned to Sonny out of a combination of love for him and Beau and the vow she'd made to them? That felt most likely. And, of course, she'd been happy. Lily was certain of it. Surprisingly, that gave Lily a sense of longed-for peace.

But there was more to the photograph.

A young boy of about ten or twelve stood in

front of the couple, both arms spread wide as if he was saying, *"Ta-da!"* He had thick, wavy brown hair and a smattering of big freckles across his cheeks.

Lucas.

Lily smiled. Her half brother seemed to have a personality as large as Ford's. She imagined she'd like him. The question was... Would Lucas like or accept her? Or rather... Did she want him to?

Wanting Lucas to accept Lily implied she wanted a relationship with Rowdy. The old coot didn't make that an easy decision, either.

Knowing the truth doesn't always make life better.

Sonny's words of wisdom were spot-on. And Lily could imagine she knew the well those words had sprung from.

She carried the picture out to the living room, where Rowdy was holding Cady and staring lovingly at her face.

Lily sat on the couch near him. "Why don't you talk about Lucas?"

Rowdy considered her before answering. "Do you want me to?"

Lily nodded. "What's he going to think about me?"

"Who cares? He left." The grouch was back, scowling at Lily.

She wasn't buying his tough-guy act, anymore. "I think you care. I think you care a lot." Lily set the photograph on the coffee table. "I love this picture, by the way. I'd like to see other family pictures you have and hear your stories, including why Lucas left. And don't tell me that ranch he used to live in is bad luck."

"I've told you stories," he said gruffly.

"About horses."

Rowdy shushed Lily.

Cady squirmed and protested her sleep being interrupted.

Rowdy rocked the baby side to side, murmuring nonsense.

Lily waited.

Finally, Cady settled back into slumber.

"You should go. I don't need a charity cleaning. I do just fine on my own." His thin chin was thrust out, daring her to come back with a retort.

But Lily was beginning to understand her father's gruffness was just an act to cover what she suspected was a tender heart, one that had been hurt too often. "If we leave, we'll have to take the baby."

Rowdy stared at Lily suspiciously.

"I think my mother is staring at us from heaven and hoping we'll manage to figure this out."

"There's nothing to figure. You're mine," Rowdy said with volume and feeling.

Cady whimpered.

"If that's how you talked to Lucas, it's no wonder he left," Lily said in a whisper.

Rowdy began rocking Cady.

Nora appeared down the hall, clearly eavesdropping, probably both out of maternal instincts and because she wanted to hear Rowdy and Lily's conversation.

Lily stared at her half brother's exuberant pose in the photograph. "Are Lucas and I alike?"

"You have a similar sense of humor," Rowdy allowed in a sandpapery whisper.

"I hope he always wanted a little sister." Lily stared at Rowdy's smile in the photograph, then turned the picture toward him. "You had a sense of humor once, I bet." And a big heart, before two women broke it.

Rowdy narrowed his eyes. "I can tell a few knock-knock jokes."

"I much prefer jokes that start with a nun, a duck and a rodeo cowboy walk into a bar." Lily smiled.

In the hallway, Nora rolled her eyes and made a cutting motion across her neck.

"Not all buttons you push will work, you know," Rowdy said in a soft voice. "Now, you'll be wanting to get this baby fed and changed before you head back into town to pick up Ford."

"Right-o." Lily got to her feet, still smiling.

Because it felt like a lot of progress had been made today. And that meant more could be made tomorrow.

CHAPTER TWENTY-THREE

"Mom, I can't believe you came to pick me up after school with Cady." Ford was thrilled to find his mother in the front seat of Lily's truck and his baby sister in the back. "Hi, little sister. I'm going to make sure you turn out as cool as I am."

That gave Lily and Nora a laugh.

"Is it a hot chocolate day, Auntie?"

"It is, Ford." Lily inched forward in the pickup line. "Double whip. Double marshmallows." She snuck a peek at Nora to gauge her reaction.

"Since I can't have coffee that sounds fantastic." Nora gave Lily two thumbs-up.

"I guess I shouldn't have worried about dosing Ford with sugar," Lily said.

"He acts the same on sugar as off," Nora admitted, waving to a woman monitoring kids crossing the street.

"Here's your pacifier, Cady," Ford cooed. Then he reached forward to tap Lily's center console, presumably to get her attention. "Auntie, maybe Zane will be at the coffee shop."

"Let's not get our hopes up." The way Lily did.

A few minutes later, they entered Clementine Coffee Roasters.

And there was Zane, standing in line to place an order. Just the sight of him made Lily's heart skip a beat. And her heart had been getting all the feels today, from highs to lows. But when Zane turned and smiled at her, Lily's heart leaped into action.

"Zane!" Ford cried, running up to hug him. "I told Auntie you'd be here, but she didn't believe me."

"Maybe that's because you didn't tell her we secretly agreed to meet here." Zane grinned but it wasn't the unfettered smile Lily loved. There was something holding him back from enjoying the moment completely.

"What's wrong?" Lily asked after Zane greeted them.

"You can tell?" Zane ran a hand around the back of his neck.

"Of course I can tell." Instinctively, she took his hand. "On the five-alarm fire scale, how bad is it?"

"A one. You'd think I could handle it better, right?" Zane shook his head. "Someone with patience and a cool head could handle it better."

"If you're in the right frame of mind, of course you can handle it better." Not that Lily knew what had happened, but it felt right to say the truth. "I've seen you have patience with your mothers, Ford and me. Take a breath."

"Right." Zane nodded. Several times. Smiling with more authenticity. "Maybe that's it. Maybe I just needed you to remind me to breathe."

The barista asked for their order. Zane treated them all to beverages.

"Wait!" Ford cried. "We need to order a hot chocolate for Cady."

Nora drew her son over to a table near the large Christmas tree, explaining how babies couldn't have hot chocolate.

"I missed you since I saw you last," Zane told Lily, right there in front of a barista making their drinks, and a growing line of school moms and dads.

Lily felt her cheeks heat, felt her heart soar. "I missed you, too."

"It feels sappy to say, doesn't it?" Zane grinned.

Lily nodded. "But a good sappy."

And that very neatly summed up her day.

"I SURE WISH we would-a caught Solomon." Ford sat closer to Zane than Lily did. The little guy had pulled his chair next to Zane's. "I'm ready for a horse. Mouse is great but soon Cady will be big enough to ride."

Zane leaned his head toward the kid. "Does this have anything to do with the fact that Santa is riding through town soon?"

"Yes, sir." Ford nodded. "And I've been *real* good this year. You can ask anybody."

"And anybody will tell you that Ford is a good

rider, a kind older brother and a cookie lover," Lily teased. "All of which get you on Santa's nice list."

Ford beamed at Lily. And then he beamed at Zane. "I'm going to get a new horse for Christmas. Just you wait and see."

"Now, Ford," Nora began. "Remember that you didn't ask for a horse from Santa until recently. Santa might have got you something else."

Nora was definitely up for Mom of the Year.

"Yeah, right." Ford stood and raised his hot chocolate cup in the air. "Santa *knows* what I need and it's a horse."

"Okay, Mr. Enthusiastic," Lily teased. "Have a seat and let Auntie tell you a tale of Christmas Past."

"Those stories never have happy endings, Auntie." But Ford sat anyway.

Zane bit back a smile. He could listen to Lily and Ford all day.

"I remember one Christmas I wanted Santa to bring me a new lasso," Lily began, her dimples showing. "And do you know what I got?"

"A Christmas ornament?"

Lily lightly slapped her hands on the table. "No. But good guess."

"Aw." Ford sat back in his chair.

"Did you get a purse?" Nora got into the game. "You don't seem like a purse person."

Lily shook her head. Then she looked at Zane,

freckles bright and dimples showing. "Any guesses?"

Zane sipped his coffee, patiently studying Lily while he took time to breathe. She was definitely good for his equilibrium. "I know what it was."

Lily rolled her eyes. "Cut the suspense and give it to me."

He leaned back, crossing his arms over his chest. "You got socks."

"How did you know?" Lily laughed.

"Because Santa always gives at least one useful gift every Christmas, particularly ones that are affordable." Zane lifted his coffee cup in a toast to Nora. "I think parents add socks to Santa's list."

Ford pivoted in his seat. "*Mom.* You didn't."

Nora sipped her hot chocolate, trying to hide a smile.

"*Mom*," Ford said again. "Every time I wrote Santa? Every time?" He collapsed onto the table, extending his arms and nearly knocking over Zane's and Nora's drinks, as well as his own. "*Mo-om.*"

"Ford." Nora removed his cowboy hat and ruffled his hair. "You know that no matter what Santa brings you, you should be grateful."

"He's bringing me socks." Ford banged his head on the table but only for effect.

And nothing they could say consoled him.

Afterward, Zane found himself thinking he wouldn't mind being part of Lily and Ford's family.

CHAPTER TWENTY-FOUR

The Tenth Party of Christmas:
The Not Fruitcake Cake Dessert Party
Hosted by: The Burns Ranch

"So. Much. Cake. This is the best party ever!" Ford stared at all the tables set out on the front yard of the Burns Ranch. And then he bolted toward the red tablecloths and sparkling white lights on the dessert buffet, shouting, *"Weeeee!"*

"Should we worry about his sugar intake?" Zane asked Lily, taking hold of her hand as they entered the Burns Ranch proper and the gathered crowd.

"As his aunt, the answer is always no." Lily liked the way their hands fit together. She liked how they joked and teased. She liked coming to events as his date. But a part of her held back a little bit of herself. She'd been hurt before.

Zane checked in with his mamas, filling out a ticket for the grand prize drawing while Lily glanced around.

"Silver Bells" was playing from somewhere

near the main house. There were lights everywhere, illuminating the yard and the arena. Several trees had been strung with holiday lights, too. Cowboys and cowgirls of all ages were clustered about eating cake, cake pops and cupcakes, wearing holiday sweaters and sprigs of what looked like holly in their hatbands.

"We're supposed to try different cakes and variations of cake and then vote on our favorites," Zane told her when he was done, taking her hand once more. "Was I supposed to bring cake?" No one had told Lily that.

"Folks signed up for the competition long ago." Zane peered past a cowboy's shoulders to eye the array of sweet offerings. Then he smiled at Lily in a way that made her heart beat faster. "I see our young chaperone is choosing everything that he can eat with his hands."

She spotted Ford and his messy fingers. "Makes sense. A fork will only slow him down." When little about herself and Zane did. Lily shut the thought away. Because when it came to Zane, thinking made no sense, only feeling did. "But now that we aren't chaperoned, would you do anything different?" she asked, her curiosity piqued.

Zane's smile widened. "I'd take the opportunity to tell you how much I like spending time with you. And I'd bring you closer..." He curled his arm around her waist.

Lily's breath caught.

"And then I'd..." Zane's lips lowered toward hers.

A male voice called out, "There's my right-hand man now!" Both Zane and Lily turned, putting distance between them.

Without having kissed.

Lily wasn't sure whether she was relieved or disappointed.

A tall cowboy with gray at his temples and a grinning cowgirl with white-blond hair wearing a pair of reindeer antlers on her head came to stand behind them in the cake line. Introductions were made and Merry Christmases exchanged.

"I'm his boss," Chandler told Lily.

"Which means he's the one to talk to if you're looking for a job come spring." Zane gave Lily's hand a little shake. "If you're staying."

"If I'm staying," Lily echoed in a small voice. She hadn't decided if she was staying. A part of her wanted to. Both for Zane and for Rowdy. But...

There was always a but.

"I haven't seen you at the feedstore," the smiling cowgirl, Izzy, said to Lily. She wore red Christmas bulb earrings and a T-shirt with a cat tangled in Christmas lights. "I work there. If you need a Christmas gift or anything stock related, we've got it or can get it for you." And then she laughed. "I didn't mean to give you a sales pitch. It can be hard to find your footing in a new town."

"Are you new to town?" Lily wondered aloud.

"No." Izzy laughed once more. It was a nice, friendly laugh. "But every new cowboy—and cowgirl—finds their way to the feedstore eventually."

"And Izzy's there to welcome them." Chandler ducked beneath Izzy's cowboy hat and kissed her fast, earning a blush and shoulder nudge from Izzy.

"Ignore the mush. They're getting married soon," Zane said softly to Lily. "Hopefully, after they get married, they won't be so touchy-feely."

Lily thought Chandler's kiss was sweet and said so.

"We've found our common ground when it comes to affection in public," Chandler said approvingly. "Didn't happen overnight. And it wasn't like that kiss you two had at the ornament exchange."

Now it was Lily's cheeks that were heating. She wasn't going to admit that there had been no more kisses, like that one or otherwise, since then. That would destroy the dating ruse.

Thankfully, there was no more need for relationship discussion. They reached the first table, each taking a plate, fork and napkin and scanning the plethora of cake offerings.

Each item had a small card in front of it stating what kind of cake it was, ingredients and the baker's name.

A few of the names were familiar to Lily now, especially Willa Tarkenton, a single mom trying to navigate a tough divorce, whom the community was rallying around.

"I have to try a slice of Willa's cake." Lily cut a

small slice of the white cake with cheerful green frosting and snowflakes made from powdered sugar on top. As Lily moved on down the line, she noticed Zane, Izzy and Chandler all did the same.

Four tables of cake options later and Lily's plate was full of holiday decadence.

"Let's go over to the arena." Zane led the way. "I hear there will be teams of kids racing piglets."

"Our kids are participating." Izzy followed along. "See the two kids wearing red cowboy hats? Technically, Sam is Chandler's and Mae is mine but—"

"They're ours in every way that matters." Chandler was getting romantic again.

And Lily was here for it.

This is how a couple should be together.

Nothing fake.

Lily's gaze drifted to Zane walking a half step ahead of her.

He turned, and smiled at Lily, as if knowing she was thinking about him, hoping…that someday they'd be as cheesy and adorable together as Chandler and Izzy.

But first, there were hurdles to get over, the most unpredictable of which was his grudge against Rowdy.

ZANE FOUND A spot on the edge of the arena large enough for the four of them to stand, eat cake, talk and watch cute piglets and kidlets have fun.

"Perfect." Lily smiled at Zane, as if he were perfect.

"Zane always finds a way to get front-row seats." Chandler leaned a shoulder against a fence post. "Good job, cowboy."

"Oh, no." Lily covered her mouth, having taken a bite of something. "I wasn't expecting that."

"What?" Zane tried to figure out what she'd eaten that had garnered a negative response. He'd taken most of the same items she had, thinking at the time that they liked the same things. But maybe not.

"Try Willa's cake," Lily whispered, still covering her mouth.

Chandler, Izzy and Zane took a bite.

"Oh," Izzy said, making a face. "Oh, that's too bad."

The taste of Willa's cake wasn't just too bad. It was bad. Period.

Zane coughed on the dry texture.

"I think she used salt instead of sugar," Chandler said in a quiet voice.

"Yep." Zane swallowed thickly.

"Regardless of how her cake tasted, Willa's got my vote," Lily said staunchly. "But I could use some water before that happens."

"I'll get water for everyone." Chandler handed his plate to Izzy and returned to the buffet area.

"Hey, Auntie!" Ford ran up to Lily and Zane. He had chocolate rimming his mouth and streaks of it on his blue jeans. "My friend and me are going to race piglets. Will you watch?"

"Of course." Lily took a moment to wipe his face before letting him go.

It struck Zane then. Lily had a big heart to go with her wit and cowgirl smarts. She was community minded, like others in Clementine.

Like me.

CHAPTER TWENTY-FIVE

The Twelfth Party of Christmas:
Ghost of Christmas Past Barbeque
Hosted by: Rolling Prairie Ranch

THE LAST PARTY of Christmas was a lunch at Rowdy's ranch. Nora and Lily had come with a group of volunteers early in the morning to decorate. Lily had wanted to make sure Rowdy was on his best behavior for his guests, so she did more Rowdy-sitting than decorating.

Rowdy had moved his horses into barn stalls the day before. He and Lily had put signs up outside the barn that stated *Trespassers Will Be Removed.*

Lily wouldn't let him write *shot*.

Rowdy hadn't wanted anyone to enter his home, not even to use the bathroom. But that plan hit a snag when he and Lily couldn't get the water turned on in his bunkhouse. Rowdy wanted to sit at the front door and escort each bathroom user to and from the bathroom.

Lily found some duct tape and cordoned off his living spaces instead.

While they were busy, Nora and the other volunteers had set up several grills and a collection of Christmas trees, hung wreaths on his front porch and set up tables and chairs for folks to eat. The theme was Ghosts of Christmas Past and everyone was encouraged to bring a photo of someone they'd lost to post on a collection of large bulletin boards leaning on the walls of Rowdy's porch.

After all the other volunteers had left, Rowdy walked Lily and Nora to Lily's truck. "I suppose you're going to be hanging on to that Duvall boy when I see you again."

"Yes." Lily refrained from rolling her eyes. "And you're going to be nice to him and to everyone else who annoys you."

"It's easy to be nice," Rowdy began. "Because I'll be sitting in the barn making sure no one noses around where they don't belong."

"You'll sit with your family," Nora told him, having adopted the same no-nonsense tone Lily used with him. "That means me, Beau, Ford, Cady, Lily and Zane."

"That Duvall boy?" Rowdy harumphed.

"That Duvall boy is serious about your Smith girl." Nora wasn't pulling any punches.

But this punch went a bit too far for Lily. "Seems like most people want to go from first meet to the altar. Slow down, Nora."

"Yeah." Rowdy looked less harangued. "Slow down, Nora."

Nora shook her finger at both Lily and Rowdy. "We will all sit together *and* we will all get along."

NORA KNOCKED ON Lily's bedroom door. "It came." She held out a plastic dry cleaning bag. "It's your Santa suit. The Santapalooza Parade committee just dropped it off."

"Twelve Christmas parties and one Santa-themed parade." Lily took the hanger, gave it a proper inspection, then put it in a closet in between some of Beau's clothes. "Somewhere along the line, Zane's mamas got me into the parade. In for a penny, in for a pound, I suppose."

"It'll wrinkle if you store it all scrunched up in there." Nora moved hangers out of the way and shook out the suit. "I've never ridden in the parade, so I'm a little jealous."

"No one offered to loan you a horse?" That seemed odd.

"I never asked." Nora smoothed the suit once more. "We've only been here a few years. Somebody's got to be in the crowd, right?"

"Nora, you can ride Jet in my place."

Someone gasped behind them.

They turned.

"Auntie, you said Jet is a horse boss." Ford stomped his foot. "Mom can't ride a horse boss. She's never had a horse of her own."

"That's true." Nora backed away from the Santa suit. "Thanks for the offer." She walked out, raising her voice, "Is everyone ready to go?"

"Auntie." Ford frowned at Lily. "I'm disappointed in you. Mom doesn't ride. Ever."

"Ford." Lily frowned back at him. "Have you ever thought that your mother might want to try to ride?"

"I..." Ford looked sad. And then he ran down the hall. "Dad! We have to get Mom a horse for Christmas... Yes, this Christmas! I can teach you how to ride, Mom. You can try to ride Mouse if you get scared."

Lily smiled as Ford continued to tell his parents what to do. Then she turned to look at her reflection in the mirror. This was the last party of the season. The last time she'd agreed to pretend to be Zane's girlfriend. But they were so far past pretend. It was just that they'd never acknowledged their feelings for each other.

Lily tugged the cuffs of the Christmas sweater she'd borrowed from Nora. Other than the loaned sweater, she looked the same. Blue jeans, brown curly hair, brown freckles and those happy dimples.

Happy dimples.

Her mother had always called them that. Had she seen the picture of Rowdy's mother? Did she associate the dimples with her time with Rowdy?

There were still so many unanswered questions

about her past and about her future. And Lily didn't know if she'd get any answers tonight... or ever.

"Mom, I thought you'd left for the party already." Despite Zane's slightly cranky greeting, he hugged his mother in the Done Roamin' Ranch's yard.

He was heading over to meet Lily at Rowdy's ranch, a place he'd never thought to visit and a topic he'd never had the courage to address with Lily—dating for real. It felt like they'd been moving slowly toward that reality for the past week.

His mother sighed. She seemed so frail in his arms, not like the dynamo who'd tried to corral him in his youth. "I'm still hopeful you and Lily will take the next step in your relationship before I leave."

"I like Lily, Mom." A lot. "But I'm not going to propose today." He'd consider it a win just to get through the barbecue without losing his cool around Rowdy.

Mom eased out of his embrace. "When your father and I broke up, I thought I could give you what you needed. But you had it in your head that what you needed was that ranch and your father."

"Mom. You were never the problem. I was." Zane didn't want to rehash the past today. Now. Before he spent hours at Rowdy's ranch.

"I just think if I'd done something differently or given you more love..." She hugged him tight.

"Your life hasn't been what I wanted for you. All this restlessness inside you."

"You did fine, Mom. Some people are just born to be restless." He set her away from him, holding on to her shoulders. "I may never live on that ranch again. I know that now." He'd thought about that every time he filled out a ticket for the grand-prize drawing. "I know I'm not going to be a race car driver or an astronaut. But I'm a good person and I'm comfortable in my own skin. You can be proud of that, whether I end up engaged by Christmas or not... Can't you?"

His mother's face was pinched and her eyes filled with unshed tears. "It's hard being a parent. I just want you to know that I never gave up on you."

Oh, that stung.

Unbidden, a memory returned. Teenage Zane shouting at his mother that he didn't love her or need her or want her in his life.

It stung his nose as tears collected in his eyes.

Zane drew his mother into another hug. "You never deserved the trouble I gave you. I was lucky to have you as a mom. I still am."

"Flattery will get you everything," Mom said in her wobbly voice. "Everything I can give you. Always."

"Does this mean I can tell Eileen that I'm your favorite child?" Zane teased, because if he didn't joke, he might shed a few tears himself.

"You can tell her you're my favorite *son*." Mom

squirmed out of his embrace and wiped her eyes. "You'd best get a move on. Don't want to keep Lily waiting."

"Why don't you ride with me?" Zane offered. "I'm meeting Lily at the party." Heaven only knew why she'd volunteered to help. Rowdy wasn't her favorite person, either.

"No. You go on. I'm riding with Mary and Frank." Mom backed away. "I'm so proud of you."

Levity was called for. "Flattery won't get you a marriage proposal for Lily, Mom."

"Oh, but it will keep it top of mind, son." She turned and walked back toward the main house.

"I love you, Mom," Zane called.

"I love you more."

And Zane had no doubt she did.

LILY WAS WATCHING for Zane to arrive. Anxious.

She hadn't told him they were going to be sitting with Rowdy.

It was one of those unseasonably warm days of winter where there was little wind, lots of sun and the temperature was in the sixties. A day filled with promise if one was hopeful.

Lily wanted to be hopeful. It was just… She wasn't the type of person who had happy endings.

She saw Zane walk up the road with long strides. He looked so handsome in black jeans, a black sweater and a black hat. She waved. She waved like they were a seventh-grade couple with too much bounce and enthusiasm.

This isn't me.

But maybe it wasn't the Lily Smith of the past. Maybe this was Lily Smith of the future.

She waved harder, laughing.

Zane's long-legged stride brought him close quickly. He was laughing, too. "What's got you jumping like a kernel of popped corn?"

Nerves. Hope. Something that feels an awful lot like love.

Lily hugged him, unable to speak.

"Hey. Are you okay?" Zane held her at arm's length, peering at her face.

"I just got carried away." Lily could feel the blush heating her cheeks. But she didn't care. "The burgers are starting to come off the grill and I'm starving." She took Zane's hand and led him to the buffet table. "Beau and his family have already sat down to eat."

"Sorry I'm late."

"You're not late. Loads of people have yet to show up." Rowdy's place was on the outskirts of town. Lily had faith in the residents of Clementine that they wouldn't skip this party just because her father was a curmudgeon.

They filled their plates and then she led Zane over to their table.

"Zane's here," Ford announced. He'd taken a seat by Rowdy and had been asking him questions nonstop. "Mr. Rowdy, did you know Zane's going to ask my auntie to marry him?"

Rowdy scrunched his face and shoveled potato salad into his mouth.

Zane said nothing.

Hoo boy. Not the best of starts.

"How's business, Beau?" Zane asked, taking hold of his burger.

Lily bumped him gently with her shoulder, as if to say, *good job.*

"Business is trending up." Beau had on his accounting hat today. Literally. He hadn't worn a cowboy hat, choosing instead a baseball cap with the words *Smith Accounting* written on the front. "Tax season is ahead of us. I've got a stack of new regulations and guidelines to read before the new year. And I might be able to hire a bookkeeper next summer."

"That would be me." Nora lifted Cady to her shoulder. "Beau has always dreamed of having a large, family-run business."

"Hang on." Ford did a dramatic double take. "Am I going to work for Dad?"

"When you're old enough, yes." Beau nodded. "It's your legacy. I'm working hard to create generational wealth."

"Watch out," Rowdy muttered. "Here come the buzzwords."

"*Dad*," Ford said in his most dramatic voice. "When I grow up, I'm going to be a working cowboy like my auntie."

Beau frowned at Lily.

Hoo boy. Lily ducked her head and pretended to be obsessed with buttering her Hawaiian roll.

"You should learn a trade," Rowdy said in a louder voice. "Be a blacksmith. Folks always need horseshoes."

Lily caught Beau frowning at Rowdy.

"Maybe Ford should follow his heart," Zane said. "Not everyone knows what they want to do or what will make them happy when they're five or thirty-five."

Lily caught Beau frowning at Zane.

"I'd hope you'd know how to make a living by thirty-five." Rowdy was winding his way up to a mild roar. "A steady paycheck will keep a roof over your head."

"And sometimes, a steady paycheck will drag a man's spirit down." Zane had a good set of lungs on him, too.

"Why are they fighting?" Ford asked. "Do they hate each other?"

"No," Zane said at the same time that Rowdy said, "Yes."

The two men scowled at each other.

"Can we all just eat and not argue?" Lily asked, noticing she'd buttered the entirety of her roll, inside and out.

"He started it," Beau muttered.

"Just calling it the way I see it. Oh…" Rowdy accepted baby Cady from Nora.

"She's napping and doesn't need to hear loud

voices." Nora marched off. "I'm going to get cake."

Everyone but Rowdy continued to eat. More partygoers arrived. Many looked around the ranch with curious gazes.

When she and Zane were done eating, Lily gathered up their trash. "Let's go look at some of the memory pictures. You know, the relatives of Christmas past." She didn't like the "ghosts" designation.

"Glad to." Zane got to his feet and put his arm around Lily, drawing her away from their table. "Why did we eat with Rowdy?"

"Oh… Nora thought it would be nice." Inwardly, Lily cringed at the lie. "You did really well with him."

"I was patient. It was the best I could manage," Zane said cryptically, leading her up the stairs to the porch. "I didn't bring a picture. Did you?"

"Yeah. My parents." She and Beau had selected a photo of their parents in front of their Christmas tree. "There aren't as many photos as I thought there'd be."

"Maybe folks haven't had a chance to post their pictures yet." Zane greeted another couple coming up the steps. "Can we talk somewhere? In private?"

LILY LED ZANE along the path toward one of the barns, specifically where Rowdy was not on patrol. "What did you want to talk about?"

Zane paused, taking in Lily's hesitant smile that only hinted at those dimples and freckles he could spend hours staring at. And the warmth in her eyes seemed to encourage him to get on with it.

But he still felt tense, like something was wrong. It had to be that he was standing on his nemesis's property. How he wished they were somewhere, anywhere, else.

Zane cleared his throat. "Well, you know…"

"Is this about our fake dating?" Lily fidgeted. "I've been thinking about this being…you know. Our last day."

He nodded. "Even though we've been through some hard times, I think it worked out pretty well."

Lily's brow furrowed.

If that wasn't what she expected him to say, she wasn't alone. He hadn't expected to say it, either. "Um… What I meant to say was that we've survived my mamas and there's no reason to fake date anymore."

The furrows in Lily's brow deepened.

I'm screwing this up.

"That is, the fake dating part can stop—"

Lily was scowling now.

"—and the real dating part can begin."

It was like a switch had been flipped. Lily's frown turned upside down and she was suddenly in his arms and kissing him.

That took a minute or two.

But there were still things Zane wanted to say.

So, he eased them apart, gave Lily a tremendous smile and said, "I don't want there to be any secrets between us," since he was planning to tell her that he'd had more than one talk with Chandler about career opportunities at the Done Roamin' Ranch, the last of which had been the most successful. Then he planned to follow that up by asking her if she'd be open to staying in town and continuing to date.

But before he got all that out, Lily said, "*Secrets?*" in a way that was a tad shocking, probably because she took a step back from Zane and had a wary look in her eyes.

"Not *secrets* secrets. As in I want to uncover information, get to know you. More," he added lamely, although the entire conversation had drifted into the lame department. "So that there aren't any sort of surprises about each other, you know?"

Lily was nodding slowly, looking at him but with that dazed expression that indicated she might not be seeing him.

I really should have dated more and learned to be less upsetting.

Because for some reason he couldn't fathom, Lily was clearly upset. Not angry upset but shocked upset. The only reason Zane could think of for why she'd be upset was that… *She's keeping a secret from me.*

"Holy smokes, are you married?" he blurted, because that was the worst secret he could imagine.

"No!" She actually laughed, although not with dimples.

So, he waited for her to expand.

Instead, Lily dragged him to the barn door, opened it and shoved him inside, closing the door behind them. "You can't tell anyone."

"That you're married?" Because suddenly, it seemed like a possibility.

"No." Lily kissed him, all too briefly in his opinion. And then she said, "Promise me you won't tell anyone what I'm about to reveal."

"I promise?"

A horse neighed near them. The two horses in the barn answered back, quick and restless in their stalls. All the barn doors were closed, even the ones leading to paddocks. It was dark in there.

Lily grabbed hold of his hand. "I need to show you something." She led him to the first stall. "Don't be mad."

A horse poked its head over the stall door. A white horse. In Rowdy Brown's barn.

"What the..." Zane's mouth went dry. "Solomon?"

The stallion looked at Zane. And then he nudged his shoulder, almost playfully. Teasingly.

Like I'm the butt of a joke.

"Explain," Zane demanded, frowning at the horse and then Lily. "And talk fast, because I feel as if the entire time we were out looking for Solomon, you knew he was right here."

In the barn of the man who'd ruined Zane's life.

"I didn't know," Lily began, filling Zane with relief. "At least, not the first time we rode out."

Zane's chest felt crowded with tension. He dropped Lily's hand.

"I need everyone's attention!" Rowdy shouted from the ranch yard. "I have an announcement to make!"

"Oh, no," Lily said, just above a whisper.

"Quiet down!" Rowdy shouted to his guests.

"Lily, I want answers." Zane stood rigidly in the dimly lit barn, feeling like he was five and not getting his way.

"Zane." Lily placed her palms on his cheeks. "I need to tell you something."

"Yes, about Solomon." Zane hoped she'd hurry.

"My daughter is here tonight," Rowdy said in a booming voice.

"His daughter?" Zane muttered. "Since when did he have a daughter?"

The crowd buzzed with chatter.

"Zane…" Lily's palms pressed harder on his cheeks. "You should know. I… I'm… Okay, yes, we've been fake dating. And I realize I shouldn't have, but I… I've fallen in love with you."

There was something desperate about her confession.

Zane opened his mouth—perhaps to repeat those words back to her or perhaps not, given she still hadn't explained about Solomon.

But Rowdy beat him to the punch. "Lily, where are you? Come on up here."

"*Lily?*" Zane wheezed, drawing back so fast that he almost fell over his own feet.

Making him feel as if he was truly falling, falling into an abyss where all his worst nightmares had come true.

Lily said her father wasn't really her father.

Lily said someone had written her a letter claiming to be her father.

Lily didn't say Rowdy Brown was her father.

Just like she didn't say Solomon is Rowdy Brown's horse.

"Lily?" Rowdy cried. "Where did that girl get to?"

"He's talking to you." Zane felt gutted. He could barely breathe. And his patience... "*Are you* Rowdy Brown's daughter?"

"Does it matter whose daughter I am?" Lily reached for him but Zane held his hands away.

"It matters to me." It shouldn't. On some level, Zane knew it shouldn't. "The lies matter to me. You knew what he'd done to me. How things he did led to my family falling apart. You knew that I wanted Solomon. And... I don't know how I can trust you after this."

"But, Zane—"

The barn door was flung open.

"All those who enter my barn will vacate the premises!" Rowdy roared. "Now!"

Zane didn't budge.

But Lily did. She ran.

CHAPTER TWENTY-SIX

"You!" Rowdy pointed at Zane. "Out!"

Then he turned and pointed to the crowd. "All of you! The barn is off-limits! Back to your tables!"

The white horse in the stall blew a raspberry.

Zane was surprised he heard anything. His ears were buzzing.

Rowdy addressed Zane. "Move your boots, boy."

And Zane did. He even tried to move his boots past the old coot.

"We need to have words," Rowdy grumbled, each syllable spoken like a pointed threat.

"Ha!" Zane tried to laugh. "After what I saw in there, it's you who needs to talk."

Rowdy set his hand against the closed barn door and shook his head. "I don't know what she sees in you…"

Blood pounded in Zane's temples. "Whatever she sees is none of your business."

"Oh, but it is my business." Rowdy's expression

turned crafty. "She's my daughter, you see. And for that reason alone, you'll listen to me."

"Zane, are you all right?" That was his mother.

"We're just checking on him, Rowdy." And that was his foster mother.

Zane stared at Rowdy, two actions warring within him. He wanted to walk away. It would feel so good to turn his back on the man and never lay eyes on him again. But he also wanted answers. Answers regarding Solomon. Answers regarding Lily.

"We're golden over here. Tell everyone to enjoy the party." Zane planted his feet. "Talk fast, mister. My patience has reached its limit."

"I'll talk at my own pace." Rowdy drew a deep breath, drawing himself up to his full height, which was just about Zane's height. He could see now where Lily got her lanky frame. "And I'll start with your father."

Zane's head flung back as if he'd been struck. "Don't you dare—"

"Badmouth your papa?" Rowdy's smile was more like a fanged snarl. "I have put up with your whining for nigh on twenty years because your father lied to you."

"I swear, Rowdy, if you say another word, I'll—"

"I bought the ranch before the bank got involved." Rowdy leaned in closer. "Your father took that money and used it to start over. New town. New ranch. New wife."

Zane couldn't say a word. His brain was spinning off in all directions.

"The deal was that I wouldn't tell your mother or either of his kids." Rowdy tipped that white ten-gallon hat back.

And Zane could swear he saw regret in the old man's eyes.

"It's a shame what happened to you and I felt guilty about it."

"Not guilty enough to help us," Zane ground out, fully aware that two people had apologized to him today about their contributions to his volatile childhood.

"Well, *my daughter* wanted me to make peace with you. A fella can get on in years and still learn to change his ways." Rowdy smacked his lips together. "But it doesn't count for much unless another fella takes the hand that's extended to him and believes the apology is sincere."

Zane hadn't noticed Rowdy extend his hand. He was of a mind not to take it.

But then, he clocked a large freckle among the age spots on Rowdy's face. And that freckle brought Lily's face to mind—her dimpled smile, her unfettered laughter, how her brown eyes seemed to soften after they kissed.

And without realizing it, Zane found his hand in Rowdy's strong grip.

"You're packing?" Beau leaned against Lily's bedroom doorway. "You're not the type to run from a little dustup."

"Oh, but I am." Lily continued to transfer clothes from the dresser to her suitcase. "Whenever things get hard or awkward, I move on. And this... What happened today was more than hard and awkward. It was painful. The way Zane looked at me when..." When he saw that white horse. "That was bad enough. But when Rowdy made his announcement. I knew it was over for us."

Too bad I told him first that I loved him.

"Lily, you can't leave two days before Christmas." Beau calmly closed her suitcase, then cleared a spot for her to sit on the bed. After a moment, he sat next to her. "Look. I'm not a fan of Zane. I think he swooped in on the new girl in town and moved way too fast."

"Beau, it wasn't like that."

He gently squeezed her hand. "Hear me out. I'm not a fan of Rowdy, either. He's manipulative and maybe you should consider having nothing to do with him."

"Beau, he's not like that." Under her brother's withering gaze, Lily added, "All the time."

"But here's the thing. If you keep running, you'll never know for sure, and maybe you'll have missed out on something really great. Stay until Christmas, Lily." Beau gave her a stern look, but she could see the humor shining through. "As the oldest in the Smith family, I'm telling you that it's best you stay."

"Yes, stay." Nora pushed the door open, holding Cady. She was a good eavesdropper, if unwelcome when she used her powers on Lily's business. "What will we tell Ford if you go?"

"Auntie's not leaving?" Ford entered, right on cue.

Lily wanted to leave right away. But she couldn't disappoint Ford. No way. No how.

Or Nora.

Or Beau.

CHAPTER TWENTY-SEVEN

CHRISTMAS EVE MORNING dawned crisp, clear and cold.

As soon as it was light, Lily went outside and saddled Jet, eyes sore and puffy from a night spent crying into her pillow. She rode him around the perimeter of the pasture.

"This is my placebo for not hotfooting it out of town," she admitted to her trusty steed.

A familiar beat-up truck pulled into the driveway towing a horse trailer.

Lily galloped to the pasture gate, hopped out of the saddle and looped Jet's reins around the rail.

"Merry Christmas," Rowdy hailed her as he climbed carefully from his truck.

"What are you doing here?" Lily slipped through the gate. "I would have come to say goodbye if I was leaving."

The front door opened at the house. Beau stepped onto the porch looking disheveled in jeans and a gray hoodie.

"Merry Christmas." Rowdy gave him a wave

as he tottered past the Santa on the front lawn. "I'm not here to cause trouble."

"Six words I imagine you've never said. Ever." Lily crossed her arms over her chest.

"Can I just have a word without all the guff you try and put between us?" Rowdy came to a stop a few feet away from her. "I'm used to doing things how I want them, but you have pushed me to my limits and—"

"You'll be better off without me," Lily interrupted. "Yes, I know."

"I was going to say," Rowdy ground out, "that you've reminded me of the things I loved about your mother and the things that she loved about me."

Lily's mouth went dry.

"I used to be good with people." Rowdy shook his head. "I was known to cut a rug at the Buckboard on a Saturday night. Had a sense of humor and a tortoise shell for a back. Comments I didn't like just rolled right off me." He peered at her, sniffing. "I had patience and empathy. I actually cared about people enough to volunteer in town. But all that was tested when Linda left me."

The front door opened and closed. Now Nora stood with Beau, bundled up in her slippers and thick blue bathrobe.

"And then Dawnice came into my life, battle-tested by a marriage where she didn't feel valued. And I felt like myself again." His nose was red and it wasn't from the cold. He was blinking back tears. "But when Sonny arrived, apologizing and telling Dawnice he loved her... When she left to do right by your brother, I became broken and bitter. I said and did things that I couldn't stand. I withdrew to the ranch because I was safer there with Lucas and my horses." He sniffed louder, as if sniffing was the only thing keeping him from falling to pieces.

And Lily... Lily's eyes were filled with tears and she hated it because she'd felt at rock bottom yesterday, only to be dragged farther along the jagged rocks this morning. Her heart ached for her father.

"Lucas left after that. The years have passed slowly, and I've felt every day. And so, when I read that Dawnice died, it was too much. I could have given up the ghost then and there." Rowdy drew another shuddering breath. "But there was that picture of the Smith family—that picture of *you*. And suddenly, I had the stupidest hope." Rowdy stared at Lily as tears spilled over his cheeks. "The hope that I could find myself again if my daughter came home." He held out his arms.

And it seemed natural to rush into them.

And cry, although not alone. Rowdy was crying, too.

"I've been so dumb," they both said at the same time.

And cried harder.

"Hey," Ford said, coming to join them in his

cowboy boots, jacket and pajamas. "Why are you crying? It's Christmas Eve!"

Lily and Rowdy stopped hugging and crying and had a good laugh.

"Mom says she's going to make pancakes cuz that's Auntie's favorite." Ford headed back toward the house. "Come on."

"Wait." Rowdy held out a hand to Ford, not Lily. "Santa's got an early Christmas present for you."

Ford turned and looked at Rowdy, then at Lily. "Is it a joke? Are you going to give me socks?"

"It's no joke." Rowdy shook his hand in Ford's direction. "I forgot my cane. I need someone to lean on. Your present is in my truck."

"No way." But Ford came over and let Rowdy lean on his shoulder as they walked together toward the truck.

Lily followed. Beau and Nora also came to join them.

Ford slowed at Rowdy's driver's side door.

"Keep going. We can't quit now." Rowdy moved on and Ford resumed helping him keep his balance. "Your present is in the back."

A horse whinnied.

Ford froze. "If you say I'm getting socks when there's a horse in there, I'm going to be so disappointed in you, Mr. Rowdy."

"You won't be disappointed." Rowdy disappeared around the rear of the trailer. There were sounds of locks being removed and then the trailer doors were opened.

Ford ran to the back. *"Two horses? Auntie, come quick!"*

Everyone came quick.

There were two white horses in the trailer. One was visibly larger than the other.

"Only one of these is for you," Rowdy said, nearly bursting with pride.

Lily had never seen her father's smile so wide.

"Her name is Daisy." Rowdy entered the trailer and guided the filly outside. "She's a gentle, patient girl but she still has a lot to learn, which is why your auntie is going to help you work with her. Isn't that right, Lily?"

Lily was taken aback. She had been planning to depart the day after Christmas. But she had so many questions for her father. So many discussions she wanted to have that weren't antagonistic.

"She can stay for as long as it takes." Beau slung his arm over Lily's shoulders. "Can't you, sis?"

Lily numbly nodded. "It'll be fine."

I'll just stay away from the coffee shop and the Buckboard.

Any place she might run into the man who'd stolen her heart.

ZANE PULLED INTO the Smiths' driveway but not very far.

Rowdy was parked there, closing the door on a horse trailer.

Ford was leading a young white horse over to

the pasture, followed by his parents and favorite aunt.

Zane got out and approached Rowdy. "Did you swear the Smiths to secrecy, too?"

The sly dog laughed. "As far as they're concerned, I bought that horse for Ford, seeing as how he's my great-nephew."

Zane didn't want to waste time arguing. He headed over with several gift boxes underneath his arm and a coffee cup in his other hand. "Merry Christmas."

"Zane!" Ford ran up to him, leading the filly, who dutifully trotted along after him. "Look at what Mr. Rowdy brought me. This is Daisy but I think I should call her Lightning. She looks like she could be the daughter of Solomon, right?"

Daisy came to a stop when Ford did, then looked at Zane with innocent brown eyes that seemed to say, "*You swore an oath to keep the secret of Solomon.*"

"I don't know, Ford." Zane moved closer to inspect the horse. She had perfect confirmation. "Look how small she is. And Rowdy told me he bought her for you."

"Oh." Ford's expression fell. "But... I can always pretend, can't I?"

"Of course you can." Lily came to stand on the other side of Daisy. "You can pretend but when your friends ask you about Daisy, you should always say that she was a gift and no relation to Solomon."

"Should I ask more questions about this gift?" Beau asked, looking from Lily to Zane to Rowdy.

They all assured him that he shouldn't.

"Lily, can I have a word?" Zane gestured with his head toward her truck. "Over here." Away from all the ears.

"I'm going to check on Cady and make pancakes." Nora went inside the house.

Ford, Beau and Rowdy continued to the pasture with Daisy.

"I suppose you want me to unsaddle your horse," Beau called back to Lily.

"Please," Lily said. She had her arms wrapped around her waist, looking standoffish. "Zane, if those are the baby gifts your mamas talked about for Nora, you can head on up to the house."

"No… This is for you." Zane balanced the gift boxes on top of her truck hood while holding the coffee cup in his other hand. He wanted to draw Lily into his arms and apologize. But he knew he had to say the words first. "I'm sorry. I've been a fool."

Lily nodded. "Okay."

"I've been looking at you through a fogged-up lens. You sat down next to me at the bar that first night and I couldn't look away." He gave a wry laugh. "There was that moment when you smiled at me that I thought you were extraordinary."

Lily's eyes widened.

"The next few days, I'd smile just thinking about something you said or remembering the way you laughed. But I was preoccupied with not falling prey to my mamas' romantic schemes and I had been feeling—as my mother put it—restless, as if something had to change in the new year to shift my fortunes." He wasn't laughing anymore. "The point is that there were sparks at first and because I'm a fool, I chalked that attraction up to you being a great wingman, a good drinking buddy, a perfect fake date."

Lily pressed her lips together.

"That wasn't fair to you," Zane admitted.

Lily stared at her boots.

"I brought you a vanilla latte." Zane handed Lily the coffee.

"Thanks." Lily took the drink from him. "This reminds me of those women bringing you cups of coffee that time before Thanksgiving."

"Yes. Those ladies all hoped to win my heart. Except now I've realized there was only ever one woman who could have done that. You." His attention shifted to the gift boxes. "But there's more to this. To honor my mothers, I'm courting you with the special gifts they thought would light a spark of love." He selected one of the boxes and handed it to her. "Truffles bought for the sweetest woman I know." He'd called Izzy and asked her to open the feedstore early this morning.

Lily accepted the pretty box. Her dimples were fading in and out. "This is an ode to your mamas?"

"And you. You've been with me through most of their...*encouragement* to help me find love."

"It's ironic," Lily said, sounding sniffy, looking teary.

"It's not ironic. It's fate." Zane handed Lily another gift box. "All paths connect and lead to you."

Lily opened the box slowly. "Oh... Solomon." She held up the white horse ornament that had been so popular at the gift exchange party.

Zane had no idea what happened to his ornament that night. It hadn't come home with him.

"We got to know each other better on our search for Solomon," Zane said quietly, gaze drifting to the pasture where a white filly trotted around the perimeter. "You convinced me to think through the implications of catching him. And Rowdy... The lore of Solomon is important to your father. It's important to you, too. And if you let me, I'll be a part of keeping that legend alive moving forward." With her.

Lilly's eyes filled with tears. She placed the white horse ornament back in its box.

Next, Zane tugged a Christmas card in a red envelope from his back pocket. "I know I didn't open mine the day we met but feel free to open yours."

Lily took the envelope and carefully removed the card. "'Tis the season for forgiveness. I hope you'll find it in your heart to forgive me. Love,

Zane.'" She wiped away a tear from her cheek. "Oh, Zane…"

"I love you, Lily." Zane had one last gift to give. "I've never been in love before and I hope you can love me despite all my quirks and flaws."

"Despite all your quirks and flaws," Lily whispered, placing the gifts he'd given her on the hood of her truck.

Zane placed a felt heart in her hand, then encased her hand in both of his. "When you took off yesterday, you took my heart with you. Honestly, I hadn't even realized I'd given my heart to you. Love snuck up on me."

Lily frowned, subtly tugging on the hand he cradled. "Maybe it isn't love, then. Maybe you're just fond of me."

Zane wouldn't let her go. "Fondness isn't defined by feeling as if your heart was ripped out when the woman you care for runs away." Releasing her hand, Zane tucked the felt heart in Lily's jacket pocket "Fondness isn't defined by a deep sense of guilt every time you remember that look on her face when you freaked out about learning the identity of her father."

Lily's eyes filled with tears. "I've never had any man start out as a friend who fell in love with me."

"I've never fallen in love with a friend, so I guess we're even." Zane eased his arms around her. "I love you, Lily. I fell in love with you while laughing, eating cake, swapping stories and dancing at twelve Christmas parties where I kept looking toward the horizon for something I had in front of me all this time."

"A horse? A ranch?" She was teasing. Her dimples gave it away.

"I have a horse, Lily. And I can buy a ranch where we can make a fresh start."

"And what about Rowdy?" Lily looked right at the man Zane had blamed for ruining his life.

But that was then. Zane nodded. "Rowdy's welcome for Sunday dinner."

Rowdy trundled over, darn him.

"Speak of the devil," Zane murmured. "Merry Christmas, Rowdy."

"The jury is still out on that." Rowdy reached Lily's truck and leaned heavily on it, winded. "Lily, your man and I made our peace yesterday. And to seal the deal, I'd like to give him something. But only with your blessing."

"I see where you're going with this," Lily said cryptically. "And you have my blessing."

Rowdy nodded, then looked toward Zane. "I've been without a ranch foreman on my spread for quite some time. And ranch hands, too." He cleared his throat and seemed to stand up taller. "Zane, I was wondering if you might consider a position working for me at the Rolling Prairie Ranch."

"We're a package deal." Zane put his arm around Lily's shoulders, hoping it was true. "She might be the better ranch foreman."

"We're a package deal." Lily repeated Zane's

words, staring into his eyes with what looked like love. "But I'm not ranch foreman material. Can't stand math."

Rowdy chewed on that for a few seconds, then nodded. "I suppose you'll both need to learn the books. You can argue about who is the official ranch foreman...for as long as you like."

"We accept your terms." Lily's smile grew until her dimples deepened.

He loved Lily so much. He hadn't known how things would turn out this morning. But now... Zane's pulse quickened and his heart melted.

She still loves me.

"I've got a signing bonus," Rowdy said, smiling at Lily. "But I only planned on one."

"Zane deserves it," Lily said emphatically.

And then the pair led Zane to the horse trailer. Lily helped her father bring the horse outside.

It was a white horse. A beautiful white horse with legs longer than a quarter horse.

The animal glanced back at Zane, revealing the delicate lines of a Thoroughbred, perhaps with some Arabian bloodlines.

"Merry Christmas," Rowdy said in a less rough voice than usual. "This is Star."

Lily slid her arm around Zane's waist. "Nice signing bonus, don't you think?"

"It's nice." Zane gathered Lily in his arms, uncaring that they had an audience. "But the only thing that really tempts me is the thought of a lifetime loving you." And then Zane kissed her.

"Is this what it's going to be like when you two work for me?" Rowdy closed the trailer doors. "I can't wait to retire." Lily guffawed.

Zane grinned and went back to kissing the cowgirl in front of him, glad and grateful he'd finally found love for real.

EPILOGUE

Christmas Day

LILY AND FORD rode over to the launch point for the Santapalooza Parade. The sun was out but it was cold enough to sting their fingers, noses and toes. They both wore long johns beneath their red velvet Santa suits. They had their white beards hooked to their saddle horns.

Ford hummed along to the tune of "We Wish You a Merry Christmas." It was his first time riding in the parade and his first long spell on Daisy. He'd been sad to leave Mouse but he was excited. "Do you think Santa was cold last night when he delivered presents?"

"You know he wears mittens."

"We need to get mittens for next year." Ford blew on his hands.

"Red or green?"

"Let's go for sparkly ones." Ford giggled. "Silver and gold. Mom said Zane's mamas are crafty. They can make them."

They were joined by other riders also headed

toward the parade's gathering spot. Several noted Daisy's resemblance to Solomon.

"Only because she's white," Ford told them.

Lily allowed herself a private smile.

They all formed ranks dressed as Santa or Mrs. Claus. There had to be over one hundred representing that jolly pair.

Zane rode up to Lily's side on Star. He wore a Santa suit with padding in the belly. "Merry Christmas, honey." He leaned over and kissed Lily. "And many more."

It was sweet and cheesy all at the same time, just like Chandler and Izzy at the cake party. Lily couldn't stop smiling.

"Ho-ho-ho." Rowdy rode up on a paint. "I've never joined in the parade before. Is it always so crowded downtown?"

"No. There's the grand-prize drawing," Zane pointed out. "You remember? The ranch you're giving away?"

"I'm hoping that place goes to someone who'll try something other than cattle ranching." Rowdy frowned. "That's the bad-luck part. Not enough acres to support a profitable herd."

"You really don't want it back, do you?" Lily asked Zane quietly, suddenly worried that he might.

"No. I don't want it. Really. Since I found out my father took the money for it and left us, it doesn't hold anything good for me." Zane smiled gently at her. "I found love in a different direction."

Lily liked hearing those words. Sweet and cheesy. Although, it was going to take some getting used to.

"You'll get used to hearing those words, love," Zane said as if reading her mind.

Lily smiled deeply. "And saying them...*love*."

A wagonful of Mrs. Clauses rolled up, drawn by two very large draft horses.

"Mama Mary!" Zane hailed the driver with an excited wave. "Look what I got for Christmas!"

"That's a fine-looking animal," Mary called out. "This is turning out to be a wonderful Christmas."

"The best." Rita waved, grinning from ear to ear. She'd wanted her son to have a whirlwind romance this holiday season and Zane hadn't disappointed her.

Lily's heart was full. She couldn't wait to start the new year and her new job.

Working for her dad.

THE PARADE BEGAN.

Calls of, "Merry Christmas! Ho-ho-ho!" filled the air, along with the jingle of sleigh bells from horse harnesses hitched to all sorts of wagons and carriages.

Clementine knew how to do Christmas Day right.

Instead of winding its way through Clementine nonstop as was customary, they called a halt in the middle of town where the drawing for the grand prize of the twelve Christmas parties was to be held. Rowdy stood at the podium with Zane's mamas. He drew the winning ticket, squinting as he read out... "And the winner is... Willa Tarkenton!"

Zane emitted a sharp whistle, then clapped for a long time. "That's the way it should be."

Lily was proud of how far Zane had come since they'd met a mere four weeks ago. The Bad Luck Ranch, or whatever it was to be called this time, was once again a family's home, after all.

Willa made her way up to the podium, crying, and bringing her daughter with her.

"I wrote her name on my tickets," someone behind Lily said. "A couple of us got together after the first party and decided Willa needed it more than we did."

Zane caught Lily's eye. "I did that, too."

"No. Really?" Lily hadn't watched him closely when he filled out his tickets.

"I started the night of the ornament exchange." Zane winked. "Did I do good?"

"You did good." Lily leaned over.

Zane leaned over, too, meeting her halfway between their horses for a quick kiss.

Willa took to the microphone. "Thank you. Thank you, everyone. Thank you, Rowdy. I... I'm ever so grateful to you and to this community."

Cheers went up. Ford tried to clap the loudest

and the longest. If he had his way, it would be Christmas every day.

The parade started again and wound its way through the rest of the town.

Rowdy was riding ahead of them now, getting reacquainted with some of his longtime friends. He'd mentioned wanting to visit the Buckboard soon. He may be the official secret keeper of the legend of Solomon, but he was opening up in all manner of ways. Ways that counted. He'd invited his son, Lucas, and his family to meet Lily over the New Year's weekend.

"Things turned out just how they were supposed to this holiday season," Zane said as they neared the end of the route. "You and me, for instance. Together. Forever. My mamas happy. Your daddy happy."

"And me!" Ford piped up. "I'm happy."

Lily smiled. "And I wouldn't have it any other way."

* * * * *

For more charming romances in The Cowboy Academy miniseries, from author Melinda Curtis and Harlequin Heartwarming, visit www.Harlequin.com today!

Get up to 4 Free Books!

We'll send you 2 free books from each series you try PLUS a free Mystery Gift.

FREE Value Over **$25**

Both the **Harlequin® Special Edition** and **Harlequin® Heartwarming™** series feature compelling novels filled with stories of love and strength where the bonds of friendship, family and community unite.

YES! Please send me 2 FREE novels from the Harlequin Special Edition or Harlequin Heartwarming series and my FREE Gift (gift is worth about $10 retail). After receiving them, if I don't wish to receive any more books, I can return the shipping statement marked "cancel." If I don't cancel, I will receive 6 brand-new Harlequin Special Edition books every month and be billed just $6.39 each in the U.S. or $7.19 each in Canada, or 4 brand-new Harlequin Heartwarming Larger-Print books every month and be billed just $7.19 each in the U.S. or $7.99 each in Canada, a savings of 20% off the cover price. It's quite a bargain! Shipping and handling is just 50¢ per book in the U.S. and $1.25 per book in Canada.* I understand that accepting the 2 free books and gift places me under no obligation to buy anything. I can always return a shipment and cancel at any time by calling the number below. The free books and gift are mine to keep no matter what I decide.

Choose one:
- ☐ **Harlequin Special Edition** (235/335 BPA G36Y)
- ☐ **Harlequin Heartwarming Larger-Print** (161/361 BPA G36Y)
- ☐ **Or Try Both!** (235/335 & 161/361 BPA G36Z)

Name (please print)

Address   Apt. #

City   State/Province   Zip/Postal Code

Email: Please check this box ☐ if you would like to receive newsletters and promotional emails from Harlequin Enterprises ULC and its affiliates. You can unsubscribe anytime.

Mail to the Harlequin Reader Service:
IN U.S.A.: P.O. Box 1341, Buffalo, NY 14240-8531
IN CANADA: P.O. Box 603, Fort Erie, Ontario L2A 5X3

Want to explore our other series or interested in ebooks? Visit www.ReaderService.com or call 1-800-873-8635.

---

*Terms and prices subject to change without notice. Prices do not include sales taxes, which will be charged (if applicable) based on your state or country of residence. Canadian residents will be charged applicable taxes. Offer not valid in Quebec. This offer is limited to one order per household. Books received may not be as shown. Not valid for current subscribers to the Harlequin Special Edition or Harlequin Heartwarming series. All orders subject to approval. Credit or debit balances in a customer's account(s) may be offset by any other outstanding balance owed by or to the customer. Please allow 4 to 6 weeks for delivery. Offer available while quantities last.

Your Privacy—Your information is being collected by Harlequin Enterprises ULC, operating as Harlequin Reader Service. For a complete summary of the information we collect, how we use this information and to whom it is disclosed, please visit our privacy notice located at https://corporate.harlequin.com/privacy-notice. Notice to California Residents – Under California law, you have specific rights to control and access your data. For more information on these rights and how to exercise them, visit https://corporate.harlequin.com/california-privacy. For additional information for residents of other U.S. states that provide their residents with certain rights with respect to personal data, visit https://corporate.harlequin.com/other-state-residents-privacy-rights/.

HSEHW25